LIKE COMING HOME AGAIN

Sarah saw that they'd arrived at her house . . . too soon! Before she could react, Hunter was around at the buggy door on her side and had the umbrella open.

"You don't have to walk with me," she said. "It's only a few steps."

Hunter didn't budge. "And those few steps would get you soaked," he said.

"I won't melt."

His look was serious. "Are you sure? Aren't girls supposed to be made of sugar and spice and everything nice?"

She'd forgotten how he liked to tease. "I'm hardly a girl," she reminded him, her voice cool.

Hunter's dark gaze swept her from the top of her head to her feet. "You could have fooled me," he said softly.

His voice trembled through her as if each word had touched a nerve. His warm breath was so close it stirred a tendril of hair at her temple. With a groan, he lowered his head; his lips touched hers.

She felt as if for years she'd been parched for water and now had taken the first tiny sip from a sweet, clear spring.

She wanted more . . . much more . . . .

SARAH'S CHRISTMAS

ELIZABETH GRAHAM

Zebra Books
Kensington Publishing Corp.

http://www.zebrabooks.com

For my family, with much love.
Thanks for your unfailing love and support.

CHAPTER ONE

Little Bethlehem, Missouri
1880

Hunter Winslow paused on the flagstone walk leading to his family home. He lifted his head and took a deep breath.

"Ah!" A smile spread across his face. After not quite a week away from St. Louis and back in Little Bethlehem, his appreciation for the freshness of the air here in this small town at the edge of the Ozarks hadn't lessened. At the end of November the air had a bite in it, but he liked that.

He also liked being able to see the distant mountains from his bedroom window.

He liked everything about the town.

Lowering his head, he saw a lace curtain twitch aside at a window in the front room of the house next door.

He'd forgotten how curious people were in small towns. Nosy, his mother would call it.

His smile widened as he waved toward the house. "Hello, Gladys," he called, although he knew she couldn't hear him.

The curtain panel abruptly slid back into place.

He guessed he shouldn't have let Gladys Randolph know he saw her at the window. It probably embarrassed her and she was a good, neighborly woman.

He'd take nosiness anyday over the impersonal way people treated one another in cities. And thank God, he was back here to stay where he could continue to appreciate all the things he liked in small-town life.

That is, if he could make a go of his fledgling cannery business.

"You will," he told himself as he continued up the walk, making his voice positive and firm. Little Bethlehem, surrounded by farms and orchards, was a good place to start such an enterprise.

Now, all he had to do was get the financial backing he needed. Which might not be so easy, he was discovering. Thank God he'd saved enough to tide his family over for several months.

Halfway up the steps, he noticed a large green wreath decorated with ribbon bows and holly berries and fastened to the white-painted front door. It hadn't been there when he'd left this morning to talk about his plans with a couple of the local farmers and the bank vice president.

His mother had always been the first person in town to start putting up Christmas decorations. Looked as if she still was. He hadn't noticed any other early harbingers of the coming season around town today.

The crisp, aromatic fragrance of the cedar branches hit his nostrils. Again he inhaled deeply, the smell taking him back to his childhood, with its many happy Christmases, its many happy memories.

And its unhappy ones, too.

His smile faded again. He wished he could go back in time to eight years ago and rewrite those intervening years . . . .

But he couldn't.

He brought his attention back to the wreath. It was topped by a large, red velvet bow, the same bow that had been on the Christmas wreath ever since he could remember. But something seemed different about the way it was tied. He frowned, trying to pinpoint the difference, but he couldn't.

He opened the door and entered the wide front hall, papered in a dainty floral print. A white-balustered staircase faced him, doors opening off the hall on either side. He sniffed again. Fresh bread. Nothing smelled any better than that.

He hurried down the hall toward the big kitchen.

Halfway there, he heard a merry laugh. His smile returned.

Despite his guilt over his past behavior, despite the unhappiness of these last eight years, he couldn't wish all the events erased.

If he hadn't married Beryl he wouldn't have Nicholas.

His son was more precious to him than anything else in this world.

And after only a few months of living here in Little Bethlehem with his grandmother, Nicholas was firmly entrenched.

The thought of having to take him—and maybe Hunter's mother, too—back to St. Louis made a chill touch Hunter's spine.

I will make a success of his business, he vowed again.

Hunter walked a little faster. In the kitchen doorway he stopped dead.

Nicholas was nowhere to be seen, but someone was in the kitchen.

Sarah stood by the stove, holding a loaf of bread.

She turned at the sound of his footsteps on the hardwood floor. Her hazel eyes widened, and the rosiness of her creamy cheeks paled.

Her light brown hair was pulled into a neat bun at the back of her neck. She wore a green dress that brought out the greenish flecks in her eyes. She wasn't as slender as she'd been at nineteen. Now, she had a more womanly roundness.

She'd been pretty then. Now she was beautiful.

He'd known this meeting was inevitable, but he hadn't expected to face it today. He wasn't ready for it.

"Sarah," he finally said, trying to put only friendly cordiality into his voice and not reveal the jumble of feelings the sight of her evoked.

This was the first time he'd spoken to her in private in eight years.

The first time since he'd jilted her.

He winced at the ugly cruelty of those words, guilt besieging him.

They'd known each other all their lives, played together as children, gone to school together, been nothing more than friends until that day . . . that day their glances had met and . . . something had flared between them.

And nothing was ever the same again.

"Hunter," Sarah at last answered, a slight tremble in her voice. Her hands also shook a little, he noticed.

This sudden encounter unsettled her, too.

Why did that knowledge give his heart a lift?

Turning aside, she set the loaf pan she held down beside another one on the back of the kitchen range. She lined them up precisely before turning to face him again.

Her face was still pale, and she'd clasped her hands together in front of her, so he couldn't tell if they were steady now.

He cleared his throat. "I didn't expect to find you here at Mama's," he said, then could have kicked himself.

That sounded as if he'd been trying to avoid her since his return to Little Bethlehem.

Hadn't he? As he'd done all these years on his infrequent visits here? Just as she'd avoided him? What else could either of them have done?

She drew herself up straight and raised her chin a bit. "I didn't know you were coming home for dinner either," she said, her voice firm. "I'm helping Faith with the cleaning and baking."

He nodded, acknowledging a fact he already knew, realizing how lame his earlier statement had been. Of course she'd be here on Saturday, since she taught school all week.

Another thought occurred to him. Would she think he'd come home for dinner *because* she was here?

Of course he hadn't. He'd just been preoccupied with his business.

You can't deny you've thought about Sarah a good bit these last months, his mind said. *Tried to think of some way to tell her how sorry you are for the mess you made of things.*

"I got all my business tended to early. Mama told me what a help you've been since Nicholas came to stay with her. It's very kind of you. I want to thank you."

His voice sounded stilted, as if she were merely an old family friend he hadn't seen in a while.

Instead of the woman he'd been engaged to for three years. The one he'd planned to share the rest of his life with.

His jaw tightened.

"Faith has been like a mother to me since my own died," Sarah answered, her voice as even as his. "It's the least I can do."

Of course he knew that, too, knew how close his mother and Sarah had grown, but the mention of Sarah's mother forced him into the past again, made him remember the night of their last, terrible argument.

The night that had changed both their lives forever.

The tightness in his jaw spread down to his neck, then into his chest.

"Mama loves you, too."

Another peal of childish laughter rang out from the sunny back room off the kitchen and then Nicholas appeared in the doorway.

"Daddy!" He ran across the room and flung himself into Hunter's arms. Hunter hugged him back, his love for this child of his flooding over him.

"Grandma Faith and me have been making paper chains for the Christmas tree!" he announced, his small face aglow. He tugged at Hunter's hand. "Come and see them!"

Hunter took his son's hand and swung it between them as they walked.

Still shaky from the unexpected encounter, Sarah watched the two of them enter the other room—the tall, broad shouldered, dark-haired man beside the equally dark boy. Hunter looked older now, fine lines radiating from around his brown eyes and tension etched around his mouth. Not surprising, considering all that had happened since last they'd talked.

Her mouth twisted. *Since Hunter had left her for another woman.*

Nicholas looked so much like his father.

The first time she'd seen Nicholas last summer, except from a distance, her heart had squeezed with pain. Now it did again. Nicholas could have, *should* have, been her son. Hunter should have been her husband.

A flash of anger mingled with the pain.

She wanted to scream at him. Beat her fists against his chest. Ask how he could have left her.

She forced the thoughts and feelings away. There was no undoing the past. And Hunter was back here to stay. Just as had happened now, she'd be bound to encounter him often.

Especially since she intended to continue helping Faith with the extra work her grandson made. Faith wasn't as strong as she used to be, and Sarah would never forget the older woman's kindness when she most needed it.

After Hunter left. After her mother's death only a few months later.

Why hadn't Faith told her Hunter would be coming home for noon dinner today?

Had the other woman *wanted* them to meet? It was possible.

Nicholas was one of Sarah's second grade pupils so she'd have to talk with Hunter from time to time about his son's progress in school. Even more than usual, because Nicholas needed extra help.

He loved his grandmother and liked living here in

Little Bethlehem, but it was obvious from the way he'd greeted his father just now how much he'd missed him these last months.

"That bread smells so good I could make a meal out of it."

Faith's voice brought Sarah back to the present. She pulled herself together and smiled at the older woman, trying to detect a hint of awareness or guilt in her face, but failed.

As usual, Faith's white hair was untidy from her play with her grandson. Her small frame was a trifle bent. But her dark eyes, so much like Hunter's and Nicholas's, snapped with spirit and humor.

"It isn't as good as yours," Sarah said, thankful she could still manage to keep her voice light and natural as if this meeting were one that took place every day.

"Oh, yes, it is. You're just too modest. You can cook rings around me anyday."

Sarah gave Faith a sharp look. Was that remark meant for Hunter's ears?

The other woman's expression was serene and guileless.

Nicholas and Hunter emerged from the back room, Nicholas still very close to his father. Sarah clenched her hands together at her sides, fighting a new wave of pain and anger.

"I don't see any rings around you, Grandma Faith," Nicholas said, his eyes sparkling.

Faith frowned as her glance caught Sarah's clenched fists. Then her face smoothed out.

She turned and gave Nicholas a surprised look. "You can't? Why, they're plain as day. But you have to hold your head just right. Tilt it to the side like this."

She demonstrated. Nicholas, completely taken in,

tilted his own the same way, gravely examining the area around Faith.

Despite her inner turmoil, Sarah had to smile. Her glance met Hunter's. He was smiling, too. For a moment, there was a connection between them, as if their thoughts and feelings had merged.

Just like it used to be . . . as if they were both part of one whole . . . each incomplete without the other.

Stunned at her thoughts, Sarah quickly denied them.

No! It wasn't like that between them anymore. It could never be again.

"I see them, Grandma!" Nicholas exclaimed. "They're kind of red and green like my paper chains."

He lifted his head and gave Faith a mischievous grin.

Sarah jerked her glance away from Hunter's, feeling her face redden.

Don't be such a fool, she chided herself. *Hunter betrayed you in the worst way possible. Everything between you was finished then.*

Faith's eyes widened. "Why, you're right! And you're so smart! Hardly anybody can see those rings."

Nicholas's grin faded. He shook his head. "Nah, I'm not smart. I'm dumb."

Nicholas's remark banished Sarah's unwanted thoughts and made her heart lurch. "You are not dumb, Nicholas," she said, making her voice very positive. "Don't you ever believe that."

"All the other kids say I'm dumb. They laugh at me at recess every day."

"That's not so," she insisted. "Only a few do, and you just have to overlook them. They don't know any better."

"That's right," Faith put in.

Again, Sarah's glance met Hunter's, but now he was frowning, a question in his eyes. She gave him a tiny nod, meaning she'd talk to him later about this. Still frowning, he nodded back, indicating he understood.

Sarah drew in her breath.

Just like it used to be. When they were so close, they could finish each other's sentences.

"Let's get dinner on the table," Faith said briskly. "I don't know about the rest of you, but I'm starving,"

It's all over between us, Sarah reminded herself again. *There can be no going back! And I wouldn't want to even if it were possible.*

"Me, too," Sarah said. She forced a smile for Nicholas. She'd grown very close to the boy in these few short months. She *wouldn't* let Hunter's return push her away from Nicholas.

"I made chocolate pudding," she told him.

To her relief, his face brightened at once. "Can I have a big dish?"

"If you eat your dinner first."

Too late, she realized she'd gone over Hunter's head with this promise. She'd spoken as if she were the one in charge of the child.

As if she were his mother. She forced down the renewed pain that thought brought.

"That is, if your father says it's all right," she amended.

She schooled her face into bland lines and once more glanced toward Hunter, avoiding a direct meeting of their eyes.

He nodded. "That's fine," he said heartily, but underneath that tone, Sarah detected another, different one. He was disturbed by the incident a moment ago.

Faith turned aside any discussion of her grandson's reading and writing problems, saying Nicholas was only seven and would outgrow it. Sarah devoutly hoped that was true, but Nicholas was miserable and she intended to help him.

Sarah waved her hand at the kitchen table. "Sit down. I'll get the food on the table."

"I'll just do that, dear," Faith said. "I'm a mite tired today." She put words to action and settled herself in her usual chair at the big round table.

"Can I help?" Nicholas asked, his face still bright at the thought of the pudding to come.

"Yes. Wait a minute and you can take the bread plate in."

Sarah tapped the bottom of one of the pans and slid the loaf onto a plate.

"I'll help, too," Hunter said, from close beside her.

Too close. Oh, yes, way too close. His clean, masculine scent came to her across the intervening inches. She could feel his warmth. He was almost touching her. And there was no way she could escape without acting like a ninny. So she kept on cutting the bread into even slices.

"You can take the roast out of the warming oven and put it on the table," she told him.

"No sooner said than done."

He reached up and opened the warming oven door.

The movement made his shirtsleeve brush against her hair. She shivered, then drew in her breath at her involuntary reaction and hoped he hadn't noticed.

Sarah kept her head bowed over the bread plate. Hunter drew out the roast with browned potatoes circling it.

"Mmmm . . . I don't know if I can wait until I get it to the table."

Across the room, Faith laughed. "You sound just like you did when you were ten years old, Hunter Winslow!"

Oh, but he's not ten years old, Faith, and you're well aware of that, Sarah thought, her anger and incredulity rising again. This time at herself.

How *could* she feel like this? After what Hunter had done to her?

Could she plead a sudden headache and flee? Not share the meal as she always did? No, she decided. She had to get through this ordeal without letting Hunter realize how she felt. She couldn't *bear* for him to know he still affected her so strongly.

Especially since he didn't seem to be affected at all by her nearness.

Hunter carried the platter to the table. "I'll never get too old to appreciate good food."

"I hope not," Faith agreed.

"Here you are." Sarah placed the bread plate into Nicholas's extended hands and gave him another forced smile.

His serious expression lightened. He turned and carefully carried the plate to the table and placed it on the blue-and-white-checked cloth.

Sarah drew in her breath and let it out, determined not to reveal how unnerved she felt, how much she dreaded sitting across the table from Hunter during the coming meal. She got the gravy and green beans out of the warming oven and took them to the table.

"Anything else?" Hunter asked.

But even worse than sitting across from him was having him over there by the stove, too close to her again.

"No," she said quickly. "I'll just get the coffee and milk."

"How did your meeting with Jasper Prescott go?" Faith asked Hunter when they were all seated.

Hunter served himself potatoes and roast before he answered. "Fine, as far as it went. He told me my plans sounded feasible. And I know they are. The new pressure-canning system has proved itself by now. It's safer and there's much less danger of spoilage. But Dudley will have to approve the loan, and Dudley wasn't available today."

After a moment, Faith said, "I guess we need to talk about this later."

Hunter nodded. "Yes." He turned his attention to his meal.

Of course they couldn't discuss this with Nicholas present, Sarah realized, since Dudley, as well as being the bank president, was also Nicholas's maternal grandfather.

"Of course it's a feasible idea," Faith went on in a moment. "A cannery in this town would give it a boost it needs. We're losing way too many young people to St. Louis and Kansas City because there's no way to earn a living around here except farming or fruit growing."

Hunter chewed and swallowed, then nodded. "Yes, and we have plenty of farmers willing and eager to grow the beef and pork we need to do it. And others who grow the vegetables and fruit."

"And you have all that experience working yourself up to manager of the cannery in St. Louis," Faith said, her voice rising a little.

"It will all work out." Hunter gave her a reassuring smile.

"We won't have to move back to St. Louis, will we,

Daddy?'' Nicholas asked, an edge of anxiety in his voice.

"No, chum, we won't," Hunter said firmly, turning to his son, his smile even more reassuring.

"I think it's a fine idea," Sarah heard herself saying to her own surprise. "As Faith says, Little Bethlehem needs something to keep the young people here."

Her glance met Hunter's. He, too, looked surprised.

No wonder. Her words implied she'd be glad if he stayed in town. Which wasn't the case, of course. But Nicholas was happy here and the child needed his father.

Especially now. Faith had told her this morning that the Cunninghams were threatening to go to court to try to get custody of Nicholas. Faith was too frail to raise her grandson properly, they claimed. And Hunter certainly couldn't do the job without a wife.

Sarah felt a twinge of uneasiness. There was more than a little truth in that assertion. That was why she'd been helping out here since Nicholas had come to stay with Faith.

Faith had told her Hunter couldn't manage any longer by himself. The older woman who'd been staying with Nicholas while Hunter was at work had moved away. Hunter hadn't been able to find anyone else he felt he could trust and Faith had insisted Hunter bring her grandson here.

"I'm glad you have confidence in the cannery," Hunter said after a moment.

There was something besides surprise in his voice. He sounded pleased, too.

The twinge of uneasiness intensified. Sarah looked down at her plate and carefully cut a bite of meat.

Why would Hunter care what she thought about

him living here permanently? It could have nothing to do with how they had once felt about each other. Because that was dead. Long dead.

Oh, so you have those same unsettling physical reactions to every handsome man you get near? her mind asked.

She ignored it. Of course, Hunter would rather the two of them got along. For Nicholas's and Faith's sake and to make things pleasant for the two of them when they must be together.

And for those reasons, she'd force herself to be decent to him.

"Of course she does," Faith said. "Everybody I've talked to thinks your cannery is a wonderful idea."

"So let's not worry about it," Hunter said. He glanced at Nicholas. "About ready for that chocolate pudding?"

Nicholas nodded vigorously.

"Good. So am I." Hunter turned his attention to his meal, as did Sarah and Faith.

A few minutes later, Sarah stood and began stacking plates before Hunter could suggest helping her.

Nicholas handed her his. "I didn't leave a bite."

"I see that. So here comes the pudding. With whipped cream of course."

Sarah carried the plates to the worktable and started dishing out dessert.

She heard a chair being pushed back. "I'll take the rest of the dishes off," Hunter said.

"I'd like a big dish, too," he said from close behind her a few moments later.

So close his warm breath tickled the back of her neck. She gave an involuntary shiver, then tensed at the unwanted memories that rose into her mind.

"Here, take this to Nicholas. He's waited long enough."

Managing a smile, she handed Hunter the first serving of deep brown, rich chocolate with its mound of whipped cream.

"What? I don't get the first bowl?" Hunter asked in mock indignation.

She wished he'd stop all this banter. She wished he'd hurry up and eat and leave. No, *she'd* leave. This wasn't her house.

She forced a matching light tone. "You're way down the line. Faith is next."

He shrugged, his glance fully meeting hers. "All right. I guess I know who's important around here."

The expression in his eyes didn't match his bantering tone.

Stunned, she realized he was as disturbed at this meeting as she. She tried to push down the satisfaction that knowledge gave her, but failed. She should be allowed some moments of satisfaction, shouldn't she? After what Hunter had put her through?

That mutual discomfort would make things easier. As far as possible, they'd try to avoid each other just as they had these last eight years.

And if you believe you can do that, you're a bigger fool than I thought you were, her mind informed her.

CHAPTER TWO

Sarah entered the church and paused for a moment to catch her breath. She'd gotten up later than usual, so she'd had to hurry.

She hadn't slept well last night. Her mind had been in turmoil. No matter how hard she tried to convince herself that her placid daily life would go on as it had, she knew better.

She wasn't late, but the church was filling up fast. She glanced over at the Winslow pew and her heart sank as she saw Faith, Hunter, and Nicholas already seated.

Faith sat on the far side, against the end, Nicholas next to her. And Hunter next to his son.

Sarah had been sitting with Faith and Nicholas every Sunday this last year. This was the first time Hunter had been in church here since his marriage. On his visits he'd always had to leave Little Bethlehem on Sunday mornings to return to his St. Louis job.

But no matter how much she wanted to, she couldn't sit anywhere else today. That would hurt Faith and Nicholas.

Faith might understand—in fact, if Sarah's suspicions were correct, she'd understand only too well—but Nicholas wouldn't.

That meant she had to sit next to Hunter.

Sarah straightened her shoulders and marched down the aisle, conscious of heads turning to watch her progress. When she reached the pew, she couldn't stop herself from glancing at the Cunningham pew on her left, directly across the aisle.

Dudley sat on the far side, looking straight ahead, his demeanor as stiff as his Sunday clothes. He was bluff and hearty most of the time, but church services always seemed to make him nervous.

His wife, Enid, dressed in a splendid dark blue silk dress with fine pleating, sat next to him, staring straight at Sarah, her thin lips pursed in disapproval. Or anger. Or probably both.

Their younger daughter Crystal, her lighter blue gown with its pleated silk bow not quite as magnificent as Enid's, sat next to her mother. Crystal, fiddling with a handkerchief in her lap, didn't glance up.

As always, since Crystal had grown into young womanhood, the sight of her gave Sarah a jolt.

With her blond hair and blue eyes, Crystal looked so much like her sister Beryl. Had Hunter noticed that? How could he help it? Did the sight of her make him feel his loss even more deeply, even though Beryl had died of a fever more than a year ago?

As quickly as the thought entered her mind, Sarah dismissed it. That was none of her business and would never be.

Enid suddenly gave Crystal a nudge in the ribs.

The girl jerked her head up, then smiled toward the Winslow pew, directly at Hunter. The smile looked forced, Sarah thought.

Or was it merely shy? Crystal was a quiet, retiring girl.

Had Hunter returned the smile? And what did it matter? He and Crystal certainly must have exchanged dozens of smiles before.

Stopping her woolgathering, she gave the family a polite smile and nod. Enid frostily returned the gesture. Dudley still stared straight ahead and Crystal gave her a timid smile and nod.

Sarah turned toward the Winslow pew. All three of its occupants smiled warmly at her.

She smiled back, forced her gaze away from Hunter's handsome face, and tried to ignore the tremors of awareness she felt all through her body.

"Hi, Miss Sarah!" Nicholas said in a loud whisper.

Her heart turned over. Dressed in his brown Sunday suit, his dark hair slicked back, Nicholas looked adorable.

Just as she'd always imagined a son of hers and Hunter's would look.

None of that, she reminded herself. "Good morning, Nicholas, Faith, Hunter," she answered in a low voice, as befitted the time and place.

"Sit down," Faith urged.

"There's plenty of room," Hunter indicated the space next to him.

Sarah was sure dozens of eyes were on her as she seated herself and felt Enid's gimlet gaze. She carefully arranged the skirts of her plain brown Sunday gown about her, calculating just how far away from Hunter she could sit without too many people noticing.

Of course they were busily speculating anyway. She had no doubt of that.

Sarah Calder was sitting in public next to the man who had jilted her eight years ago.

For the first time since it happened.

She could hear the buzz of discreet whispers, and she felt her face warming as she left a foot of space between her and Hunter on the pew.

"You look pretty, Miss Sarah," Nicholas whispered again, leaning forward in the seat to see her.

"Thank you." Sarah gave him another smile.

"Nicholas certainly has taken a shine to you," Hunter said in a low voice.

Sarah swallowed and glanced up. She'd forgotten how melting his eyes were. How when he looked at her his gaze was so focused no one else seemed to exist but the two of them.

What an illusion that was, her mind said. *Beryl existed for him.*

"He's an easy child to like," she said in an equally low tone, relieved her voice sounded steadier than she felt.

The low murmur of talk died out. Sarah glanced toward the front of the church. Reverend Hopkins stood behind the pulpit, every fold of his robes in place, his brown hair equally well groomed.

By the end of his sometimes impassioned sermons, his robe was often askew, his hair on end where he'd run his fingers through it.

"Good morning, all!" he boomed. "It's indeed wonderful to see such a large turnout. Especially this Sunday. Since it's time to begin planning our annual Christmas pageant. As usual, Sarah Calder will be in charge. Anyone who can help—and we hope that will be many of you—talk to Sarah after the service."

Again Sarah felt Hunter's gaze, and despite her intentions to the contrary, she couldn't keep from glancing at him. One dark brow was raised quizzically.

Before she thought, she nodded and shrugged.

Then was at once appalled.

So they take it for granted you'll do the pageant every year, he'd silently asked. Without using words, she'd answered yes.

As they used to do. As if the years were wiped away and what had happened didn't matter.

But it *did* matter. They could never go back to that innocent time.

She was jolted from her unhappy thoughts by a nudge against her arm. Startled, she looked at Hunter again to see him extending an open hymn book toward her.

"Looks like we'll have to share," he mouthed at her.

She wouldn't get that close to him. Sarah darted a glance at the hymn book receptacle on the back of the pew ahead. Empty. Faith held the other one allotted to their pew.

There was no help for it. She'd have to share or look like an idiot.

Awkwardly she reached for her side of the hymn book. There was too much space between her and Hunter. But she wouldn't move an inch closer to him.

So Hunter did, sliding toward her. He gave her a satisfied nod and raised his voice in song.

Hunter's rich, baritone voice soared above those of most of the congregation.

She'd forgotten what a wonderful singer he was. How sitting like this with him, all those years ago, she'd so enjoyed listening to him she'd forgotten to join in the hymns herself.

As she was doing now, she realized with a start. Resolutely, she began to sing, too.

She'd also forgotten how well their voices blended together.

She felt Hunter's gaze again and glanced toward him. He nodded, as if he'd read her mind and was agreeing with her.

Sarah drew herself up straight and gave her full concentration to the hymn. As it ended, she heaved a relieved sigh and removed her hand from its grasp on the hymn book.

So did Hunter. Then they both grabbed for it at the same time to prevent it from hitting the floor.

One of Hunter's big hands gripped the underside of the hymn book. The other clamped over hers on top.

Quickly, she pulled her hand out from under his and clasped both hands firmly together in her lap so he couldn't see how they trembled.

During the rest of the service she steadfastly refused to glance his way. Hunter remained where he was, much too close for her comfort. They shared the hymn book several more times, but no more mishaps occurred.

Usually, she enjoyed Reverend Hopkins's sermons, but today she couldn't wait for the service to end. After the last prayer, she slid out into the aisle, planning to exchange quick greetings with everyone and hurry back to her house.

She'd forgotten about the Christmas pageant.

She had no sooner set foot into the aisle than Gladys Randolph stopped her.

"Sarah dear, I'll be happy to be in charge of the costumes again."

Sarah smiled. "Thank you, Gladys. I appreciate that."

"I like to do my part."

"And you always do," Sarah assured her. That was true, but Sarah wished Gladys had more of a knack with her needle. The costumes invariably fit wrong—either too big or too little for the young pageant participants. But no one else ever volunteered for the time-consuming job.

With a gratified smile, Gladys moved away. Replaced by the entire Cunningham family. Sarah moved aside to let Hunter and his mother and Nicholas out of the pew, hoping to avoid dealing with Enid right now.

But of course that was impossible. Enid's and Dudley's solid shapes stood in the aisle, blocking escape. Crystal stood slightly behind them, but Enid moved aside and turned to her daughter with a frown.

Crystal stepped forward with another tight-looking smile. "Hello, Hunter," she said. "It's so nice to see you."

"Good day, Crystal, Enid, Dudley," Hunter responded a little stiffly.

He didn't address them as Mother and Father Cunningham, Sarah noticed. She wondered if he had while Beryl was alive.

Enid gave Hunter a simpering smile. "We were hoping you and Nicholas would come back with us for Sunday dinner."

Hunter was so close to Sarah that she felt him stiffen.

"That's very kind of you," he said.

"Nonsense. Why, you're part of our family and we don't see nearly enough of either of you. Especially our only grandson."

Enid's voice held a slight touch of censure. She leaned over and attempted to chuck Nicholas under the chin.

He stepped back just before her hand touched him. Enid straightened, her frown back.

"There's no need for you to bring your carriage," she said. "You can ride with us."

"Since it's such a nice day, we walked to church," Hunter said. He sounded resigned now, as if he knew there was no way he could get out of this invitation.

He glanced toward Faith, then at Sarah. "Do you mind walking home with Mama?"

"Of course not," Sarah said.

Faith laid her hand on Sarah's arm. "And you'll stay to dinner, too, won't you, dear? Even if it is leftovers from yesterday."

"If you want me to."

"You know I do," Faith said.

Sarah felt Enid's glance and looked her way. The other woman's eyes were cold with anger. Shock washed over Sarah as she realized why. Of course Enid wouldn't want Faith to show such warmth toward Sarah.

Not now. Not when Hunter was back in town and Enid was throwing Crystal at him. Enid was probably angry about Sarah sitting next to Hunter during the service, too.

You don't have anything to worry about from me, Sarah told her silently. *If you can marry your younger daughter off to him, I certainly don't care.*

And she didn't. Of course she didn't.

"We want Nicholas to stay the night with us," Enid said. "It's been such a long time since he has."

"Only a little over a week, Enid," Faith said. "He

had to miss his usual Friday overnight stay because you weren't feeling well."

Enid's smile was chilly. "Oh, really? It seems like much longer than that."

"Tomorrow's a school day," Hunter said. "That will have to wait until next Friday."

Enid's smile faded completely. She gave Sarah a cool glance. "And how is dear Nicholas doing in school these days?"

"He's coming along well," Sarah answered evenly, determined not to discuss Nicholas's problems here.

Enid raised her brows. "I must say that wasn't my impression." She turned to Crystal. "When he read to you during his last visit, he had a great deal of difficulty, didn't he, dear?"

Crystal gave an uncomfortable shrug. "Some, I guess," she said. "But I'm no teacher."

Sarah glanced at Nicholas. He was looking at the floor, his cheeks red. Her mouth tightened. It was one thing for Enid to utter veiled criticisms of Sarah's teaching. It was quite another for her to humiliate her own grandson in public.

Enid turned back to Hunter. "My daughter is too modest. You know she passed her normal school examinations at the top of her class. She's a very qualified teacher. Such a pity there's no opening here."

Sarah's drew in her breath. Never before had Enid been so open in her wish to see Crystal take Sarah's place as Little Bethlehem's teacher.

Hunter hadn't missed his son's reaction either, Sarah saw. He was frowning as he looked at Nicholas.

He lifted his head and gave Enid a straight, unsmiling look. "Go on ahead. Nicholas and I'll enjoy walking to your house."

"Sounds like an excellent plan. Fresh air and exercise are good for everyone. We should have walked, too."

Dudley Cunningham's hearty voice spoke for the first time. He sounded relieved, as if he'd had enough of this veiled bickering.

That wasn't true of the rest of the congregation. Sarah saw avidly listening people who'd paused in their exodus from the church in order not to miss out on this conversation.

Enid sniffed and turned to Crystal. "Come along, dear," she said.

Crystal obediently fell in beside her. Skirts swishing, both women headed toward the rear door, where Reverend Hopkins waited to greet his flock.

Sarah let out her breath in relief. Enid always took charge of the pageant music. She must have gotten so upset with what she perceived as a threat to her plans that she'd forgotten to inform Sarah she intended to do so again this year.

How wonderful it would be if she'd get so offended she'd refuse to work with Sarah. The church organist would be a splendid replacement.

Sarah sighed and shook her head. Wishful thinking indeed. Enid would never step down.

"I guess we'd better get started," Hunter said. "What do you say? Up to a walk with your old man?"

Nicholas nodded. "Sure, Daddy." He gave Sarah and Faith a wan smile. " 'Bye, Miss Sarah, Grandma Faith."

Sarah and Faith said their good-byes to Nicholas.

Hunter turned to Sarah again. "I'd like to stop over at your house this afternoon and talk to you about Nicholas."

Amazed, she stared at him. Did he actually think she'd allow him to be alone in her house with her?

"Of course. You can stop in at the school tomorrow after classes are dismissed," she said, making her voice coolly businesslike.

Hunter blinked, as if surprised at her response.

Did he think he could come back to Little Bethlehem and act as if they were just friends and had never been anything else?

"I'd rather talk about it this afternoon," he said.

Why was he insisting on coming to her house? Surely, he didn't want to . . . discuss anything personal.

She noticed other members of the congregation were pausing on the way out to listen. She couldn't get into an argument with Hunter here in the church aisle. And he knew that, too. Was counting on it.

She'd have to agree gracefully, make light of this. "All right. Come about three," she said briskly.

She had wanted to talk to him about Nicholas anyway. But she'd planned for it to be in the impersonal atmosphere of her classroom.

It wouldn't be hard to keep their conversation impersonal, she told herself. Hunter must be so anxious to discuss Nicholas's problems he didn't want to wait even one more day.

Hunter nodded and smiled. "That's fine. I'll see you then."

Sarah watched the two walk down the aisle. Pain went through her again, mixing with anger. How often she'd dreamed of a son like Nicholas. And Hunter had ruined those dreams.

How could she ever be friends with him again?

Faith waited for her while a few more pageant volunteers assured her of their willingness to help again this year.

As usual, the same faithful few. She guessed that was the way it always was. Finally, she and Faith were free to return to the Winslow house.

"I'm going to have to step up my praying for patience to deal with that woman," Faith said, sighing.

Sarah didn't have to ask whom she meant. Faith and Enid had never gotten along, due to Enid's bossy, disdainful ways.

"Me, too," Sarah admitted.

"Did you see how she was trying to throw Crystal at Hunter?" Faith went on, indignation mixing with incredulity in her voice.

Tension hit Sarah's stomach. "Yes," she finally said.

Faith huffed. "Crystal's always been under Enid's thumb and meekly goes along with whatever the woman says. I swear, she looks so much like Beryl it gives me the all-overs sometimes."

Sarah swallowed. "Yes, I've noticed that, too."

Faith shook her head. "I've got enough to worry about. I'm not going to let that bother me. Hunter has more sense than to get mixed up with another one of the Cunninghams."

Sarah felt the other woman's gaze and turned. Faith was giving her a speculative look.

"You know, when I saw you sitting by Hunter today, sharing the hymn book, you looked so right together. Just like before that awful mess happened."

The tension in Sarah's stomach grew. As she'd suspected, Faith hoped for things that could never be.

Faith's son had deeply wronged Sarah, but she was willing to forget that.

Still, Sarah acknowledged, Faith had been good to

her. She loved the other woman and wouldn't reveal that her anger at Hunter was still alive.

"That was a long time ago. I could never think of Hunter in that way again. And I'm sure he feels the same."

Faith didn't say anything for a few moments. Then she reached over and squeezed Sarah's jacket-encased arm. "Of course you're right, dear. Don't pay any attention to an old woman's ramblings."

"You're not an old woman, Faith," Sarah protested, uneasily. Faith had given in too quickly. Was she just biding her time?

"Let's talk about something else. The Christmas pageant, for instance. It will be here sooner than we know."

"All right," Faith agreed.

For the remainder of the walk, they did just that and Sarah tried resolutely to keep her mind on all the Christmas preparations yet to be done.

But underneath the light talk, a dark current ran through Sarah's mind, and she couldn't seem to turn it off no matter how she tried.

Hunter was coming to her house this afternoon. For the first time in eight years they would be completely alone with each other.

She should never have agreed to this meeting. She should have insisted they talk after school let out tomorrow.

But she hadn't and now she'd look like a fool if she refused to let him in when he arrived.

They'd sit on the porch, she vowed. Right out in the open for the whole town to see. No matter if it was chilly. And it would be. The wind was already picking up.

This unseasonably warm day was going to change before evening.

Never mind, she'd dress warmly and control her shivers.

You'd better, her mind said. *Especially if they come not from the cold but from something else you're trying to pretend isn't there.*

CHAPTER THREE

Hunter glanced down at Nicholas's bowed head as they walked along the sidewalk. "Nice day for a walk," he finally said.

Nicholas glanced up and shrugged. "I guess. I wish we were going somewhere else besides Grandmama Enid's house."

So do I, boy, so do I, Hunter wanted to reply. But he didn't. The Cunninghams were, after all, Nicholas's close relations and they had to visit one another.

There were other reasons, too, Hunter admitted. Dudley had a lot of influence in the area. Even with the local judges. If Dudley and Enid tried to get legal custody of Nicholas, Hunter feared they might succeed.

His mother *was* frail. Since he'd moved back, he realized that caring for Nicholas, even with him in school most of the weekdays, was too much for her. He shouldn't have let her persuade him into it. Without Sarah's help she couldn't do it.

Thinking of Sarah made those competing emotions swirl up inside him again, with guilt still the strongest. He would see Sarah this afternoon. Alone. Could he try to explain what had happened that night? Try to apologize?

Too little. Too late, his mind told him. Sighing, he silently agreed. No explanation would have sufficed before. It certainly wouldn't now.

When he and Sarah had shared the hymn book during the service, it seemed for a few minutes as if they'd gone back in time. Their voices blended as they had then, and when their hands touched, he'd felt as if a lightning bolt went through him. From the stunned expression on Sarah's face, he'd wager she felt the same.

The strong sensual attraction between them had never died.

And with him living in Little Bethlehem again, this could only cause unwanted complications.

He brought his mind back to his other problems. A judge might well think Nicholas would be better off in a house with a grandmother who was able-bodied, capable of caring for Nicholas by herself.

Not that Enid would. No, she'd never give up her myriad of activities to stay home with her grandson. If the Cunninghams got control of Nicholas, Enid's maid would be in charge of his son a lot of the time.

Or Crystal. Hunter frowned. Enid was throwing Crystal at his head all too obviously. It was embarrassing for him and Crystal, too, he thought. But the girl was so shy he wasn't sure how she actually felt.

He hoped she didn't look upon him as a potential

husband. But Enid *wouldn't* succeed. He'd do whatever it took to keep that from happening.

Nicholas tugged at his hand. "Do *you* want to go to Grandmama Enid's, Daddy?"

"We'll have a good dinner," Hunter evaded, smiling down at his son. "Chicken and dumplings, I betcha?"

After a moment, Nicholas smiled back and nodded. "Yeah, I betcha, too, but I wish we were back at Grandma Faith's and Miss Sarah was eating with us."

His son's words evoked a memory of yesterday's dinner. *I couldn't agree more, son,* Hunter told him silently, then was surprised at his thoughts.

Being with Sarah had been profoundly unsettling, but he *had* enjoyed it.

"After dinner you can play in the maze," Hunter said. Enid's recent creation, an authentic English maze, had half the town snickering, his mother had said. Behind the Cunninghams' backs, of course.

Nicholas nodded. "Yeah, that's fun. Will you play hide-and-seek with me in there?"

"Yeah," Hunter replied, grinning. That would beat sitting in the parlor, trying to make awkward conversation.

He wished he could feel closer to his late wife's family. God knew, he'd tried. But it hadn't worked from the beginning. He and the Cunninghams had nothing in common.

Except Nicholas. And he wouldn't let his son suffer the consequences of a family feud no matter what he had to do. Even if that meant taking Nicholas and his mother and leaving Little Bethlehem. Going back to St. Louis for good.

He pushed those gloomy thoughts aside. Things were still a long way from that coming to pass.

They'd gotten into the part of town where the expensive houses were located, on big plots of land that gently rose. Going uphill, they passed the Madisons' large residence. Then came Doc Lawson's large brick house.

And there it was at the top of the hill.

The imposing stone pile where the Cunninghams lived. The biggest and most expensive house in Little Bethlehem.

Hunter paused before starting down the poplar-lined drive. "Here we are," he told Nicholas.

Nicholas sighed.

Hunter barely kept himself from following suit.

A pretty young girl in a maid's uniform answered Hunter's knock at the massive front door. The Randolph girl, Matilda.

She smiled at them and stepped back so they could enter the marble-floored foyer. "They're all in the front parlor, waiting for you."

Hunter came inside, followed by Nicholas. As always, the cold, ornate grandeur of this house made him want to turn around and leave. He smiled back. "Thanks, Mattie. We're not that late, are we?"

"Not so's you'd notice it." Matilda took their coats and hats. Her smile widened into a grin, and she shrugged, rolling her eyes.

Conscious of Nicholas's all too alert ears and eyes, Hunter merely nodded, but irritation rose inside him. Enid must be making a fuss about having to wait for him and Nicholas.

Matilda opened the parlor door and ushered them into the elaborately furnished room. Everywhere you looked furniture or bric-a-brac vied for space. There was scarcely room to put your feet down. The windows were so heavily draped in velvet, little light came through, even on a sunny day like this. It always felt hard to breathe in here.

"Mr. Hunter and Master Nicholas, mum," Matilda said primly.

Enid and Dudley sat side by side on a velvet-covered wine sofa. Enid's back was ramrod straight. Dudley looked a little more relaxed. Crystal sat to the side of them on another sofa upholstered in gold velvet.

She glanced up and gave Nicholas and Hunter a nervous-looking smile.

Enid turned with a sharp look, her brows raised a trifle. "There you are, Hunter. We've been waiting for you."

From her intonation, you'd think they'd all three been sitting there for a couple of hours, Hunter thought as he greeted everyone.

Enid gestured at Crystal's sofa. "Go ahead and sit for a moment before we go in to luncheon."

Luncheon. Hunter barely restrained himself from rolling his eyes as Mattie had. He'd bet everyone else in Little Bethlehem called the noon meal dinner.

"And, Nicholas dear, you sit here between your grandfather and me."

Hunter had to admit Enid's smile for her grandson held real warmth. She did truly love him, in her own way. And Crystal, too. But her love was overpowered by her desire for power.

Nicholas smiled politely and eased himself between his grandparents. Hunter could almost hear another of his son's silent sighs.

Hunter lowered himself to the seat beside Crystal, noticing she edged away from him a little, not enough for her mother to notice. Again, he didn't know if it was from timidity or other reasons.

"You're looking well today," he told her, smiling,

trying to put her at ease, not that it wasn't the truth. She was a pretty girl and always well dressed and groomed.

She blushed and gave him another wan smile in return. "Thank you," she murmured.

He glanced over at Enid to see a satisfied expression on her face, and his jaw tightened. No doubt his merely polite attentions were being construed as interest in Crystal as a woman.

Nothing could be farther from the truth.

Silence settled over the room. Finally, Enid cleared her throat. "Reverend Hopkins's sermon was a bit long-winded today."

"He's a good man," Dudley said after a moment. "Good man."

Enid sniffed. "I didn't say he wasn't a good man. No one doubts that. But he doesn't know when to stop."

"He's just so enthusiastic," Crystal said. "He gets caught up in his sermons."

Enid snapped her head around to stare at her younger daughter in surprise. "He still ought to realize when to stop."

Hunter, glancing at the girl, felt surprise, too. Crystal's usually almost colorless voice had sounded different as she defended their minister.

Her cheeks were even rosier than they'd been a few moments before.

Could Crystal be interested in David Hopkins as a man? Hunter's spirits rose at that thought. He hoped his supposition was true.

If so, Enid certainly didn't know anything about it. And would hit the roof if she knew. Considering her newly hatched campaign to try to get Hunter and Crystal together.

"Shall we go in to luncheon?" Enid said, rising. "Come along, Nicholas." She tucked her hand into the crook of Dudley's elbow and marched toward the door. Nicholas gave his father an unhappy glance, then followed along behind his grandparents.

This was a new little formal touch, Hunter thought. A subtle way to get Crystal's hand on his arm. He rose and smiled at the girl. She bit her lip, then took his arm.

The dining room was paneled in dark wood, and it had heavy walnut furniture. Expensively furnished, of course, like the entire house, but not conducive to pleasant dining.

"Hunter, you and Crystal sit on that side," Enid directed. "Nicholas, sit over here with your grandfather and me. Since we see so little of you, we have to make the most of every moment, don't we, dear?"

Don't miss an opportunity to get a little dig in, Hunter told her silently. He pulled Crystal's chair out for her and the girl quickly seated herself, not looking at him.

Nicholas tugged at the back of his heavy chair.

"Here, let me help you with that." Dudley pulled the chair out and Nicholas slid into it. Dudley stood for a moment, glancing down at the top of his grandson's head, a fond look on his face.

Hunter's conscience smote him. These two people loved Nicholas. Why did things have to be in such an unholy mess? Why couldn't Nicholas's frequent visits with them be enough? Why did Enid have to push for more? Pretend that Hunter tried to keep Nicholas completely away from them?

He thought he knew. Beryl's elopement with Hunter had devastated Enid. She'd had another husband picked out for her favorite daughter. Dr. Lawson's son. Hunter's father had merely been the owner of a moderately successful general store at the other end of town until his death a year after Hunter and Beryl married.

Enid had never thawed toward him.

Hunter wasn't good enough for Beryl, but he was fine for Crystal. Enid was willing to use her younger daughter as merely the means to gain more control of Beryl's son.

The unspoken message was: *Marry Crystal and everything will be fine. We'll never talk about the custody issue again.*

Anger filled him at that thought, for his own sake and for Crystal's too. The girl deserved a chance to pick her own husband, and if and when he married again it would be to a wife of his choosing.

He had to admit a wife would solve his problems with Enid. He'd once more have an intact family and no judge would agree then that Nicholas would be better off with Enid and Dudley.

Of course, if that happened, Enid might persuade Dudley not to provide backing for his cannery.

He could be forced to give up the idea—at least in this town. But there were other towns. Or cities.

There are no other places your mother wants to live, his mind told him. *And you can't leave her alone here anymore. You can't expect Sarah to keep on helping her out forever.*

Sarah's face flashed in his mind's eye.

If he and Sarah married, he would never have to worry about losing his son.

He stiffened at that totally unexpected thought. He had no plans to marry anyone. Especially not Sarah.

No, he'd had his chance to marry her and he'd lost it. He'd never have the chance again.

"Dig in, everyone," Dudley's hearty voice urged.

"Really, Dudley, must you be so crude?" Enid said with a sniff.

Hunter realized he was staring unseeingly at his plate. "Everything looks wonderful," he managed, forcing his attention back to the meal. He took the big bowl of chicken and dumplings Dudley handed to him.

Enid could go only so far with Dudley; then he put his foot down. He refused to have a formal meal service or fancy food at his family table. The table was filled with plain, well-cooked food, and everybody helped themselves.

Hunter glanced over at Nicholas and winked. *See, chicken and dumplings, just like I told you.*

Nicholas winked back, lifting Hunter's spirits. He *would* enjoy the good meal and give his tumultuous thoughts a rest.

Afterward, as the group left the dining room, he decided to put his earlier plans in action. "Ready for a game of hide-and-seek in the maze?" he asked Nicholas.

"Sure!" Nicholas gave him a delighted grin.

"Oh, that sounds delightful!" Enid said, her normally sharp voice almost a squeal. "Dudley dear, let's you and I take Nicholas out and play with him."

Hunter stared at his mother-in-law. The thought of Enid and Dudley cavorting in the maze brought a picture to his mind that barely kept his mouth from hanging open.

Dudley must have had the same thoughts. He stopped walking down the hall and also stared at his wife. "I don't believe I'm up to that right now. Ate too much dinner, you know."

The whole group had stopped now.

Enid frowned, her pseudo-girlish pose wilting a bit. "That's just what you need to help you digest your food," she said. "Those heavy meals you insist we have aren't good for you."

Dudley gave her a bland look. "Enid, I've eaten this kind of food all my life, and I intend to keep on doing so for the rest of it."

Enid didn't say anything for a moment. Finally, she laid her hand on Dudley's arm and smiled up at him. "We need to do more things with Nicholas," she said, her voice unnaturally sweet. "After all, he is our only grandchild."

Dudley looked at her. Finally he reached over and patted her hand, still resting on his sleeve. "All right, my dear. But you're not big enough to carry me inside if I keel over."

"Oh, for heaven's sake, you're not going to keel over," Enid said, her voice still dulcet.

She turned to Hunter and Crystal. "This will be a perfect opportunity for you two young people to sit in the parlor and get better acquainted. Why, Hunter, Crystal was only a child when you and Beryl married. You never got to know her."

Laying it on with a trowel, aren't you? Hunter silently asked Enid. *But I'm not going to let you get away with this.*

He patted his stomach. "I also ate too much of that delightful meal and need some exercise. And I promised Nicholas. What about you, Crystal?" he asked, turning toward the girl.

A relieved smile lit her face, making her startlingly pretty. "That's a splendid idea," she said eagerly.

Frowning, Enid looked from one to the other. "But I really think—"

Dudley tucked her arm in his. "Nonsense, my dear.

The young people need exercise as much as we do. Come along now.''

He strode briskly down the hall. Enid, a thwarted frown still on her face, her arm pinned in his, was forced to trot along beside him.

Hunter gave Crystal a conspirator's grin. She looked startled, her eyes wide. Then she blushed and turned away.

What did that mean? That Crystal was no more interested in him than he was in her?

Or merely that she was embarrassed by his maneuvering?

It was quite possible he'd misread the little incident in the parlor and Crystal *was* interested in him as a husband. After all, she was about twenty, and most girls her age were already married or at least engaged.

Too late, he realized he should have taken this chance to get her alone and talk frankly with her. He'd have to make an opportunity to do that—but without Enid knowing and misinterpreting.

Until then, he'd have to avoid Enid's ploys.

And then what? If Enid gave up on this plan she might decide to get serious about the custody issue.

Would Dudley stop her?

Or go along with her all the way?

CHAPTER FOUR

Shivering a little at the sudden drop in temperature during the last hour, Hunter opened Sarah's front gate and let himself inside her neatly kept yard.

The gate's hinges didn't squeak, and it and the picket fence had a fresh coat of white paint. Neither the white clapboard house nor the dark green shutters had any peeling paint.

When they'd been engaged, he'd kept up the yard and the outside of the house. God knows Sarah'd had enough to do to take care of her ailing mother.

Guilt struck him at that thought, as it always did. He told himself to stop those thoughts. There was no undoing the past.

But maybe he could make the future better.

He took a deep breath, strengthening his resolve.

This afternoon, as he'd played with Nicholas in the maze, then walked home with his son afterward, his mind wouldn't leave him alone.

It kept telling him he had to try to make Sarah understand what had happened that night eight years ago. Try to get her forgiveness.

They both needed that if they were going to live in the same town for the rest of their lives.

Halfway up the cobblestone walk, the rain that had been threatening began, and the wind gusted. Still shivering, he hurried onto the porch. Another gust hit the green wooden swing on the left side and made it bang against the porch railing.

Memories rolled over him. He and Sarah had spent countless hours in that swing holding hands, his arm around her waist. She'd been so soft, so sweet . . . he'd wanted to do more than hold her hand and steal an occasional kiss . . . .

Quickly, he stopped that line of thought.

They'd planned their future.

Later, always later. When her mother finally got well.

But Mrs. Calder hadn't gotten well. She'd died. Only a few months after he and Beryl had married.

He turned those thoughts off, too, and knocked on the door.

Sarah opened it at once, as if she'd been standing there waiting for his knock.

She'd changed from her church clothes to the green dress she'd worn yesterday. And she looked every bit as lovely in it as she had then.

Don't think about how she looks, his mind advised him. *You're not here to rekindle anything between you. Just to try to ease the tension you both feel when you're together.*

"Good afternoon, Sarah," he said, making his smile of greeting casually friendly.

"Good afternoon, Hunter," she answered stiffly.

"I thought we could sit on the porch but it's raining now."

It was obvious she didn't want to let him in the house. Not a good start to his plan to resolve their past.

"Yes, and the temperature has dropped quite a bit."

He saw her swallow. "It would be better if we talked tomorrow at the schoolhouse."

Tomorrow, in the impersonal atmosphere of the schoolhouse, he wouldn't be able to talk to her about their past. He had to convince her to let him inside now.

"Sarah," he said, making his voice very firm. "I had no idea Nicholas was having trouble in school. I want to discuss this now and get started on ways to correct the problems. It's still daylight, if you're worried about what the neighbors will say."

She frowned. "I'm not worried about the neighbors," she said as he'd hoped. "I guess we'll have to sit in the parlor."

He had to try to put her at ease—at least a little. He smiled again. "The kitchen's good enough for me. I'm cold. I could use a cup of coffee. Or cocoa if it's not too much trouble. You always made the best cocoa."

She didn't comment on his remark. A faint flush staining her cheeks, she moved aside so he could enter. "Come on then."

He stepped over the threshold into the front hall. It also looked just as he remembered it. Neat, the hardwood floors polished, the cabbage-rose wallpaper a bit faded now, but still unstained.

"You've kept the place up well," he said to her

straight, retreating back as he followed her down the hall. "Is Hiram still the town handyman?"

They'd reached the kitchen. Sarah stopped in the doorway and turned to him. Her cheeks retained that touch of becoming pink.

"I suppose so. I wouldn't know."

Surprised at her answer, another thought occurred to him. What if she had a new man in her life, doing all these things he used to do? Wasn't it conceited of him to think that an attractive woman like Sarah wouldn't? It was a miracle she wasn't married.

"I do my own work."

He gave her an even more surprised glance, feeling his spirits rise, even while he knew it would be better for both of them if she was married. But of course she didn't have a serious beau. His mother would have told him.

"You do all the repairs and painting?"

She shrugged. "Yes."

Hunter frowned. "But that's too much for you with teaching school and now helping Mama out, too."

He briefly considered offering his services. No, she'd refuse instantly.

"I don't have much choice," she said crisply, turning again and entering the kitchen. "A teacher's salary doesn't stretch very far."

"That may be remedied soon. Mama's resigned from the school board and I've been appointed to finish out her term."

Dudley, president of the board, had approved his appointment, even though Hunter had just moved back to Little Bethlehem. The other members had agreed, his mother had told him yesterday. She'd said she hadn't expected anything different. He'd been gone for a long time, true, but he was still well liked in town. And the Winslow family was respected.

She hadn't added that he was also Dudley's son-in-law, which couldn't hurt, although both of them were well aware of that fact. And Hunter was uncomfortable with it.

"What do you mean?"

"Mama told me what your salary is and that you've worked for the same amount for the last five years. It's high time you had a raise."

The pink in her face increased. She straightened up and her chin went up. "I don't expect any special favors."

She was as thorny as a porcupine. Not at all how she used to be. He gave her another friendly smile. "It's no special favor. Teaching is a hard, demanding job. You certainly deserve a pay increase."

She stared at him. "You've got a lot to learn about how teachers are regarded. I'm lucky to own my house. If I didn't, I'd have to move from family to family, staying with one for a while, then another. Since women teachers must be unmarried—most of those with no families have to do that. Our salary is much less than the male teachers'."

He stared back at her, chastened and jolted by her words. He guessed he'd sounded pretty cocky.

Women teachers must be single. Was that why she'd never married? She hadn't started teaching until a year after he'd left town, so that question had never arisen during their engagement.

Sarah abruptly turned and went to the big cast-iron range across the room. She lifted a stove lid, stirred the embers with the lifter, then put in two pieces of the slab wood from the box.

Curled up in the old rocker close to the stove's

warmth was Sarah's white cat, Snowball, who glanced up, then yawned and went back to sleep. Lord, how that took him back. Sarah loved that cat. She must be getting very old by now.

Sarah reached up to the warming oven over the range and took out a blue-speckled tin saucepan. The same one she'd used all those years ago.

Her graceful movements brought another flood of memories. How many times had he watched her at the stove making some delicacy that might tempt her mother's appetite?

Or cocoa for her and him. He watched as she spooned the cocoa powder from the round red canister he remembered so well.

And how many times had his desire for her flowered as her movements stretched her dress tight across her breasts? Her rounded backside?

Hunter swallowed, pushing down these thoughts.

That wasn't why he was here, he reminded himself again.

That night there'd been no time . . . afterward . . . to talk to Sarah. Besides, anything he could have said would only have hurt her more.

And he'd been angry with her, too. Believing that part of what happened was her fault. He'd married Beryl. They'd moved at once to St. Louis . . . and then Nicholas had been born.

Over the years he'd never made an opportunity to talk to Sarah. It hadn't seemed the right thing to do. Nothing could be changed.

But things were different now. He was a widower and he was back in Little Bethlehem to stay—if that was possible. They needed to try to clear the air so that they could at least be civil with each other.

Maybe then there wouldn't be this pervasive physical awareness between them that kept them both tense and wary.

The delicious aroma of the cooking cocoa wafted to his nostrils. He sniffed appreciatively.

"Smells just the same as it always did," he told her. "You haven't lost your touch."

She flicked a glance at him. "No reason why I should have. I make cocoa all the time."

There was no nostalgic softness in her matter-of-fact voice. *Good*, he told himself. If he could achieve his goal of merely being friends with her again, that was all he wanted.

But first they had to try to lay the past to rest.

Sarah poured cocoa into two cups and moved the saucepan to the far side of the stove.

Hunter hurried forward and picked up his cup. "I can't wait to taste this."

He smiled at her with a warmer smile than any he'd given her these last two days, hoping to elicit a return smile of some warmth.

He didn't get it. Sarah picked up her own cup and took it to the big table. After a moment, Hunter followed, his mind made up to start this discussion.

He sat down, looking at her across the expanse of blue tablecloth. Her head was lowered; she was gazing into her cup as if it fascinated her.

Or to keep from looking at him.

He took a deep breath to fortify himself. "Sarah, I'd like to talk to you."

She finally raised her head. "I know. That's why you're here. We need to discuss Nicholas's learning problems."

He nodded. "Yes." He paused and took another breath and let it out. "But I want to talk about something else first."

"What?" Her voice was wary and challenging, as if she knew what he was going to say.

"About us. About what happened eight years ago."

Her face tightened. "All that's over and done with."

Hunter held her gaze. "It's over, but it isn't done with."

Two bright pink spots of color appeared on her cheeks. "What do you mean?"

"I'm sorrier than I can say that I hurt you."

Sarah pushed back her chair and got up, her hazel eyes dark with emotion. "It's eight years too late to tell me that!"

His heart sank. Just as he'd feared, deep anger still simmered beneath her calm surface. No wonder. He should have tried to talk to her a long time ago.

Hunter rose, too, and placed his hand on her arm. Even through her dress, her skin felt warm and vibrant and made him remember other times he'd touched her.

"Please sit down and listen to me," he pleaded.

Sarah shook his arm off, her eyes flashing. "Why should I? You have nothing to say that I want to hear! You decided you wanted Beryl Cunningham instead of me and you married her. Now you think you can just say you're sorry and that will make what happened all right?"

He winced at the incredulity in her angry voice. "It wasn't ... it's not that simple," Hunter said, floundering for words. "Let me try to explain."

She still stood there, glaring at him. "No," she said, each word bitten off. "The only reason I agreed to see you was to talk about Nicholas. If you don't want to do that, leave."

She wasn't going to be budged, he saw. Not now anyway. He'd have to wait until another time. And he'd have to try to smooth things over now or there might not be another time.

"I do want to talk about Nicholas," he agreed, forcing his voice to sound calm. He sat down again.

After a moment, Sarah also returned to her seat. The pink spots still burning on her cheeks, she lifted her cup and sipped her cocoa.

Hunter did the same. After a few more silent moments, he said evenly, "Nicholas's teacher last year never mentioned any problems. I wasn't aware he had any."

He heard the defensive tone in his voice and winced. "Maybe I didn't pay enough attention to him. Things were pretty rough for a while."

He winced again, not wanting her to think he was trying to play on her sympathy.

Sarah took another sip of her hot drink, then set the cup down. She gave him a direct look, her emotions under control again, her anger suppressed.

"I know. Faith told me what a struggle you had, trying to handle Nicholas and your work. Last year Nicholas was just getting started in school. But by now, the middle of second grade, it's obvious he needs extra help. Which I'm giving him. But he also needs the right kind of encouragement from you and Faith. She always brushes my concerns aside."

Hunter felt chastened. "What kind of encouragement does he need?"

"He needs to be told that he's as smart as the other children. Of course Faith does that. But he also needs to admit that he needs more help than most of the other children."

"And he doesn't?" Hunter asked. "Yesterday, he seemed to."

"Thinking he's dumb isn't accepting that he needs

help," Sarah said crisply, her level glance meeting his with no hint that only a few minutes ago she'd been so angry at him she was ready to throw him out of her house.

"Right now, he just thinks he'll be this way forever."

Hunter frowned. "I know how Mama is," he admitted. "She made me toe the line growing up, but she'd accept no criticism of me from anyone else."

Sarah bit her lip. "I don't want to say anything against Faith. She's been like a mother to me, and I love her dearly. But, yes, that's how she is with Nicholas. She just can't admit he has problems in reading and writing that need correcting while it's still relatively easy to do."

Hunter nodded. "What do you want me to do?"

Some of the tension in Sarah's face eased. "Have him read to you every evening. Faith thinks he shouldn't have to do any schoolwork at home. And have him write. He makes some of his letters backward and doesn't realize it."

"Backward?" Hunter asked, his frown deeper. "What do you mean?"

"It's like you were seeing his writing reflected in a mirror."

"I never heard of such a thing," he admitted. "But you don't think it's serious?"

"I didn't say that. I think it could be very serious if it's ignored."

Hunter felt he was in over his head. "I didn't realize Nicholas had these kinds of problems. I thought it was just a matter of him being a little slow in learning."

Sarah shook her head emphatically. "No. He's a very bright child. It has nothing to do with slowness."

"Then what does it have to do with?"

"As I said, I don't know. I haven't encountered this

before. But I believe it can be overcome, if we work with him."

"But that's just your own opinion," Hunter persisted. "You don't know for sure."

"No, I don't," she admitted. She firmed her lips again. "I work with him all I can at school when time permits. But I have the other pupils. I just can't give him all the attention he needs."

"And Mama resists the idea of you or anyone helping him at home. Thinks he should be out playing like the other kids. Is that about it?"

"Yes, it is."

Hunter lifted his cup and finished the cocoa. He'd like to stay longer. He'd like to ask for another cup. But he wouldn't. Not tonight. He didn't want to overstay his welcome.

His mouth twisted. What welcome? Sarah was truly concerned about Nicholas, but that was all. She wanted nothing to do with him on a personal level.

Personal level? That wasn't why he wanted to try to lay old ghosts to rest. They just had to get along if they were going to live in the same town.

He rose. "I'd better be going. I'll get started with Nicholas this evening. And I'll talk to Mama. She'll come around."

Sarah got up, too, relief plain on her face—some of which was because he understood about Nicholas and would help.

The rest was because his own back would soon be going out the door.

But if she thought he'd agreed to bury their past, and never refer to it again, she was wrong.

She followed him to the door. He opened it to find the wind and rain hadn't slowed down any.

"You'll get soaked," Sarah said. She went to the hall tree and took down a dark green umbrella.

"Here, take this."

"What if it's still raining tomorrow? You'll need it to go to school."

"It will probably stop. It's not far, in any case."

An idea came to him. Another opportunity to talk to her.

"Far enough to get you wet. If the rain hasn't stopped, I'll pick up in the buggy. What time do you leave?"

Her face tensed again. "You don't have to do that. I'll be fine."

He shrugged. "Then I can't take your umbrella."

Sarah huffed out her breath. She extended the umbrella toward him. "If it's raining you can pick me up. I leave about eight."

Satisfaction went through him. Hunter took the umbrella, noticing how careful she was that her hand didn't touch his.

Not that he cared. No, that was certainly best.

He suddenly became aware of how close she was to him.

It would be so easy to reach for her, to pull her into his arms and taste the sweetness of her lips against his own . . . just as he remembered their kisses from long ago . . . .

His mind froze in shock at his unbidden, unwanted thoughts.

As if she'd read them, Sarah backed up a step, her face closing down again.

They stood, looking at each other for a long moment. Hunter seemed to see something deep in Sarah's eyes besides wariness, hurt, and repressed anger. Something that used to be there . . . for him.

No, he didn't. And he didn't want to.

"Good night, Hunter," Sarah said evenly.

"Good night, Sarah."

He headed down her steps, aware she still stood in the doorway, watching him.

He'd go home, have Nicholas read to him, write for him.

And he'd pray for rain tomorrow.

CHAPTER FIVE

Her emotions in a turmoil, Sarah pulled the curtains on the front window aside and watched Hunter walk away.

He hadn't lost his confident stride, telling the world he could handle anything that came up. Even if he didn't feel cocky inside, he still gave that impression.

And maybe he did feel that sure of himself. She didn't know.

Or care, she told herself firmly. How Hunter Winslow felt was none of her concern. Which was why she'd refused to listen when he'd wanted to explain what had happened eight years ago.

She dropped the curtain. She knew she still had a lot of hidden anger, but she hadn't expected to lose her temper like that. It wouldn't happen again. Her anger could stay inside where it belonged.

She'd built a new life for herself as Little Bethlehem's schoolteacher. She was happy and content. She loved teaching and had never even been tempted to give it up for any of several would-be swains who'd wanted to court her.

She *wouldn't* let Hunter disrupt that life. Those bitter memories were buried deep inside with her anger, and they were not going to be dragged out again.

But despite her avowals, her mind insisted on returning to the night Hunter had left.

She finally stopped fighting it. All right, she'd think about it one more time, then bury the memories again. Forever.

They'd had a terrible argument. He'd begged her to marry him right away. Told her he couldn't wait any longer. They'd work something out about her mother. She refused, telling him she thought her mother was improving and would soon be well again. And then they'd be able to marry as planned.

Hunter angrily said he'd heard that a hundred times. And he didn't think it would ever happen . . . .

Sarah's heart contracted with pain. She couldn't bear to think about this even now.

She'd known Beryl had an eye for Hunter. Beryl didn't bother hiding that. But Beryl flirted with all the good-looking single men in Little Bethlehem. So Sarah didn't think anything of it.

Because she hadn't known Hunter also had an eye for Beryl.

The pain in her heart worsened.

She hadn't known Hunter had fallen in love with Beryl.

Hunter had stormed out of her mother's house. The same night he and Beryl had eloped.

Anger again surfaced from the roiling mix inside.

What hurt worst was that Hunter hadn't meant a word of what he'd said that night.

He couldn't have, since he'd left her house and, only a few hours later, run off with Beryl. His supposedly impassioned pleas for Sarah to marry him were only an act.

He knew Sarah would refuse, *must* refuse.

None of it made sense. It never had.

He wanted to talk to you tonight, explain what happened. Maybe you should have listened to him.

No! He could have no explanation that would satisfy her.

And now she would put all these hurtful memories back in a far corner of her mind and forget them.

Resolutely, she returned to the kitchen and put their cups in the dishpan. There was cocoa left. She'd have it for breakfast instead of her usual coffee. She couldn't afford to waste anything.

That thought brought back what Hunter had said about a raise in her salary. Having a little extra money to put aside for emergencies, for things she needed, maybe even for Hiram Slocum to do a few repairs would be wonderful. She couldn't deny that.

How did Hunter think he could influence the school board to raise her salary? He must know most of the members were under Dudley Cunningham's thumb. Or rather, Enid's, she amended.

Enough of this, Sarah thought. *To bed with you.* Mondays were always difficult, the children restless and more mischievous than usual after two days away from school.

After undressing, she put on her flannel nightgown, then plaited her long hair into one thick braid.

Sarah got into bed and raised the shade. If the rain had stopped, she could open the window for some

fresh air. She drew in her breath, her spirits rising.
It was snowing! How she loved the first snow. She
wished it had started earlier so she could have gone
out, her head raised to catch snowflakes on her face
and let them melt on her tongue.

Although she'd helped Faith make her front door
wreath yesterday, she hadn't had any Christmas spirit.
She'd only done it to please Faith so she could, as
usual, be the first person in town to start decorating.

But now, with the snow, she started thinking about
sleigh bells and snowmen and all the rest of the things
that added up to Christmas. For the first time since
she'd seen Hunter yesterday, a genuine smile curved
her lips.

And the rain had stopped. The snow was melting
almost as fast as it hit the ground. Hunter wouldn't
have to take her to school tomorrow morning.

Her relief should have been complete. But somehow it wasn't. It was mixed with something that felt
strangely like disappointment.

Humming to herself, Sarah slipped her cloak
around her shoulders. Most of the snow had already
melted.

Hunter wouldn't come.

She picked up her satchel, heavy with papers she'd
brought home to grade over the weekend, and went
out to the sidewalk.

Once there, she drew a breath of the fresh wintry
air and heard a buggy coming down the street at a
brisk pace. She glanced toward the sound.

Her stomach tensed as she recognized the Winslow
buggy, with Hunter holding the reins. He'd come
anyway! And alone. Where was Nicholas?

Hunter stopped before her house. Smiling, he reached over and unfastened the door on her side. "Good morning, Sarah."

His smile and expression held no hint he remembered yesterday's argument and her anger.

Fine. That was just the way she wanted it.

"Good morning, Hunter," Sarah said briskly. "You don't need to bother taking me to school."

"Oh, it's no bother," he assured her. "There's snow on the ground and I'm going that way."

He was going to be stubborn. "I'm wearing my Arctics. It's a nice day and I'll enjoy the walk."

"You're carrying a heavy load," Hunter pointed out. He kept on giving her that expectant look.

From the corner of her eye Sarah saw Tabor Reid come out of his house next door and glance her way. Like a lot of Little Bethlehem residents, Tabor shared his wife Irene's lively interest in everything that went on in town.

Sarah didn't want him listening while she argued with Hunter.

"All right," she said ungraciously.

"Good." Hunter's smile widened. He moved to his side of the seat.

Sarah got in and glanced at Tabor. He stood stock-still on the sidewalk, staring toward the buggy. Too late, she realized accepting the ride had also given him something to discuss with Irene. And probably with half the townspeople as well.

She couldn't do anything about it now. She smiled and waved at Tabor as they passed. So did Hunter. Tabor waved back, his eyes bright with interest.

"Nothing like the first snow of the season," Hunter said.

"No," Sarah agreed, easing over toward her door.

Although they weren't sitting nearly as close together as in church yesterday, the buggy's close confines somehow gave Sarah an uncomfortable feeling of intimacy.

"I looked out my window as I was getting into bed and saw it coming down and it gave me a lift," Hunter continued.

Just as she had. Just as she'd felt.

They used to bundle up and walk through the first snowfall together, holding hands and laughing.

"Not much to this one," she finally said, thankful her voice was steady.

"Nope," Hunter agreed. After a moment he said, "Mama's got company. A cousin who's staying until after Christmas. She offered to walk Nicholas to school and he jumped at the chance to get out in the snow."

Hunter's unexpected statements so surprised Sarah she glanced over at him. So that was why Nicholas wasn't with Hunter.

"When did she come? Faith didn't mention to me any relatives were planning to visit."

"Mama didn't know about it. Angela was there when I got home last night. Came in on the afternoon train, she said."

Sarah frowned. "I don't remember Faith talking about any cousins named Angela."

"Seems this one is really distant and by marriage. She's a widow, I gather. Sounds like she has no home of her own, poor soul, and just moves around from one family member to another."

"Oh. That's sad for her," Sarah said, still frowning. "But I hope Faith won't do too much to entertain her and get herself worn out. That always makes her rheumatism flare up."

Hunter laughed. The rich, full sound sent a shiver down Sarah's spine. She'd always loved Hunter's laugh. Just as she'd enjoyed hearing him talk and sing.

That was then. Now is now, she reminded herself.

"You don't have to worry about that. This woman is a little whirlwind. She had supper cooked and waiting and insisted on doing the dishes. Good cook, too."

"Oh," Sarah said again. She was no longer worried about Faith overdoing it, but something else seemed to be bothering her.

"Nicholas took right to her. He was reading to her when I got there and Mama was listening."

This woman sounded too good to be true. "Did you talk to Faith about Nicholas?"

"Yes. She agreed, but wanted to be sure Nicholas had enough outdoors playtime."

"Of course." Sarah cleared her throat. "Angela must be a young woman to have that much energy."

Hunter laughed again. "Nope. She's middle-aged, I guess. Hard to tell. She's got kind of silvery blond hair and bright blue eyes and she's round as an apple. Amazing how fast she moves around though."

The bothersome feeling vanished. "I guess she couldn't have come at a better time. Since your mother does so many extra things at Christmas, Angela will be a godsend."

"Just what I was thinking," Hunter agreed.

He drew up on the reins and the horse stopped.

"Here we are," he announced.

Surprised, Sarah realized they'd arrived at the schoolhouse. The trip she'd dreaded so much was over. And she and Hunter had talked together like old friends. Which they used to be.

What were they now? They couldn't go back to that

friendship after . . . loving each other. After Hunter's betrayal of her.

Heaviness descended on her heart again.

"Yes," she said. She turned to Hunter, forcing a smile. "Thanks for driving me."

He smiled back, his dark gaze lingering, holding hers. "You're quite welcome."

For a long moment, she couldn't draw her gaze away. Again, that little prickle moved down her spine. With a mental wrench, she jerked her head around and reached for the door handle.

"Wait a minute and I'll let you out."

"No, don't bother," Sarah said over her shoulder, determined not to look at him again. She got the door open and left the buggy so hurriedly that if anyone was glancing their way she must have looked as if someone was after her. She hoped no one was. She'd already given the town enough to gossip about for one day.

"Wait. You forgot your umbrella," Hunter called.

She turned and took it from him, careful their hands didn't touch then she hurried up the walk to the schoolhouse.

Behind her, she was conscious of Hunter's clucking to the horse and the clatter of hooves as he left.

Her fingers fumbled with the key as she tried to insert it in the lock. Finally, she dropped it, just grabbing it before it slid through a crack between the planks of the small porch.

"What is wrong with you?" she scolded herself, scooping the key up. Forcing her movements to be slow and careful, she at last got the door open and walked inside.

Compared to the warmth of the buggy, the musty chill of the unheated room hit her and she shivered.

It seemed so much colder than it had last Friday when she'd left.

It had been so cozy in the buggy. It had seemed so right to be sitting next to Hunter again on that seat she'd occupied so often in the past . . . .

Stop it! she told herself. Of course it was chilly in here. The weather had turned a lot colder.

She hurried to the front of the room and dropped her satchel on her battered old desk, then found kindling and wood and made a fire in the equally ancient cast-iron stove.

An ember shot out and hit the well-oiled plank floor. Sarah hastily stamped it out with her boot. The floor around the stove was scarred with black burn marks from similar incidents.

Shivering, she warmed her hands as the stove heated.

"Maybe I still have some physical feelings for Hunter," she said to the empty room. "That's only natural. He's the only man I ever kissed. The only man who ever held me in his arms. The only man I ever loved."

The last words echoed in her mind as well as in the room. A lump rose in her throat. Tears came to her eyes. Angrily, she brushed them away.

She squeezed her hands into fists at her sides. She *wouldn't* cry over Hunter. She *wouldn't*. All her tears had been shed years ago.

She heard the door open behind her. "Good morning, Miss Sarah," Nicholas's voice sang out.

Nicholas was always the first pupil to arrive. Frantically, she swiped at her wet cheeks and tried to draw herself together. She heard his quick steps as he came toward the front of the room.

"Good morning, Nicholas," Sarah said, turning and hoping her face was back to normal.

Halfway up the room, Nicholas beamed at her.

A short, round woman with silvery hair and bright blue eyes trotted along behind him. She gave Sarah a wide smile.

"I'm Angela Garland, a cousin of Faith's."

Nicholas reached his desk in the front row and put the reading book and lunch bucket he carried on top; then he sat down.

Angela Garland had arrived at the front of the room now and extended her hand. Sarah took it, surprised at the strength and warmth of the small woman's grip.

"I'm Sarah Calder," Sarah answered, relieved. She must look all right. The other woman's expression didn't show any curiosity or shock.

Angela nodded. "Oh, I know who you are. Faith spent all evening singing your praises."

Sarah felt uncomfortable.

"According to Faith you've helped her out so much this last year. I hope I can take some of the burden from you. What with the Christmas pageant to manage along with teaching school, you must not have a spare minute. Now you just tell me what you need help with."

Sarah stared at her, feeling a bit overwhelmed at the other woman's volubility and willingness to work. "I wish there were more people like you in Little Bethlehem," she blurted.

Angela laughed, a robust sound that made Sarah feel warm inside. "Oh, I bet you're going to be amazed at how many people volunteer this year."

"Angela says I can be in the pageant," Nicholas said, pride in his voice.

Surprise again went through Sarah. As shy as Nicholas was, as uncomfortable as he felt with the other children, she hadn't even thought about offering him a part.

And it wasn't Angela's place to do that, but strangely, Sarah didn't feel annoyed. Somehow, she knew Angela had only Nicholas's welfare at heart.

She glanced at him, not knowing what to say. Nicholas's smile was as proud as his voice had been.

"He'll do just fine," Angela said, her voice confident.

Sarah turned to her, not able to keep a worried frown from her face.

Angela's blue eyes gazed straight into Sarah's. "He needs to have someone believe in him so he can believe in himself," she said softly.

Sarah realized her thoughts and feelings had changed from a few moments ago. "You're right," she said, nodding. "You're absolutely right."

She glanced at Nicholas again. "I know just the part for you. One of the Wise Men."

Out of the corner of her eye, she saw Angela's approving nod.

The door opened again, and several children trooped in, laughing and talking. They stared at Angela curiously.

"I'd better be getting back to Faith's," Angela said, smiling warmly at the children.

They smiled back just as warmly. Even Walter Darby, the worst troublemaker in school.

"Remember, I'm ready and willing to work. Do you need help with the costumes? I'm pretty good with my needle, if I do say so myself."

Sarah closed her eyes. Her prayers had been answered.

"Mrs. Randolph always does the costumes. It would be so kind of you to give her a hand."

"Ah, yes—a good-hearted soul if ever I saw one."

"She is that," Sarah agreed, wondering how Angela had already managed to meet Gladys.

"Well, good-bye for now." Angela gave Sarah and the children another smile and left, leaving Sarah staring after her.

Despite the turmoil of emotions that had been roiling inside her when Nicholas and Angela came in, for some reason now she felt calmer, as if things weren't really as bad as she'd thought. How could she feel that way? she asked herself, astonished.

Hunter was back to stay. How would she be able to live here, knowing she'd see him often and have to be polite and not let him realize how much she still hurt inside.

How much she was still drawn to him despite everything that had happened.

She could do it. She had to—or move away. She'd avoid him as much as possible and wait for these unwanted feelings to disappear.

Avoiding him would be difficult. She was committed to helping Faith on Saturdays. And Hunter would be there for the noon meal. A meal Faith would certainly insist she share after cooking it.

She firmed her mouth. She'd get everything ready early and, despite Faith's protests, leave before noon.

It would be awkward, but she'd manage.

A thought struck Sarah. Angela was helping Faith with the housework and cooking.

Maybe she wouldn't have to go to Faith's house for a few weeks . . . wouldn't have to worry about encountering Hunter . . . .

What about after Angela leaves? her mind asked. *You'll get back into your regular routine again.*

Yes, and besides, she couldn't just stop going to Faith's house. Faith's feelings would be hurt and Sarah would miss her too much to stop seeing her.

Never mind. She had a few weeks' reprieve. She'd figure out something else when she had to.

CHAPTER SIX

"You won't have to stand still much longer."

Angela gave Nicholas a wide smile. She knelt beside the boy in the back room of the church, pinning up the bottom of a length of tan fabric that was draped around him.

"I don't mind." Nicholas smiled back at her.

Angela's smiles were so comforting, Sarah thought, glancing up from a sheet of paper listing the pageant volunteers, they made a person feel good inside.

It was strange how, after only a few days, it seemed as if Angela had been here in Little Bethlehem forever.

She'd somehow met practically everyone in town already. And everyone liked her. How could anyone help liking her?

Nicholas seemed to regard her as a favorite aunt and she treated him exactly as if she were.

Amazingly, everything to do with the pageant was working as smoothly as clockwork this year. Angela had somehow persuaded Gladys Randolph to let Angela go ahead with all the fitting and measuring for the children's costumes. Angela was much better at the job than Gladys.

Even Enid was easier to get along with when Angela was around.

Sarah knew she should be content. She should be happy. And she was. Of course she was. In a few weeks she'd feel better. Once she got used to the idea of Hunter being here to stay.

How you lie, her mind told her. *You'll never be happy or content again with Hunter living in Little Bethlehem. Not that you were happy when he wasn't here either, no matter what you say.*

"Is something wrong, Sarah dear?" Angela asked, concern in her voice. "You must be tired after teaching most of the day and then coming over here afterward to work."

Sarah glanced up, forcing a smile. "I'm fine. Just woolgathering."

"I don't see any wool that you're gathering," Nicholas said, looking puzzled.

Nicholas was the only child here at the moment, and he was a different boy from when he was in her classroom. He got along so much better with adults than with other children. Probably because adults never teased him.

"It's invisible wool," Sarah answered, trying to lighten her mood by joking with Nicholas. "Only a few people can see it."

Nicholas nodded. "Oh, like the rings Grandma Faith says you can work around her?"

Sarah had to laugh, remembering last Saturday in Faith's kitchen. "Yes, kind of like that, I guess."

"Woolgathering. Now I wonder how that expression originated," Angela said.

Her wise blue eyes seemed to take in all the implications of the scene and understand everything without being told.

"I haven't the slightest idea," Sarah confessed.

Behind Sarah, the room's door opened and closed. Sarah tensed, hoping it wasn't Enid. If so, she'd probably try to take Nicholas home with her. And Hunter didn't want that unless he knew about it first.

"You look busy. Nicholas, that robe makes you look wiser already."

Hunter's voice made Sarah start and her tension grew. She hadn't expected him to come for Nicholas. She hadn't even realized he knew Nicholas would be here. Most fathers didn't keep such close tabs on their children.

But then, Hunter wasn't like most fathers. And maybe he was trying to make up for the months he had been in St. Louis and hadn't seen very much of his son.

"I don't feel any wiser," Nicholas said, his voice echoing Hunter's light, bantering tone.

She heard Hunter's footsteps on the bare wood floor and in a few moments he'd reached their little group.

Sarah turned her head toward him and forced a smile. "Hello, Hunter."

"Hello."

His smile looked easy and natural. Did he feel that way or was he only pretending? Deep inside, was he tied up in knots just as she was, anger battling with attraction?

No, no reason for him to be angry. *She* hadn't betrayed *him*.

"Oh, my, yes. He's plenty wise," Angela agreed. Her smile, too, looked effortless and as warm as her voice.

Hunter's dark eyes gleamed and his hair glistened in the late afternoon light coming through the windows. Glistened too much. Sarah glanced toward the west window and saw rain slanting against the panes.

"I've come to take everyone home," Hunter said. "Cold rain coming down—may turn to snow."

"We're about finished," Angela said. "Just let me put in a few more pins."

"Of course. I don't mind waiting." Hunter glanced around, then seated himself beside Sarah on the small settee she occupied.

His coat sleeve brushed her dress sleeve, sending a small shiver through her. He was much too close. She started to move away from him the few inches possible, then changed her mind.

Angela was looking right at her. Sarah forced her smile to stay in place, praying it wasn't all too obvious how unsettled Hunter's nearness made her feel.

Unless Faith had told her, Angela knew nothing about Sarah and Hunter's past. She'd like to keep it that way.

But Angela's bright glance was disconcerting. Maybe Faith had told her after all. Or Gladys. Or any of a dozen other people. Sarah's tension eased a bit when Angela returned to her pinning.

Hunter's warmth seeped into Sarah. It felt so good . . . so comforting somehow. How could that be? She didn't know and didn't care. She just wanted to keep on sitting here. She wanted Hunter to turn to her . . . to fold her in his arms . . . to kiss her . . . .

"There, all done for the moment."

Sarah came to herself with a start, horrified at her

thoughts. Either she or Hunter had moved because they were now so close together their bodies touched all along their sides. She felt warmer and somehow more comforted than she had in years.

Quickly, she rose, stuffing her list into the satchel of papers she had to grade that evening. No use arguing with Hunter about riding with him. She hadn't brought her umbrella and she'd look like a fool refusing the offer in this kind of weather.

Today, Hunter had an umbrella, and a few minutes later they were all bundled on the buggy seat. Sarah gave thanks that Nicholas sat beside his father, with Angela next. She herself was against the door, all ready to slip out when he reached her house.

No matter how she tried, she couldn't keep her thoughts from returning to those moments that had just passed in the church. She'd felt as she used to when she and Hunter were engaged. All that had happened since had vanished from her mind. She'd wanted nothing more than to stay there close to him forever . . . .

"Here we are," Angela's cheerful voice announced, bringing Sarah back into the present.

She reached for her satchel, then glanced up. The buggy sat before the Winslow house, not hers.

Hunter had already slid out of his seat and Nicholas and Angela did the same from his side.

After their good-byes, Hunter held his umbrella over Angela's and Nicholas's heads and escorted them to the front porch.

He'd arranged that very cleverly. Well, there was a wide space between them on the seat, and it would stay wide while he drove her home.

Angela and Nicholas went inside and Hunter came

back to the buggy, looking pleased. He seated himself, then got the horse going again.

"Hope this turns into snow," he said cheerfully. "Sunday's could hardly be counted." He chuckled. "Guess I'm crazy. Snow just makes it hard to get through the streets."

He smelled of fresh air and rain. Along with his own masculine essence. Sarah realized she was drawing deep breaths, enjoying the scent.

She felt his glance on her and couldn't stop her head from turning toward him.

His smile still lingered. His glance moved over her face. "We always used to enjoy the snow, didn't we?"

Pain returned as memories assailed her. "I don't want to talk about anything in our past." Her voice was sharp. Good.

Hunter's smile faded, but he didn't turn away. "I know you don't, but we'll have to eventually."

"No, we won't!" she refuted.

"Yes, we will," Hunter insisted. "I wish you'd agree it could be now."

Sarah's heart began thumping. Her hand settled on the door latch. "Just pull over to the side and I'll get out and walk the rest of the way."

Hunter huffed out his breath. "I won't say any more now. Just relax."

As if she could. Sarah drew a few shallow breaths, trying to get her emotions under control.

"Nicholas has been reading and writing for me the last couple of days," Hunter said after a few moments of silence.

"Good," Sarah answered, relief filling her at the change of subject.

"He doesn't like to do either of those things, but

he enjoys listening to stories. And he's good at arith-
metic.''

"Yes," Sarah agreed. "That's why I think he'll be
fine once he gets over this problem."

"You don't know how grateful I am that you're
here," Hunter said.

Sarah threw him a startled glance when she found
him looking at her again. With a different expression
on his face, in his dark eyes.

"To help him so much," he went on.

Sarah shrugged, looking down at her lap. "Of
course I've tried to help him. After all, I'm his teacher.
That's my job."

"But not every teacher would spend extra time with
a student," Hunter insisted. "If you hadn't recognized he was having problems, he might have convinced himself he was just dumb and could never
learn."

Sarah glanced up at Hunter again. The intent
expression was still in his eyes. "That's what worries
me. He has those feelings already."

"But they're not bone deep yet," Hunter said with
conviction. "And with both of us working on it, we'll
get him over them."

With both of us working on it. Hunter's words sounded
so much like something he might have said all those
years ago when they were engaged.

Stop it! she told herself sternly. "Yes," she finally
said.

"Good. I'm glad we agree. Here we are," he said
again, pulling up on the reins.

Sarah saw they'd arrived at her house. She pushed
down an absurd feeling of disappointment they were
here so soon.

Before she could react, he was around at the buggy door on her side and had it and the umbrella open.

Sarah picked up her satchel and got out. "You don't have to walk with me. It's only a few steps to the porch."

Hunter didn't budge. Had she really thought he would? "And those few steps would get you soaked."

"I won't melt," she snapped.

His look was serious. "Are you sure? Aren't girls supposed to be made of sugar and spice and everything nice?"

She drew a sharp breath. She'd forgotten how he liked to tease . . . how he used to say things like that to her . . . .

A smile hovered over his mouth again. How she'd loved the shape of his mouth. She'd often traced the outline of his lips with her finger . . . .

Stop that! she told herself again, dismayed at her lack of control over her thoughts.

"I'm hardly a girl," she reminded him, her voice cool.

Hunter's dark gaze swept her from the top of her cloak-covered head to her booted feet. "You could have fooled me," he said softly.

His voice trembled through her as if each word touched a nerve.

"Here, let me take that."

Before she could protest, he'd taken her satchel. She could do nothing except walk beside him under the umbrella's shelter.

For some reason the umbrella seemed awfully small now. They kept bumping against each other all the way up the steps and across the porch. Each time they touched, Sarah flinched and trembled again.

At the door, hoping he hadn't noticed, she forced a smile and reached for the satchel. "Thanks so much."

Hunter didn't relinquish his hold. He gave her a hurt, surprised look. "Aren't you even going to ask me in and offer me a hot drink? After all, it is a cold and rainy afternoon."

Yes, let him come in, some weak part of her urged. *You want that—you know you do.*

No! She didn't. She wasn't that big a fool.

"I've a lot of papers to grade this evening." She fought the tremor creeping into her voice as well as her body. "And I'm sure Faith will have a hot drink waiting for you."

Hunter closed the umbrella with a snap. Drops of water flew out of the folds and landed on Sarah's face.

He moved a step nearer. "Sorry about that." He reached in an inner pocket and drew out a big white handkerchief. "Let me dry you."

"It's all right," Sarah protested, moving a step back.

Hunter followed, his hand already touching her face.

Even through the handkerchief, the warmth of his hand flowed into her, following nerve paths all the way down her body. As she savored the sensation, her eyes involuntarily closed.

Hunter's touch felt so wonderful. How she'd missed it . . . . How she had longed to feel it again . . . .

"Sarah," he said softly.

His warm breath was so close it stirred a tendril of hair at her temple. She shivered. His hand moved from her cheek down to her mouth. One finger traced the outline of her lips, just as she'd imagined touching him a few moments ago. His finger left a trail of fire in its wake.

Step back. Go inside, the sensible part of her mind urged. Yes, she should do that. Instead, she moved closer to him.

"Sarah," he said again, an unutterable longing in his soft voice.

She responded to that instead of her prudent inner voice. Her eyelids fluttered open as she lifted her head. The expression on his face took her breath away. The yearning in his voice was also in his features.

"Hunter," she said, her voice even softer than his.

With a groan he lowered his head. His lips touched hers. She felt as if for years she'd been parched for water and now had taken the first tiny sip from a sweet, clear spring.

She wanted more . . . much more.

Hunter's arms enfolded her. He pulled her against his damp coat, and his mouth covered hers, the kiss deepening and deepening . . . until they were lost in that private world they used to share . . . .

Sarah's fingers moved over the rough wool of his coat. She heard his quick, shallow breaths . . . felt the bunching of his muscles as he strained to pull her closer into his embrace . . . .

A loud noise came from somewhere close by. What was it? A whistle?

Sarah left her dreamworld with a gasp. She jerked out of Hunter's arms and stepped away from him.

For a long moment she stood staring at him in shocked disbelief.

He didn't look at all shocked. No, he looked as if he was going to come after her and pull her into his arms again.

Turning, Sarah jerked open the unlocked door, hurried inside, and closed the door. She leaned against it, her breath coming hard and fast.

Hunter didn't try to enter. He didn't pound on the door or say anything. After a few moments, she heard his footsteps go down the steps and then the *clop-clop* of the horse's hooves as the buggy moved away.

Sarah kept on standing against the door for a while after the sounds had died away.

"You are a fool, Sarah Calder," she scolded herself. "A complete, utter fool."

She began to shiver, as if from deep cold. She needed a hot drink herself. Starting for the kitchen, she remembered her satchel.

It was right outside the door, where Hunter had left it.

Who had passed by whistling? Had the person seen her standing shamelessly on her front porch embracing the man who'd jilted her so cruelly by marrying another woman without so much as a word?

Old, familiar pain ground through her again.

Sarah glanced around and saw no one. She didn't even see a curtain move at any of the nearby houses on the street.

She snatched up the satchel and walked to the kitchen, head up, back straight.

She'd cook herself some supper and spend the evening grading these papers. She'd forget that kiss had ever happened.

And she would never accept another ride from Hunter or let him get as far as her porch again.

In the kitchen, she lifted the stove lid, stirred the ashes through the grating, then built a new fire, all the while conscious of doing these same things when Hunter had been here a few days ago.

Hunter . . . . Oh, how good, how right, it had felt

to be in his arms again. To have his lips pressed against hers . . .

Forcibly, she closed those thoughts off. It wasn't right. It could never be right again.

She couldn't take the chance of having to bear that kind of pain again.

It would kill her this time.

What makes you think Hunter wants to renew anything? the sensible part of her brain asked coldly. *He only kissed you . . . and you kissed him back. All that proves is that you're still sensually drawn to each other.*

Which she already knew—and which didn't mean anything important. So that was fine. All she had to do was make sure nothing like this happened again.

And she'd be safe.

She grabbed a pan and poured apple cider in it to heat, vainly trying to close out the taunting voice that told her she'd never be safe again as long as both she and Hunter lived in Little Bethlehem.

CHAPTER SEVEN

Sarah glanced toward Nicholas, who was standing under a tree.

It was the noon recess and all the children were in the schoolyard. Nicholas was playing by himself as usual, but at least none of the boys was teasing him. She had to force herself not to go stand with him, but knew she mustn't single him out as her favorite or he'd have an even worse time.

Her glance swept the schoolyard. Some boys were shooting marbles. Girls stood around and talked and giggled in small groups. Everything was all right.

Thoughts of yesterday evening drifted through Sarah's mind: Hunter's lips on hers . . . warm and soft and yet seeking . . . .

She forced the thoughts away for the dozenth time today. Hunter hadn't dropped off Nicholas this morning. Angela had, instead.

What did that mean? That he wanted to avoid her?

That the kiss was an impulsive act he now regretted? Wasn't that what she wanted him to feel?

Stop this nonsense and tend to your business, she told herself.

Sarah again glanced over toward Nicholas. He was fine.

A commotion across the schoolyard drew her attention.

Roger Kane had Walter Darby down and was flailing at him while an interested group of children gathered around.

"Walter! Roger! Stop that this instant." Sarah hurried toward the two boys.

In a way, she hated to intervene because Walter was bigger than Roger and a bully. Apparently, Roger had finally had enough of being teased and taunted and had decided to do something about it.

But since she was the teacher she had to stop the fight. If you could call it that. Walter was squalling to high heaven while Roger pummeled him.

Sarah reached the group. "That's enough now," she said, forcing sternness into her voice as she pulled Roger off Walter.

Walter had a bloody nose, but otherwise seemed none the worse. It would probably do him good. She hoped so anyway.

She knelt and wiped the blood off Walter's nose and face with her handkerchief.

His squalls had subsided to blubbering "You gotta paddle Roger, Miss Sarah," he said. "He knocked me down and wouldn't stop hitting me."

Sarah gave him a level look. "Are you sure you didn't do anything to him first?"

"No, ma'am. I wasn't doing nothing," Walter said, a look of wide-eyed innocence on his face.

"Liar! You were, too." His fists still balled up, and glowering like a thundercloud, Roger started toward the other boy.

Walter shrank back. "Don't let him hit me again, Miss Sarah," he begged.

Sarah bit her lip to hide a smile she couldn't stop. She made her voice commanding. "Roger, that's enough."

Roger subsided, but now that he'd overcome his fear of the bigger boy, he was clearly ready to continue his triumph.

"Come on, Walter. Get up. You're not really hurt," Sarah said.

Walter shot one more apprehensive glance toward Roger, then struggled to his feet.

A scream suddenly came from the group of onlookers, which now seemed to include nearly all the children.

Lily Hawkins, Sarah thought, sighing. Lily screamed at frequent intervals about anything she considered remotely threatening.

"What's wrong, Lily?" Sarah asked, glancing at her.

The girl's eyes were wide, her mouth hanging open. She pointed to the school building. "Miss Calder, look at all the smoke! The schoolhouse is on fire!"

"What?" Sarah turned her head, expecting to see only the usual plume of smoke coming from the building's chimney.

Her breath caught. Dark smoke billowed out the open door and windows.

Oh, Lord, Lily was right. Were all the children accounted for?

Quickly, Sarah glanced around the group, then toward the tree where Nicholas had been standing.

He was gone.

Sarah's heart lurched with fear. "Have any of you seen Nicholas?"

"I saw him go back inside the schoolhouse," Lonnie Brown said.

Sarah ran toward the building, her heart pounding with fear. The children ran behind her. Nicholas must have slipped away while she was settling the fight. It seemed to take forever to reach the one-room building.

At the door, she stopped, her fear increasing as the black smoke billowed out, making her cough. She couldn't see a thing inside. But Nicholas must still be in there. She had to get him out.

"Stay back, children!" Sarah told the hovering group.

She took a deep breath, held her handkerchief to her nose, and crouching, moved cautiously inside, searching for a glimpse of Nicholas.

Stronger fear clutched at her. She could see him nowhere. "Nicholas!" she called. "Where are you?"

Only silence answered. "Nicholas!" she called again, fighting the panic threatening to overwhelm her. "Can you hear me? Answer me!"

A cough came from the direction of the cloakroom. "Miss Sarah . . . I'm in here."

Thank God he was still conscious. Sarah took a few shallow breaths, then plunged toward the cloakroom and inside. For a few moments she could see nothing; then she made out a huddled shape against the far wall.

Crawling, staying as low as she could, she hurried toward the shape. Smoke slid down her throat and into her lungs. Time slowed to an agonizing creep. Would she ever get there?

Finally, she reached the shape. Nicholas, thank God!

He was too heavy for her to carry. She found one of his hands and pulled him to his knees. Even through the smoke, she could see the fear in his eyes.

"Hold on to my hand," she said urgently. "I'll lead you out."

Nicholas coughed again; then to her relief his grip on her hand tightened.

"Stay low and hang on tight. Hold this over your nose and mouth." She handed him the handkerchief.

Taking in tiny, shallow breaths, Sarah crawled toward the doorway. Smoke was so thick now she couldn't see the door and had to rely on where she thought it was.

Behind her, she heard a crash that sounded like part of the roof. Again, she fought panic, thankful none of the other children had ventured inside after her.

Or had they? Would she even have known if any of them had?

Over the crackling of the flames she heard shouting outside. Through the smoke, she made out a shape where she thought the door should be.

Oh, no! One of the children was coming into this inferno.

"Go back!" she shouted, then coughing overcame her. She felt blackness threatening and desperately gripped Nicholas's hand.

"Don't let go!"

"I won't," he answered; then a coughing fit hit him, too.

"Sarah, where are you?" a voice shouted.

Hunter's voice? How could that be? Sarah wondered fuzzily. Hunter wasn't here.

Strong arms suddenly gripped her. "Let's get out of here."

It *was* Hunter. Relief filled her. "Have you got Nicholas?" she whispered.

"Yes."

Sarah coughed again and felt herself sagging against Hunter; then everything in her head went as black as the smoke surrounding her.

" . . . Sarah, wake up," a voice said, its tone commanding. It seemed to be far away. Too far to pay any attention to . . .

She didn't want to wake . . . too much effort. It was so easy just to lie here in this dark warmth . . . .

Suddenly she was turned onto her stomach. Strong hands pounded roughly on her back.

"Stop. That hurts," she mumbled; then a coughing fit came again. She coughed until it took her breath away, and once more everything started going black.

"Take some deep breaths to clear out your lungs," a voice said.

Hunter's voice. Where was she and why was Hunter telling her these things? She tried to do what he'd said, but the deep breaths hurt her chest.

"That's fine," the voice approved. "Take more breaths."

She did and it didn't hurt so much this time. Gradually, the blackness faded away, and her breathing evened out.

Sarah turned over on her back and opened her eyes. Hunter leaned over her, a worried frown on his face.

With a rush, everything came back. The roar of flames was deafening. She glanced toward the school. The fire wagon was there, and men were throwing buckets of water on the flames, to no avail. The building was completely engulfed.

When she struggled to get up, Hunter gently but firmly restrained her.

"Nicholas! How is he? Are all the children safe?"

Hunter nodded. The worried expression faded and was replaced by a relieved smile. "Yes, no one was hurt. Nicholas is fine, thanks to you. See, here he is."

He nodded to one side and Sarah saw Nicholas standing a few feet away. His face and clothes were soot streaked, but he looked all right otherwise.

"How are you, Miss Sarah?" His voice trembled.

Sarah's fears receded. She managed a smile. "I'm fine," she assured him before another coughing fit caught her.

Hunter's strong hands gently held her until the paroxysm was over. Sarah struggled to sit up and this time he allowed her to.

A crowd of people milled about the schoolyard. Children cried, and mothers had their arms around the smaller ones, comforting them.

It looked like everyone in town was here.

Including Enid and Crystal, searching the crowd with frightened eyes.

Enid's glance found their group. She grabbed her daughter's arm and hurried toward them.

Enid stooped before Nicholas, flung her cloak-clad arms around him, and drew him tightly against her ample chest. "Oh, my poor baby!" she wailed. "I just heard you almost died in there!"

"I'm fine," Nicholas mumbled. He struggled to get out of her confining grip, and finally Enid let him move back a little.

Enid stood and glared at Sarah. "How could you allow such a thing to happen?" she demanded. "Your carelessness could have cost the lives of not only my grandson, but of all these children!''

Sarah gaped at her, speechless with shock at the unexpected attack.

"Enid, that will be enough." Hunter's face was set in tight lines. "If it wasn't for Sarah, Nicholas could have died in the fire."

Enid flung her head back. "If Sarah was properly taking care of things, there would have been no fire in the first place."

Sarah gasped, her shock deepening. "It was noon recess," she said. "I was out in the schoolyard with the children. A spark must have started it. The floor is old and dry."

Enid sniffed. "Then you should never have left the building with the fire going full blast."

A sudden wave of dizziness hit Sarah. She felt as if she were going to lose consciousness again. No, she couldn't. Not now. She fought the feeling and it finally receded.

"The fire wasn't going full blast. And I have to watch the children when they're outside," Sarah finally said, hearing the unsteadiness in her voice.

"Why was Nicholas in the school building with everyone else out here?" Enid demanded, still glaring at Sarah. "And why didn't you know he was in there? Doesn't sound like you do a very good job of supervising."

"There are twenty-five children," Sarah said, desperately trying to hold herself together. "Two of the older boys were fighting. After I settled that, I noticed Nicholas was gone. By that ti—"

"Never mind trying to explain your incompetence, *Miss* Calder," Enid interrupted, her voice even frostier. "We pay you to be responsible for these children and you're supposed to do your job, not whine about how you can't.''

His face stony, Hunter stepped in front of Sarah, blocking her from Enid. "I said that's enough. Sarah could have died herself rescuing Nicholas. Stop haranguing her.''

Sarah couldn't see Enid now, but she heard the other woman's outraged gasp. "How dare you talk to me like that, Hunter Winslow.''

Hunter folded his arms across his chest. "This is no time to barge in here and spout all this nonsense. Nicholas and Sarah need rest. I'm taking them home right now.''

Again, Sarah heard Enid's gasp of outraged disbelief. "If you think this is the end of the matter, you're sadly mistaken, Hunter. Sarah isn't a fit person to teach in this school. And I'm going to see that she doesn't teach another day here.''

Sarah's heart stopped, then started beating furiously. She tried to push her way around Hunter, but he reached out an arm to stop her.

"Leave it be, Sarah. You're in no condition to get into an argument with Enid about her ridiculous accusations.''

"Ridiculous? We'll see how ridiculous they are when I have Dudley call a meeting of the school board. I'm sure everyone will see the wisdom of appointing a truly qualified teacher like my Crystal.''

"I doubt that very much,'' Hunter said, his voice cold as ice. "I'm a member of the board now, too, in case you've forgotten, and I certainly won't vote in any such manner.''

"Yours will be only one vote,'' Enid said, her voice still furious. "The other members will see how sensible our plan is. Especially when we can offer them a building to use as a schoolhouse since this one is totally destroyed.''

Sarah turned her head toward the burning building. She'd known even before Enid's words that the building was gone. Flames still shot up, but only the chimney and part of the roof were left. Even while she watched, the roof tumbled into the flames with a crash that turned her stomach over.

Her life was crashing down, destroyed as the fire had destroyed the schoolhouse. How could she hope to fight against the power and influence the Cunninghams wielded in Little Bethlehem? Her family had lived here for generations and were of respectable stock. But they'd never had any power or influence or much money.

And none of them were left now except her.

"Mama, I don't want to teach school." Crystal's light, high voice, now agitated, came to Sarah's ears.

"Hush your mouth, child. You don't know what's best for you. That's what your father and I are here for.''

Hunter suddenly turned toward Sarah. The lines of his face were hard. "Let's go.''

Sarah nodded, tight lipped, trying to hold back the tears that threatened to overflow.

"Come along, son," Hunter told Nicholas.

Sarah stepped forward, swaying a little. Hunter put his arm around her waist, supporting her. The trio walked by Enid and Crystal. Enid still glared.

"You're not going to have the last word on this, Hunter Winslow, and don't you forget it," she flung at their backs.

Hunter didn't answer, but his hand curved around Sarah's waist tightened. She shivered.

"Are you cold? Here, take my coat.''

His coat slid around her shoulders before she could protest. It was still warm from his body. She shivered again.

Hunter didn't miss it. "I'd better get Doc Lawson over to take a look at you. I'm amazed he isn't here. Half the town seems to be."

Yes, or more than half, Sarah thought. And all of them had heard Enid's angry words. Did they, too, believe she'd been careless, neglectful of the children's lives? Some would, of course. Others would accept Enid's judgment just because of who she was.

"I'm fine," Sarah said, trying to inject firmness into her voice. "I don't need the doctor."

"You're getting him. I don't intend to take any chances."

They'd reached Hunter's buggy. Carefully, he helped Sarah onto the seat, then Nicholas. In a few moments they were heading down the street. They passed people hurrying the other way, toward the fire, anticipation of excitement in their faces.

Sarah's mood darkened. Little Bethlehem usually offered its inhabitants little drama in their daily lives. This would be talked about for months. And right now, Enid would have more people to bend to her views.

Another, even more depressing thought went through Sarah's mind. Would people think she'd left in a hurry because she couldn't face anyone? That she *had* been careless and irresponsible?

"Daddy, why is Grandmama Enid so mad at Miss Sarah?" Nicholas's voice, trembling with bewilderment and exhaustion, asked.

For a moment, Hunter didn't answer. Then Sarah heard him draw in a breath and let it out in a sigh. "Don't worry about it, son. Your grandmother was upset about you maybe being hurt, just like Miss Sarah and I were. She'll get over it and everything will be all right."

How she wished Hunter's words were true. Not just soothing reassurances for Nicholas. She didn't believe that though, and she didn't think Hunter did either.

But despite her raw, burning throat and her emotional turmoil over Enid's threats, comfort was seeping into her shaky body from Hunter's warmth so close beside her.

If she was honest, more than comfort. The memory of yesterday's kiss crept back into her mind . . . her heart and her soul.

She didn't have either the emotional or physical strength to banish it. Instead she let the memory, the feelings the kiss had aroused, spread inside her. Warm her even more.

"Miss Sarah, are you all right?"

Nicholas's small, scared voice jolted her out of her musings. She realized her eyes were closed and quickly opened them and forced a smile as she turned to the child.

His face was set in anxious lines as he stared at her.

She squeezed his shoulder. "I'm fine, honey. Just a little tired and shook up, I guess."

He nodded, his face clearing. "Me, too."

"You're both going to rest," Hunter said, his voice decisive.

Rest? How could she rest, knowing she probably would no longer have her teaching job?

What would she do?

Hunter pulled on the reins and the buggy stopped.

Bleakness filled Sarah at the thought of entering her silent, empty house. A wave of the shaky light-headedness hit her again and again she fought it off.

She took off Hunter's coat and turned to him. "Thank you."

Then she saw they were at the Winslow house.

Her eyes widened. She shook her head at Hunter.

He gave her a firm look. "Don't argue. I'm going to have Doc Lawson look you over. Nicholas, too. And I don't want you by yourself until he does."

She started to protest, then closed her mouth as a wave of fatigue swept over her. Truth to tell, she didn't want to be alone today either. Or tonight.

"All right," she agreed.

Angela was at the front door before Hunter had it open. She clucked at the sight of Sarah and Nicholas, but didn't look surprised at their bedraggled appearance.

"Let's get you two to bed, where you belong." She put her arms around both Sarah and Nicholas.

"I don't need to be in bed," Sarah protested. A renewed wave of faintness swept over her, making her last words shaky.

"Of course you do."

Sarah closed her eyes, letting Angela's soothing voice wash over her, mingle with another, stronger wave of faintness.

Then Sarah crumpled to her knees and the blackness overcame her again.

Softness and warmth enveloped her from head to foot. Sarah snuggled deeper. It felt so good, so comforting, she wanted to sink into it and stay forever . . . .

But something nagged at the back of her mind, telling her she had to get up. That she couldn't stay here. There was something she had to do . . . .

She resisted, but finally let herself swim up through the layers of consciousness.

Her throat was raw and sore. Her body ached all over. And this bed wasn't her own.

Sarah opened her eyes and gazed around at the white curtains, the blue-flowered wallpaper, the walnut bureau across the room.

This wasn't her house or her bedroom, but it wasn't unfamiliar either. She'd dusted and swept this room many a time. It was one of Faith's two spare bedrooms. Angela slept in the other one now.

Vague memories drifted into her mind. Angela had put her to bed here, Faith hovering nearby. And Hunter had been somewhere nearby, too. Then Dr. Lawson had bent over her, telling her to wake up for a minute. He'd taken her pulse . . . lifted her eyelids . . . .

Then everyone had gone away and left her to sleep again, but she'd known they weren't far away . . . that if she cried out, someone would be here in a moment. It had given her such a warm, comforted feeling.

She wasn't alone anymore, as she'd been since her mother's death. She was surrounded by people who loved her, were concerned for her.

Sarah swam up through the last layer into full consciousness. She remembered the fire, Enid's angry threats.

The warm feelings dissipated.

Bleakness replaced them.

She glanced over at the side window. Early morning sun streamed through. She must have slept all the rest of the day and night.

What had happened while she slept? Had Enid made good on her threats?

Sarah pushed the covers back and slid her legs,

covered with one of Faith's voluminous flannel night-gowns, over the side of the bed.

The door opened. Angela bustled in, beaming. "You're awake. Good, good. And you're looking much better this morning. I saved some breakfast for you. Do you feel like coming down? I can bring it up here if you'd rather."

"No. Of course I'll come down. But I'm not very hungry."

Angela's beam didn't waver. "You will be when you're up and about for a few minutes and smell the food."

Sarah slid her feet to the floor and stood. Her head swam for a moment and her knees felt shaky, but she pressed her lips together, determined not to let Angela see any signs of weakness.

"I have to get home. Snowball will be starving."

"Don't worry about your cat. Hunter went over and fed her yesterday evening. She's just fine."

"Oh. Well, I have to get home anyway."

Sarah swallowed the sudden lump in her throat. With an effort of will she kept herself from swaying.

"I have to go home," she repeated.

Angela had reached her side by now. Gently, she eased Sarah back down on the side of the bed.

"There, there. Don't fret over that. Dr. Lawson said you need to rest for a few days. And that he thought it was a fine idea for you to do your resting right here in this bed where we can look after you."

"I don't need anyone to look after me," Sarah protested. "I've been taking care of myself for a long time."

"Maybe too long," Angela said softly. "Everyone needs to be looked after sometimes. Now you don't want to disobey the doctor's orders, do you?"

"I'm *fine*," Sarah said, trying to make her voice firm and forceful and failing. It sounded as wobbly as she felt.

She heard a noise from across the room and looked up.

Hunter stood in the doorway. He looked pale and tired and the smile on his face seemed pasted on. "Good morning, Sarah."

"Enid had her way, didn't she?" Sarah asked. "They gave Crystal my school."

Hunter's smile didn't waver. He shook his head.

"No, Sarah. Nothing's been decided. I'm sure everything will turn out all right. Stop worrying and get some more rest."

His voice sounded too hearty. And his dark gaze was evasive. He didn't believe what he was trying to convince her of. Bleakness again swept over her.

"Why don't you lie back down for a little while longer?" Angela's soothing voice asked.

"All right," Sarah said. And heard the deadness in her voice.

All the purpose in her life had been swept away in those minutes the fire had ravaged the school building yesterday.

The life she'd so carefully and painstakingly built for herself over the years since Hunter had left her.

Leaving nothing but emptiness behind.

She should go home. But there was nothing for her to do at home. No papers to grade for the next day. No new assignments to write down for the children.

Nothing . . . there was nothing for her to do.

Nothing to look forward to anymore.

Maybe there would never be again.

CHAPTER EIGHT

Hunter smiled reassuringly at Sarah, trying not to let her see how despondent he felt. She looked so small in the bed, so pale and exhausted. She needed to be held and comforted.

And he'd like to be the one to do that. He wanted to kiss her again . . . just as he had the other day . . . .

No, you don't, the sensible part of him protested. *That was a mistake and you know it. You'll never get her to believe you only want her friendship if you keep on like that.*

And what if he wanted more than her friendship?

That errant thought had been trying to surface since the kiss. He banished it again. He had to concentrate on helping Sarah keep her job.

Tonight there would be an emergency school board meeting supposedly called for by Dudley Cunningham, but Hunter was sure Enid was the moving force behind it. Left alone, Dudley was a decent enough man. But his wife seldom left anything alone that she could use her husband's power to influence.

"Yes, you'd better rest awhile longer," Hunter said. "You went through quite an ordeal yesterday."

Sarah pulled the quilt up to her chin and turned toward him again. "How is Nicholas?"

Even when she felt this bad, she was still concerned about his son. She loved Nicholas . . . almost like a mother. Sarah was a wonderful woman.

Pity you didn't have sense enough to realize that eight years ago. That she was worth waiting for, his mind told him.

Yes, wasn't it? He didn't need to be reminded of his foolish youthful mistakes.

Memories returned of those moments on her porch when she'd been in his arms, and they made his heart speed up. She'd been so warm and sweet. She'd felt just as she had those years ago, with something added. Some new dimension of womanhood.

And that was none of his concern. Not now. Not ever again. She wouldn't even listen to him try to explain what had happened those years ago.

"Nicholas is fine," he said. "He ate enough breakfast for two boys and now he's playing outside."

His words brought a fleeting smile to Sarah's pale lips. "I'm glad. I was so worried about him. You don't know how scared I was when I realized he'd gone back into the schoolhouse yesterday."

Maybe he should keep on talking about Nicholas for a few more minutes. Sarah needed more rest, but she needed some interest, some hope, too.

"I can imagine how you felt. Do you know why he went back in?"

He saw the rise and fall of her breasts under the quilt as she drew in a deep breath and let it out.

He wished he could crawl under the covers and take her into his arms. He wanted that so badly he had to force himself to stand still in the doorway.

"Yes," Sarah said. "He's always shy with the other children at recesses. A fight broke out between two older boys, one of them a bully who teases a lot of the children. Nicholas hates fights. He was probably just trying to get away from the yelling and screaming the boys were doing."

Her words pierced his heart like a knife. Yes, he knew Nicholas hated fights. How many times had he found the boy hidden in a corner after Beryl had screamed at him or at Hunter. Beryl had been such an unhappy woman. Nothing he could do had ever seemed to please her for long.

They should never have married. He knew that after the first week. But there had been no other choice—at least not for him.

"I shouldn't have taken my eyes off him," Sarah said, pain in her soft voice.

Hunter took a step forward before he could stop himself. "You had all those children to oversee. It wasn't your fault. Stop blaming yourself."

"But he could have died in there!"

Her voice was so full of anguish Hunter couldn't stand it. He took another step forward. "But he *didn't* die. You saved him. Not many women—or men— would have been that brave."

Angela gave Hunter an approving glance, which also held a bit of caution, and motioned toward the door.

She patted Sarah on her quaking shoulders. "Hunter's right, Sarah dear. You were very brave. And now you must rest."

Angela's kind and cheerful words seemed to lessen

the tension in the room. Hunter felt himself feeling a little better despite everything that had happened— and all that was still to come.

"I'll see you later, Sarah. You sleep some more," he said, surprised at the lift in his voice. Then he left the room.

Faith was washing dishes in the big kitchen. She looked up, her lined face creased with worry as he entered. "How is she?"

Hunter crossed the room and gave his mother a hug. The momentary lift he'd felt was fading as the reality of the situation sank in again. "She's still feeling yesterday's effects. But she's going to be . . . all right."

He couldn't help hesitating and of course his mother caught it. She gave him a sharp look.

"You think she's going to lose her job as teacher, don't you?"

Hunter hesitated again. He didn't want to worry his mother any more than necessary, but she could see through any evasions he tried. Finally, he nodded.

"Yes, I do, Mama. I'm afraid the Cunninghams have too much influence."

Her dark eyes flashed. "Yes, they do. Oh, I'd like to wring Enid's neck! Or Dudley's for being so henpecked."

She gave him a quick glance. "But you're going to give them a fight, aren't you? Even if you shouldn't."

He knew what she meant. He shouldn't be risking his in-laws' ire—not if he wanted to stay in Little Bethlehem.

"Yes, Mama. I'm going to give them a fight. Sarah's a good teacher. She doesn't deserve this."

His mother smiled. "Good. Don't worry, son. Whatever happens, we can handle it."

Hunter smiled back. "You bet. I'm going to talk to a couple of the farmers on the school board who are interested in my cannery. Maybe I can have some influence, too."

But an hour later, sitting in Burt Williams's kitchen, he realized that wouldn't happen.

Burt gave him a troubled frown. "I've known Sarah all her life. The Calders was good people. I've never heard nothing against Sarah, but I got my own worries. Dudley's loaned me money several times. And this wasn't a good crop year. I'll have to ask him for another loan for spring planting."

Hunter's spirits sank. Jim Tuttle had told him much the same thing less than an hour ago. He couldn't blame either man. Burt couldn't risk going against Dudley and Enid. There was too much at stake for his own family's future.

Hunter rose, as did Burt. "I understand. And I don't hold it against you."

He offered his hand, and Burt shook it, relief in the lines of his weathered face. "You're a good man, Hunter. Glad you decided to come back here to stay."

"So am I," Hunter said. He hoped he'd be able to stay, but that might not be possible.

"Wish things weren't like they are," Burt said. "But that's the way of the world, I reckon."

As Hunter drove back to town, anger and frustration filled him. He pounded his fist against the buggy door.

"Damn the way of the world! It's not fair and it's not right."

He'd let Sarah down. And there was nothing he

could do about it. His vote might well be the only one in favor of keeping Sarah on as teacher.

A few hours later, seated around the polished oak table in Dudley's handsomely furnished office at the bank, he found he was about correct in that assumption.

Hunter's and Dr. Lawson's were the only dissenting votes against firing Sarah. Crystal Cunningham was appointed the new teacher. Enid and Dudley were donating books, desks, and even a school building.

The board members, with the exception of Dr. Lawson, hurriedly left, not looking each other in the eye.

Hunter was glad he'd chosen to walk instead of driving the buggy because he badly needed the exercise to work off his anger and frustration.

He was tempted to resign as a board member, but he knew that wouldn't do Sarah any good. If he stayed he might be able to help.

Dr. Lawson walked to the door with him, his expression as dark as Hunter's. "Bad thing, this," he said tightly.

"Yes," Hunter agreed.

The doctor strode off to his buggy.

Closing the door, Hunter caught Enid's hard look and knew his actions tonight had made her furious, and she'd find some way to punish him.

But that wasn't the worst of it.

The worst would come when he must face Sarah tomorrow. Was it only a few days ago he'd told her he'd do his best to get her a raise in salary?

His mouth twisted. That would never happen now. What would she do? he suddenly wondered as his long strides ate up the distance to his family home.

What a sad Christmas she was going to have.

And all Sarah's problems had indirectly been brought about by his actions years ago. If he'd waited for Sarah and married her as he'd promised, she wouldn't be going through this now.

She'd be married to him. She'd be raising their family.

His jaw clenched. It was up to him to straighten out this mess. How, he didn't know. She wouldn't even listen to him explain what had happened that long ago night.

He reached his house. A light shone in the front window, the one his mother always left on when he went out at night. But none in Sarah's room. She was exhausted and needed to sleep.

But tomorrow was another day. She'd be rested. He'd take her home and make her listen.

Why is that so important? his mind asked. *You're supposed to be concentrating on trying to help her.*

The front door opened. Angela's head, with its halo of silvery hair, poked around the frame.

"There you are, Hunter," she said, as familiarly as if they'd known each other all their lives. "I just made a pan of cocoa."

"That sounds wonderful." He hurried up the walk. After the meeting, sitting around the kitchen table with Angela and his mother was a welcome prospect.

Angela held the door for him, giving him her usual warm smile.

Hunter smiled back. "Angela, just the sight of you always makes me feel better."

Her smile widened. "Good. That's my job." She turned and bustled off to the kitchen.

Hunter followed, wondering what her last words meant. He guessed she felt as if she must always be cheerful and helpful at the various relations' houses she visited so they'd allow her to stay.

He didn't like that picture of her life. But Angela was naturally friendly and optimistic. He knew his mother wished she'd stay permanently. Maybe they could talk her into it.

Angela was at the stove, ladling cocoa into a cup.

His mother sat at the table, a steaming cup before her. Hunter sniffed appreciatively. The kitchen was filled with the aroma of cocoa and spices.

His mother smiled at him. "Molasses cookies," she said, gesturing to a plate on the table. "Angela has the most wonderful recipe."

Hunter sat down across from her and Angela put his cup before him and seated herself.

"How's Sarah?" Hunter asked.

"She went to bed early. I think she'll be fine by tomorrow."

"Good." Hunter sipped his hot drink. Both women were looking at him expectantly. No more putting it off. He'd have to tell them the bad news.

When he'd finished, his mother gave a sharp, indrawn breath. "I was afraid they'd not have enough backbone to stand up for what's right."

"I guess that's the way the world works, as Burt told me today." He heard the bitterness in his voice.

"We're not the world," his mother answered, her voice trembling with anger. "This is Little Bethlehem. I thought our town had good, decent people."

"It does, Faith dear," Angela said. "Don't give up hope in them yet."

His mother glanced at Angela. "It's awfully hard to believe in their goodness with this happening to Sarah. Especially at Christmas time."

"Yes. But you know the old saying that it's always darkest before the dawn."

"I wish the dawn would hurry up and get here then. Because it seems awfully dark right now."

"Indeed it does," Angela agreed. "Let's try to lighten things ourselves. Does Sarah have savings to tide her over for a while?"

"I don't see how, with the pitiful salary she was getting," his mother said. "And her mama didn't leave Sarah anything but doctor bills. Doc Lawson was real decent and wiped the slate clean. Sarah wanted to pay a little each month, but he wouldn't let her."

His mother didn't glance his way, but guilt smote Hunter just the same. If he'd kept his promise to Sarah, waited for her, married her, none of this would be happening.

But Sarah had been so stubborn, so sure her way was right. He'd let that drive him to making the biggest mistake of his life. But if he hadn't made that mistake he wouldn't have his son.

Angela smiled and patted Faith's hand. "There, you see, your townspeople are good underneath. Things will work out all right in the end."

His mother's face smoothed out a little. She managed a return smile. "I hope you're right."

"I will be," Angela said, her voice positive. "Now how can we help Sarah in the meantime?"

"She knows she'd be more than welcome to move in here. But she's got too much pride. At least she has her house, and like most everyone, a lot of canned goods put by. She'll need wood and coal oil for the lamps."

His mother glanced over at Hunter. "Do you think she'd accept wood from our lot if you cut it and took it to her?"

"I'll see to that," Hunter said. "One way or the other." He couldn't bear the thought of Sarah sitting in her little house with no fire to warm her during the cold winter.

"The worst part of this whole thing is it's darkened Sarah's good name." His mother sighed. "That could make it hard for her to find a teaching job elsewhere. There's not much other work here."

She gave Hunter a significant look. "Not that we want her to leave. We'll do everything we can to keep that from happening."

Hunter blinked. What did his mother mean by that look? Was she suggesting he try to rekindle his old relationship with Sarah?

Surely not. Didn't she believe, like Sarah, that was impossible?

What did he mean, "like Sarah?" He believed that, too, didn't he? Of course he did.

But he agreed with his mother. Sarah should stay here where she belonged. "You bet we will, Mama."

If anyone had to leave, it would be him and his family. And he'd put up a fight before he allowed that to happen.

"Christmas will soon be here and we'll all be busy," Angela said. "Managing the pageant will keep Sarah occupied. Don't worry so much. Things will work out all right."

His mother reached for a molasses cookie. "It's hard to keep low spirits around you. Even if I don't see how this mess can come right, I find myself believing you."

"I surely hope you do," Angela said.

Hunter picked up a cookie and headed upstairs. Somehow, he found himself believing in Angela's optimistic words, too.

You know the solution to Sarah's problem, his mind told him. *You want Sarah with you. The way it should have been from the beginning.*

The thoughts hit him, shocked him.

No, of course he didn't. It was far too late for that.

When he'd left Little Bethlehem with Beryl that long-ago night, he'd exiled his love for Sarah to the farthest part of his mind, determined to put the past behind him.

He'd tried hard to be a good husband to Beryl until her death. He'd tried to be a good father. He hoped he'd at least partially succeeded.

That's all well and good, but you didn't stop loving Sarah. You just never let yourself admit it.

Of course not. He couldn't have stood his life if he'd allowed that. No, he'd pushed all that away. Banished it forever.

Not forever. You can't do it any longer.

No, that wasn't true. It couldn't be.

Yes, it is, his relentless mind insisted. *You've reached the end. You can't go on like this.*

Something gave way in his mind . . . in his heart. A rush of long-suppressed feelings surged through him, making him stagger.

Your love for Sarah is still in your heart. As strong as it ever was.

What are you going to do about it?

CHAPTER NINE

"Have another biscuit, Sarah," Faith urged, handing her the still heaping plate. "Angela has outdone herself this morning."

Sarah didn't want a second biscuit. She'd had to force herself to eat one, along with a fried egg and some sausage and gravy. She took one anyway, to ease Faith's anxious expression.

"They're very good," she told Angela, forcing a smile she didn't feel.

"I do love to cook," Angela said with her usual cheerful smile. She picked up a glass dish and held it out to Sarah.

"I made fresh apple butter."

Sarah's stomach felt as if it had a huge knot in it, but she also put some of the apple butter on her plate.

Her glance met Hunter's and, despite everything she'd been telling herself, lingered.

His gaze was intent, as if he wanted her to know that he had things to say to her.

She slid her gaze away from his. Hunter had dark smudges under his eyes and looked exhausted. She'd heard him come upstairs last night after the school board meeting, but he hadn't stopped at her room.

He'd probably thought her asleep, since her lamp was out, and he was no doubt relieved he wouldn't have to tell her she'd lost her teaching job.

Angela had done that when she'd looked in on her this morning. Not that she had to say anything. The tenderness in her twinkling blue eyes was enough.

Sarah realized she must have been holding on to some hope, no matter what she'd told herself, because at that look, she wanted to slide under the covers of the comfortable bed and stay there.

Of course she didn't. She couldn't give in to this weakness. After brushing away Angela's sympathy, she had gotten up, dressed, and come down to breakfast. She had to go home and make plans.

Hunter looked pale, too. Her glance went lower still and found his mouth. It was tightly set, with none of the softness it had held when he'd kissed her . . . when he'd held her in his arms for those brief moments . . . .

Sarah lowered her head to her plate, tried to stop her thoughts, which wasn't so easily managed. That kiss was like a dream . . . .

But it wasn't a dream. It had happened and . . . she would like for it to happen again.

She felt herself reddening and quickly turned her attention to her breakfast. She buttered the biscuit, piled apple butter on it, then lifted her head again and raised the biscuit to her mouth.

Hunter was still looking at her, his glance on her mouth. As if he, too, were remembering the kiss.

Feeling her blush deepening, Sarah once more lowered her head, hoping neither Angela nor Faith had noticed any of this. And that was a useless wish. Neither of the two women ever missed anything.

"Miss Sarah, I want you to be my teacher. I don't want Aunt Crystal," Nicholas said from across the table.

Sarah's stomach tightened further. She forced a smile. "Your aunt Crystal will do fine," she told him, a false brightness in her voice. "You like her."

Nicholas didn't smile back. He slowly nodded. "Ye-e-s I like her, but I don't want her for my teacher. I want you to be. Why can't you, Miss Sarah?"

Sarah swallowed. Nicholas had heard what Enid said in the schoolyard, but she didn't know how much he'd understood. She wouldn't criticize the Cunninghams. That would be too hard on him.

Hunter suddenly rose, solving her dilemma. "It's time I took you to school."

Nicholas slowly got up, his movements reluctant. "But why can't Miss Sarah be my teacher anymore?" he asked again, his voice trembling. Sarah saw tears on his lashes.

Hunter reached for his son's hand. "Come along now," he said gently. "We'll talk about it on the way to school."

Sarah clenched her hands as she watched them go down the long hall, pause to get their coats and hats from the rack, and go out the front door.

How could she stand this? Crystal Cunningham would teach her children today. And everyone in town would gossip about Sarah. Some would be on her side, but a lot wouldn't. Many would accept what Enid Cunningham said as gospel truth.

That Sarah was a careless, neglectful teacher. That she hadn't watched the children properly and had endangered their lives.

Sarah pushed her chair back and stood. "I need to be getting home," she said, fighting the tremor in her voice.

Faith gave her a troubled frown. "We expected you to stay a few days longer. You still look weak and tired. You went through a terrible ordeal."

Sarah straightened her shoulders. "I'm fine, Faith, and I want to go home. I—I have a lot of things to do."

"Nothing that can't wait," Faith insisted, then stopped, as if realizing she'd only emphasized how little Sarah actually had to do now that she was no longer the schoolteacher.

"I wish you'd stay a couple more days and let us take care of you," Faith finally said.

Angela said nothing, but Sarah saw the concern in her eyes.

Sarah appreciated their compassion, but she couldn't stay any longer. It would only make her feel worse, less able to deal with what had happened.

"Thank you, Faith, but I don't need to be taken care of," Sarah said, firmly. Deep inside something insisted that, yes, she did. But the only person who could do that was Hunter.

And that could never be.

Half an hour later, Sarah opened the front door of her little house and went inside. She'd expected the house to be cold and clammy, since she'd been away for two days and nights.

But instead, it was warm and comfortable. Someone

must have started a fire this morning. Probably
Angela. She seemed to know when anything needed
to be done and then did it.

Snowball came running in from the kitchen, purr-
ing loudly. Sarah stooped to run her hand down the
cat's white coat. Snowball twined around her ankles
in an ecstasy of delight.

"It's nice you're glad to see me," Sarah said.

Snowball meowed her agreement and kept on purr-
ing and twining.

Finally, Sarah straightened up, looked around, and
took a deep breath. The house was neat, just as she'd
left it. She'd washed her clothes last Saturday.

As Faith had said, there was nothing urgent here
that needed her attention. She felt tears pricking her
eyelids again and blinked them away. She wouldn't
feel sorry for herself. She'd think of something to do
and get busy doing it.

She took off her cloak and hung it on the hall tree,
then laid her gloves on one of the rungs while she
thought.

Christmas. Yes, she would do all the Christmas
things ahead of time instead of spacing them out to
do on Saturdays and evenings as she usually did.

When she had a job to go to every day.

Forcing that thought away, she went to the kitchen.
Once there, she added more wood to the fire in the
range, then did the same to the parlor stove.

First, she would finish the wreath for the front door
and hang it. All it needed was shaping and a few red
and green bows. Sarah retrieved it from the back
porch, where she'd left it so the cedar branches
wouldn't dry out.

After that, she'd finish knitting the mittens she'd

started for Nicholas several weeks ago. And then there was the afghan she was crocheting for Faith.

What about Angela? What on earth could she make for her? The woman seemed to have few possessions. Since she traveled around from one relative to another, that was understandable.

She'd think about the problem of Angela's gift while she worked on the other ones.

Hunter. What about Hunter? Of course she'd have to give him a gift, too. What could it be?

A muffler—yes, she would knit him a muffler. She had that nice brown yarn. It would look well with his dark blue coat. Anything would look good on Hunter. He was still just as handsome as he'd been when they were engaged . . . .

You're not engaged now. And if you're smart, you'll stop all this nonsense, she told herself. She settled herself at the kitchen table and got to work.

A knock at the door several hours later startled her. Sarah glanced at the clock on the wall, surprised to see it was four o'clock. She'd forgotten to make herself anything for the noon meal, and now her stomach reminded her of that fact.

She laid Faith's afghan on the table and rose, the knot in her stomach growing. Who could that be? Some neighbor to offer her sympathy or at least pretend to? She didn't want to see anyone.

Angela, smiling as always, stood on the doorstep, Nicholas beside her.

Nicholas gave her a wide, delighted smile. "Hi, Miss Sarah."

Sarah greeted them and returned their smiles. She *was* glad to see these two people.

"I hope you're feeling up to working with Nicholas a little while today," Angela said.

"Of course I am." Sarah stood back to let them enter.

"Nicholas wanted to see you so badly, and there wasn't that much to do on the pageant today, so I came right over after picking him up from school."

Sarah frowned. "I should have gone over to the church, too."

"No one expected you today," Angela said. She helped Nicholas with his wraps, then turned to Sarah. "I'll come get him in an hour."

"All right," Sarah agreed, firmly pushing down her disappointment that Hunter wouldn't be the one to fetch Nicholas.

How many times did she have to tell herself she must stay away from Hunter all she could?

Would the townspeople want her to work on the pageant now that she'd been fired from her job? How could she give that up, too? The knot in her stomach grew again.

"Gladys and Millie Lawson asked about you when I was at the church," Angela went on, as if Sarah had spoken her thoughts aloud. "They wanted to know if you were all right and said they missed you."

"Thanks, Angela." Sarah felt a little better. At least those two women were on her side. But that didn't mean everyone was. Or even a majority. Her spirits plunged again.

"I'll be over tomorrow afternoon," she told Angela. But how she dreaded the thought.

"All right, if you're up to it. I'll see you two in a little while," Angela said cheerfully and left.

"Come along to the kitchen and I'll find a cookie for you," Sarah told Nicholas, forcing cheerfulness into her voice.

Sarah settled him at the table with cookies and

milk, glad she'd finished his mittens earlier and put them away.

"Now let's get to work," Sarah said when he'd made short work of the treat.

"I wish you were still my teacher," he said again, as he had that morning.

Sarah gave him a smile. "I do, too, but I can't be. And I bet your aunt Crystal did just fine today."

Nicholas shook his head. "No, she didn't. No one paid any attention to her. And Roger and Walter got into a fight."

"In the schoolyard?"

Nicholas shook his head again. "No, inside. Right on the floor. Aunt Crystal tried to get them to stop, and when they wouldn't, she cried. There isn't any schoolyard. There's just an old building with cracks in the walls. She didn't know how to keep the fire going either, so we were all cold."

"Oh," Sarah said at a loss as how to answer him. Despite her anguish over losing her job, she felt sorry for Crystal. She'd always liked the girl and didn't wish her ill. This was all Enid's doing, not Crystal's.

And this was Crystal's first day as a teacher. Of course she was having trouble. In a little while, things would settle down.

"Well, let's get to work," Sarah said again.

Nicholas sighed. "All right, Miss Sarah."

When Angela came for Nicholas, Sarah hated to say good-bye to the little boy she loved.

"I'll be glad to work with Nicholas every day," she told Angela. "If it's all right with his father."

Angela beamed. "I'm sure it will be. That would be wonderful."

Nicholas grinned up at Sarah. "I'll see you tomorrow, Miss Sarah."

She stood in the doorway and watched them go down the walk.

Back inside, Sarah leaned against the door, her blue mood returning. Her stomach rumbled, reminding her again that she'd missed dinner and now it was almost suppertime.

She made herself a quick meal and forced herself to eat it, then tried to decide what to do with the evening. Dusk was settling in and the short winter day was coming to a close. Maybe she'd go to bed and not bother even lighting a lamp. She'd done enough work for one day.

And tomorrow would come soon enough.

That thought made her mood even lower.

A knock sounded at the door again. Sarah stiffened. This had to be a neighbor and she still didn't want to talk to anyone.

Maybe if she ignored it the person would go away.

The knock came again, louder this time. *Oh, for heaven's sake, answer it,* she told herself impatiently. *You can't hide in this house forever.*

She swung the door open and her heart skipped a beat. Hunter stood there, flakes of snow sparkling on his dark head.

He smiled at her. "Maybe this one will stick."

She looked beyond him to see snow coming down heavily. "Maybe so," she agreed. "Angela already came by for Nicholas."

"I know. I'm here to see you, Sarah."

She drew a quick breath. "I'm tired. I'm getting ready to go to bed."

Her hand tightened on the door handle, but before she could push it closed, Hunter was inside.

"We have to talk," he said firmly. "I'm not leaving until we do."

Sarah's mouth firmed. "No. Talking won't change anything."

"Are you going to be reasonable? Or scream and have the neighbors flying over here?"

"Don't be ridiculous," she snapped. "I want you to leave."

Hunter gently disengaged Sarah's hand from the door knob and closed the door. He folded his arms across his chest.

"I'm stubborn. We can stand here for an hour arguing if you like, but in the end, we're going to talk."

Her hand still felt the touch of his, reminding her of the kiss they'd shared two evenings ago. A shiver went through her. He couldn't stay here. He just couldn't!

"I don't want to discuss anything that happened in our past."

"I know, but the way I see it, you have to. God willing, I'm planning to live here for the rest of my life. I can't see avoiding this subject for that many years to come."

Pain began moving to the surface from somewhere inside her. "It's over—nothing can change that. What's the use of talking about it?"

"You never knew the full story and I want you to. I *need* you to."

The pain was closer to the surface now, making it hard to breathe. Knife-edged memories began tumbling through her mind.

"What else is there to know? You begged me to marry you, and when I told you I couldn't, you eloped with Beryl. The only thing I've never understood was why you even bothered to ask me that night. When you obviously loved Beryl."

She'd never spoken those words aloud before. Deeper pain ripped through her.

Hunter moved closer, his features set in tense lines. He reached for her hands, but she retreated.

"That's where you're wrong, Sarah. I didn't love Beryl. I never loved her."

Sarah stared at him, shock running through the pain. "I don't believe you! If you didn't love her, why did you marry her?"

He swallowed as if it hurt his throat. "Because we made love that night. I'd had too much to drink. Beryl was . . . willing . . . and afterward she was hysterical . . . afraid I might have gotten her with child, and I was, too. She begged me to marry her. I was sorry and ashamed. So I did."

Sarah stared at him as if she'd never seen him before in her life. "You were only with Beryl that one time before you married her?"

Hunter's haunted gaze bored into hers. "Yes. But that was enough. Nicholas was conceived that night."

Sarah's throat was so dry she couldn't swallow. "You ruined our lives for one night with Beryl?"

She felt as if her heart were shattering. "My God, how could you? How could you hurt me like that?"

His jaw tightened. "I wasn't trying to hurt you. I was only thinking of myself. I was young and hot-blooded. We'd been engaged for such a long time. And we'd never—"

She stared at him in disbelief. "Of course not. You knew we had to wait until we were married."

"But I wanted you so much, Sarah. You were so sweet and you heated my blood to boiling. I felt we were never going to be married. That night when you refused me, I went to the Cunninghams. They were having a party for Beryl's nineteenth birthday.

I . . . had some liquor. Beryl and I went out to the gardens.''

Pictures of Beryl and Hunter together filled her mind. "Stop! I can't stand to hear any more."

She backed up until she was almost against the wall.

Hunter took a step nearer. "But you need to. You have to try to understand—"

"I have to understand you needed a woman so much that since Beryl was available you took her?"

His mouth tightened. Shame filled his eyes. "Yes, that's just what happened. Beryl had . . . wanted me. She didn't stop me . . . ."

"As I had always stopped you," Sarah finished, bitterly. "Of course I did. I had some sense even if you didn't. What would have happened if we had . . . ."

Her words faltered. She couldn't go on because the words brought another picture to her mind, one that made heat go through her, mixed with pain.

"If *we* had made love?" Hunter moved closer.

Sarah retreated another step and now she was against the wall and could back up no farther.

"You know that answer," he said softly, entreatingly. "We would have married. You wouldn't have refused me then."

"You're twisting things!" she protested, pressing her back against the wall. "You're making me sound so hard and unfeeling."

His smile was as soft as his voice. "Oh, no. You were never hard and unfeeling. Never, never that."

He reached out, gently touched her cheek with his fingertips, then stroked down it to her throat.

Sarah's anger and confusion blended, mixed with other feelings rising in her. She should move. She should run from him . . . go to her bedroom and close the door. But the touch of his hand felt so good . . . .

"You loved your mother very much. I understood that," Hunter went on, still in that soft voice that sent shivers down her arms and spine.

"You didn't think there was any solution except to wait."

"There *wasn't*," Sarah said, desperately trying to hold on to her anger, to make her voice forceful and strong so that he would take his hand away, leave her.

"I was giving all I had to my mother. There wouldn't have been enough left over of me to be a wife, too."

"I didn't agree with you," Hunter said. He stroked her neck, then went back up to the other cheek.

"You were wrong!"

"Maybe I was. But maybe I wasn't. There's no way we can ever know now."

She gasped at his last words. "No, there isn't. You married Beryl and . . . and you had Nicholas. That night our lives were torn apart forever."

He dropped his hand away from her face and moved closer. Only a few inches separated them now. He gave her a searching look.

"Why does it have to be that way, Sarah?"

She swallowed, missing his touch, watching the movements of his mouth as he talked. She'd always loved his mouth, the way his lips curved up a little at the corners, how soft they were against her own . . . .

He reached out both hands and took her face between them. His hands were so warm . . . . He tilted up her head so that their gazes met. His eyes were like dark brown velvet, soft and deep . . . .

She fought with herself, tried to summon back the

anger, but it was overcome by a yearning so strong her knees shook. By desire that had never died.

His head slowly lowered toward her.

His lips brushed hers with a feather-light touch, then withdrew, making her lips tingle, making her burn with the need for more. She tried to resist, tried to keep her hands clenched at her sides.

But instead, she moved closer to him. Her arms went upward, her hands unclenched and clasped together around his neck.

The skin of his nape, hair roughened, was warm beneath her hands. Warm and familiar . . . just as it had been all those years ago . . .

She stopped resisting, closed her eyes, and surrendered to the waves of feeling flowing over and around her.

"Sarah . . ." Hunter's warm breath fanned against her face. "Kiss me, Sarah."

"Yes," she whispered, her eyes still closed. Hunter's lips touched hers, again lightly, like a few moments ago.

But now that wasn't enough. No, not nearly enough. Sarah moved closer to him, her lips under his, parting in invitation.

She heard his indrawn breath as his arms clasped her tightly to him, his lips pressed against hers. The tip of his tongue found her own, withdrew, then circled it with slow, sensual movements.

Sarah gasped, her breath coming faster. Boldly, she returned his touches, helped him deepen the kiss until it was possible to deepen it no more. Until they were pressed so tightly together she felt every hard muscle in Hunter's body, knew he could feel all the softness of her own . . . knew it and reveled in it. She was intoxicated with sensuous delight and desire. She belonged here, in Hunter's arms. She could stay here forever . . . safe and secure in his strong embrace, wanted, loved, and needed.

Just as she had felt all those years ago . . .

Memory's wings brushed through the spell of Hunter's arms and lips and touch . . . .

But you weren't safe. He didn't love you enough to wait for you, the cold voice of reason said inside her head. *When you wouldn't give him what he wanted, he found it somewhere else . . . with Beryl.*

You trusted him with your life and he betrayed you. How could you ever trust him again?

The coldness crept from her head down into her face and her body, stiffening her lips, her limbs.

Hunter drew away first. His hands slid to her arms, holding her away from him. His mouth looked pink and a little swollen, just as hers must, too. His hair was mussed. Just as hers must be.

"What's wrong?" Hunter's voice was husky, a little rough . . . .

"How can you ask me that?" she said through cold lips. "Did you honestly think one kiss could erase the past?"

"No, of course not."

"Then what *were* you trying to do? Make me want you so much I'd forget everything else? Just as you tried to do all those years ago?"

He looked at her for a long moment. "I wasn't trying to do anything. I love you, Sarah."

His voice sounded almost awed as if he were saying these words not only to her but also to himself.

"I've never stopped loving you. I just realized that last night. I kissed you because I wanted you to feel my love and believe in it."

Sarah moved back, struggling to release herself from his grip. Hunter let his arms drop away.

"*Believe* in your newfound love?" she scoffed. "How could I possibly do that when it wasn't strong enough before?"

"Sarah, please," Hunter said.

"Please what? Please let myself be beguiled into thinking you've changed? That now you couldn't be tempted by a pretty face or a come-hither look? Why, Crystal is after you just like you say Beryl was."

Hunter frowned. "Sarah, you're talking foolish. You know Enid is throwing Crystal at my head and you also know I'm not interested in her."

"How do I know that?" Sarah demanded. "I certainly didn't know anything about you and Beryl."

Hunter's frown deepened. "There wasn't anything between Beryl and me until that night. Didn't you hear anything I said a few minutes ago?"

"Oh, I heard all right," Sarah said grimly. "It was bad enough when I believed you'd fallen in love with Beryl and couldn't bear to tell me. It's a hundred times worse to know you were so weak you couldn't wait for me. That you destroyed our lives because of your physical cravings."

Hunter's face tightened until it was as drawn looking as her own. "Yes, maybe I destroyed the lives we had planned years ago."

Sarah couldn't believe her ears. "*Maybe* you destroyed our lives? What do you mean maybe?"

Hunter drew another deep breath and let it out. "I was young and foolish then, but I was right in one thing. We could have married, but you wouldn't listen to me."

"Mama was so sick she needed my almost constant care. How could I possibly have been your wife, too?"

"My mother would have helped. Many neighbors volunteered to help, too. You wouldn't accept their offers."

"Mama was my responsibility," Sarah said, tilting her chin up. "It was up to me to take care of her."

"You have way too much pride, Sarah," Hunter said. "It's no sign of weakness to accept help from others. We all need that sometimes."

"Daddy died when I was twelve, and he made me promise to take care of Mama. Mama was never strong, not even then. I had to do it."

They looked at each other for long moments. Both faces tight and strained.

Finally, Hunter shook his head. "I know you truly believe what you said then, what you're saying now. I've regretted what I did every day for eight years. But now, we have a chance to start over and you refuse to take that chance."

"Of course I do," she flared. "How could I ever trust you again after what you've told me?"

"I'm not trying to make excuses for myself, but people make mistakes. Bad, stupid mistakes. That doesn't mean they'll make the same ones again. Answer one thing, Sarah. Do you still love me?"

She stared at him. *Of course you do. You may as well admit it,* her mind said.

No! She didn't, and even if she did, she wouldn't tell him. It would give him too much power over her.

"How can you ask that? No, I don't love you."

His dark gaze seemed to see right through her. "I don't believe you," he said gently. "You couldn't have kissed me like you just did if your love was dead."

"Lust isn't the same as love," she said evenly. "After what you've just told me, you of all people should know that."

"It's a part of love," he said. "But not the biggest part."

"It's not the same at all," she insisted. "Love includes trust and faith. I'll never trust you again. You made that impossible."

He abruptly turned toward the door. His hand on the knob, he turned back, his face somber. "I made the mistake eight years ago. This time you're making it, Sarah. We could have a happy life together."

He opened the door and closed it behind him.

Sarah stared at the dark wood of the door for a long time after he left.

Finally, she moved, heading for the kitchen. Her body felt stiff and achy, like an old woman's.

You'll be an old woman in truth, soon enough, she told herself. *And you'll be all alone. With no husband, no family. Nothing of your own.*

Hunter's parting words came back to her. *We could have a happy life together,* he'd said.

No! They couldn't. And it was entirely his fault. She could have made no other choice. Maybe some-day she could forgive him—even after finding out the whole truth.

But how could he expect her to forget what he'd done?

How could he expect her to ever trust him again?

CHAPTER TEN

Crystal stood behind her battered desk at the front of the makeshift schoolhouse, which was an old storage building. Her parents would have it fixed up over the Christmas holidays, but that was almost three weeks away.

Her mother had hurried her in here to show everyone how good she was, so there'd be no complaints about Sarah losing her job. Crystal felt bad about that, but didn't see what she could do. When her Mama was set on something, she nearly always got her way.

Crystal nervously cleared her throat and faced the roomful of young faces. She could feel herself stiffening with tension.

"Children, it's a nice morning," she said, forcing brightness into her voice. "Did you get your sleds out yesterday to enjoy the snow?"

No one said a word or even smiled. Not even Nicholas, her own nephew. She liked him and had always thought he liked her. The children just stared at her as they'd done since her first day as teacher. Which was only three days ago, she reminded herself, glumly.

It seemed more like three years.

Crystal sat down and cautiously eased open the top left desk drawer, where she kept the roll call book.

The first day there'd been a frog in the drawer. She'd screamed and it had leaped out and all around the desktop, croaking loudly. Finally, one of the older boys caught it and put it outside.

The children had laughed so hard she didn't think she'd ever get them settled down. She was pretty sure Walter Darby had done it. But he'd never admit it. And of course none of the other children would tattle on him.

She didn't tell her parents. It wasn't the only incident and she couldn't face Mama's tirades about not keeping order. Her mother expected her to be a better teacher than Sarah. She'd never be as good as Sarah, let alone better.

Today, the drawer didn't hold anything that moved, she saw, relieved. She should know a lot of the children by name—she'd seen them around town all her life—but she didn't. Mama hadn't encouraged her to associate with most of the families. If she had, maybe then they wouldn't act as if she was some stranger they didn't want anything to do with.

She took a deep breath and opened the book. "Walter Darby," she said, wincing at the wobble in her voice.

Walter sat in his usual seat in the last row, but he didn't answer. None of the boys would answer the roll call. Not even Nicholas, after the first day, when he'd asked if Sarah would ever come back and she'd said she didn't know.

They all wanted Sarah back even if they didn't say so.

"Roger Kane," Crystal continued. Again, silence greeted her. She felt her cheeks warming and heard a few snickers.

Thank goodness a girl's name was next. "Dora Lowfield," Crystal said. Dora, in the front row, just looked at her with a blank face.

Crystal sucked in her breath. Dora was one of the older students and she had given Crystal no trouble before.

Her glance fell on Nicholas. He was holding his hand over his mouth to suppress a smile.

Things were getting worse.

Closing the book with a snap, she forced herself to look steadily at what by now was just a sea of faces. "Since I know everyone, there's no reason to call your names every morning. Let's proceed with our work."

She opened her dog-eared copy of McGuffey's *Eclectic Reader*. Where had she left off yesterday? Frowning, she tried to remember.

"Luther and Maynard ain't here today," Roger's voice piped up. "Ain't you going to mark them absent?"

The ever present knot in Crystal's stomach got bigger. She hadn't even noticed they weren't here.

"Of course," Crystal said.

Walter stood up. "I don't feel like school today either." He glanced across the aisle. "What about you, Roger?"

Roger also got up. "Nope."

Both boys swaggered insolently to the door and left.

Crystal knew her face was as red as fire. She didn't want to think about fire. If the old schoolhouse hadn't burned, Sarah would still be teaching, and she'd be at home, helping Mama run the household as she'd done since she was twelve.

The thought brought tears. She blinked them away. How she *hated* this job!

Somehow, she got through the day. After school, the children left like a herd of cattle turned loose, with not a good-bye or a backward glance, except for Nicholas, who went outside to wait for Angela or Hunter, and Lorna Miller, the oldest girl in school.

The tall, dark-haired girl walked to the front of the room. She stood there, biting her lip.

Crystal smiled. She liked Lorna.

Lorna smiled back, and that seemed to give her courage to speak.

"Miss Cunningham, if you'd use your paddle on a few of the boys that would settle them all down."

Crystal stared at the girl, who was only a few years younger than she was. "I couldn't do that."

Lorna's gaze didn't waver. "If you don't, they'll never respect or mind you."

To her mortification, Crystal again felt sudden tears. "They won't anyway. They don't like me."

"That's not why they're acting up. They just know they can get away with it."

To her horror, Crystal blurted, "I'm no good at this job. I never wanted it in the first place."

Lorna looked wistful. "I'd love to teach."

"Why don't you?" Crystal no longer cared what she said. She had to talk to somebody and her parents wouldn't listen.

"I'd have to finish the academy in Spring Grove first."

"The law doesn't require that," Crystal said. "You could take over right now and do a better job than me."

Lorna frowned. "You don't give yourself enough credit, Miss Cunningham. You're plenty smart."

The girl's words warmed Crystal. She couldn't remember when anyone had given her a word of praise. "Thank you, Lorna. I must be going. You probably should get home, too."

Crystal watched the girl hurry off, then pulled herself together. She neatened the room, then swept the floor, glad of the familiar physical work she could do easily and well.

She went outside just as Hunter pulled up in his buggy. "There's Daddy!" Nicholas said happily and ran toward the buggy.

Hunter leaned over and unlatched the door. He waved. "Hello, Crystal."

Crystal waved back and watched them drive off toward the Winslow house. Hunter's voice had sounded friendly but a little reserved. No wonder, the way her mother kept pushing her to make up to him. She knew he'd never be interested in her and she didn't want him to be.

After locking the door behind her, she stood on the step a moment, breathing in the fresh wintry air. Down the street, she saw children on sleds.

She wished she was still a child and out there playing.

No, she didn't. She wished she had her own house to take care of.

She wished she had a husband. But not Hunter.

She blushed at that thought as a man's face came into her mind's eye.

Crystal sighed and headed for the church. Besides teaching school, her mother said she was supposed to run the pageant, since she was now the schoolteacher.

Sarah didn't know that yet. She hadn't worked on the pageant since the fire. Dr. Lawson had made her rest.

Crystal's steps slowed. But today, Sarah would probably show up, ready to take over again.

Mama would be there, bossing everyone around, just like yesterday, when two of the women had gone home in a huff. And she'd embarrass Sarah in front of everyone.

Crystal's steps slowed more. Sarah had enough trouble. And she'd run the pageant for years and could do it better than anyone else in town.

Reaching the white clapboard building, Crystal paused for a moment before she went in. The front yard of the rectory next door, even under its new coating of snow, looked bare and a little neglected.

Reverend Hopkins wasn't much interested in flowers or shrubs. His mind was always on higher matters. He gave the most stirring sermons Crystal had ever heard. She loved to watch him behind the pulpit, getting so carried away he moved back and forth and ran his hands through his thick brown hair . . . his brown eyes flashing with fire . . . .

Sometimes, when she sat in the Cunningham pew, she wondered what it would feel like if she could slide her fingers through his hair . . . .

Crystal came to herself with a start. What in the world had made her think such thoughts about David?

David?

Clapping both gloved hands to her cheeks, she could feel the heat even through the leather.

She glanced quickly around to see if anyone was nearby and had noticed her dawdling like a ninny. To her relief, she saw no one. Then she hurried up the walk and through the church into the small room in back.

Although a welcoming fire crackled in the stove, no one else was there. Crystal hung up her wraps. Her boots were damp and her feet cold. She drew a chair up to the stove, sat down, and held her feet toward the stove. Closing her eyes, she basked in the warmth.

The door behind her opened, then closed. Crystal tensed, hoping it wasn't her mother. *Please let it be Angela or one of the other women who are helping with the pageant.*

"The fire feels good today, doesn't it?"

Reverend Hopkins's voice behind her was so unexpected Crystal started, her feet falling to the floor with a thump. The sudden movement made her chair slide backward, and before she could catch her balance, all of her slid off the chair onto the floor.

She landed on her behind and a sharp pain shot through her tailbone and up her back.

"Did you hurt yourself?" Reverend Hopkins, his voice full of concern, asked from close beside her.

Crystal realized her skirts were hiked up her legs halfway to her knees, revealing her heavy gray wool stockings. Ugly stockings. Why hadn't she worn her nice silk ones?

She gasped at her wayward thoughts and quickly pulled down her blue woolen skirt.

"I'm fine," she said, struggling to get up. The movement made another pain shoot through her tailbone and she staggered.

"Here, let me help you."

Reverend Hopkins reached out and took hold of her arms in a steadying grip.

Through the cloth of her dress, his hands felt warm on her arms. She'd known he'd have warm hands. How could he help it, considering the fire banked inside him?

Crystal gasped again at these thoughts. What was wrong with her? Why, this was their *minister*. The man whose sermons she listened to every Sunday morning.

He's also a man. And handsome. And his name is David. David is a good name. Strong and masculine. And he isn't married.

Desperately, Crystal turned off these thoughts. "I'm fine now, Da—Reverend Hopkins," she said, hoping he hadn't caught her near slip. She managed a small smile.

He smiled back, still holding her arms. "I want to be sure. That could have been a nasty fall. This old floor is hard."

He had a wonderful smile and white teeth. One of the front ones was a tiny bit crooked. She found that endearing.

Oh, stop this! she told herself and moved backward a step. Her face felt so hot, she knew it must be brick red by now. She hoped he didn't realize why or guess her shocking thoughts.

Shocking? Why are they shocking? He's a young, single man and you're a young, single woman. He's taken no vows of celibacy.

"I'm just fine," she repeated.

David let go of her and stepped back himself, wondering why he'd felt so strange when he had grasped

Crystal's arms. Waves of pleasant warmth had moved all through his body. He'd suddenly become aware of what a pretty young woman she was.

"I guess you're here to work on the pageant?" he asked so she wouldn't wonder why he was standing there gawking at her.

Crystal nodded. "Yes."

She had a sweet, musical voice, too. He'd never noticed that either.

"I love the snow, don't you?" he went on, changing the subject so abruptly she blinked. He winced inwardly, realizing he wanted to make a good impression on her, as if she were a woman he'd just met.

That thought made him feel even more strange. "Makes me wish I was a boy again and out sledding."

Crystal gave him a surprised look, as if she couldn't picture him sledding. Maybe that was because she hadn't known him as a boy. Another odd thought entered his mind.

He wished he'd known her as a girl.

"Yes, that's just what I was thinking," she said, then blushed again.

Which was most becoming to her pink-and-white complexion, David thought.

Their glances met . . . and held. He felt himself drawn into the glance, deeper and deeper . . . .

The door behind them opened and closed again. "Good afternoon, Reverend Hopkins," Enid Cunningham's brisk voice said.

Not waiting for his reply, she continued, "So here you are, Crystal. We stopped by for you at the school. Didn't you remember you were supposed to wait for us because of the snow?"

David frowned. Mrs. Cunningham talked to her

daughter as if she were a child. Instead of an attractive young woman.

Crystal tore her gaze away from Reverend Hopkins and turned toward her mother. "No, I guess I forgot."

Her mother shook her head. "I swear, sometimes I don't believe you'll ever grow up."

Humiliation swept over Crystal. How could her mother say such a thing in front of Dav—Reverend Hopkins? She lifted her chin a little, not glancing his way.

"It's not snowing now, Mama," Crystal answered, surprised at her nerve in talking back to her mother. "I just felt like walking."

Her mother blinked as if she couldn't believe her ears and opened her mouth.

The door swung open again and Angela came through, as usual, a beaming smile on her face. "Isn't the snow delightful? Just perfect for snowballs."

Crystal's mother closed her still open mouth and turned to Angela with a sniff. "I wouldn't think at your age you'd be entertaining such notions."

Angela's merry gaze fell upon the other woman. "Why not? Age has nothing to do with enjoying a snowfall or relishing the idea of tossing a few snow-balls."

"How right you are, Miss Garland," Reverend Hopkins said. "I was just telling Crystal I'd like to be out in this."

Her mother glanced at him. Then her gaze went back to Crystal and she frowned. Crystal knew what the frown meant. Mama just realized her daughter and their minister had been alone in the room before her arrival.

And thoroughly disapproved, Crystal thought, her embarrassment increasing. Oh, surely, her mother wouldn't let Reverend Hopkins see how she felt. Or actually say something to him. As if he could ever have any kind of a personal interest in *her.*

Why not? her mind asked. *You're pretty enough. And he's a robust young man. Maybe he's thinking it's time he considered doing a little courting.*

Crystal closed her eyes. She'd given up trying to figure out what had come over her. She wasn't herself at all. Her mind kept telling her these shocking things.

Maybe it's time you did your own thinking, instead of letting your mother do it all for you.

Mama pulled herself up ramrod straight, her lips thin and unsmiling. "It's high time we got busy. Reverend Hopkins, I brought some new music for you to look over in view of using it for the pageant."

Crystal gave her a surprised look, glad to put her mind on something besides her own disturbing thoughts. They always used the same familiar, well-loved carols.

Reverend Hopkins looked as surprised as Crystal felt.

Mama held out some sheets of paper.

The minister walked over and took them. "Thank you, Mrs. Cunningham."

"Since we're starting afresh this year with my daughter Crystal directing the pageant, I thought it might be nice to make a few changes."

The minister's surprised look changed to bewilderment. "Crystal is going to direct the pageant? Sarah hasn't said anything to me about that."

Mama sniffed for the third time. "She's only done it all these years because she was the town's schoolteacher."

Reverend Hopkins looked at her for a moment.

"I've only been here three years. I just assumed Sarah did it because she's so good at organizing things."

For the first time, her mother smiled. But it looked forced, Crystal thought, as if she could hardly bring herself to do it.

"My daughter is every bit as good, if not better, at organizing such affairs. I'm sure no one will have any complaints."

Angela stood to one side, her bright gaze taking everything in. Crystal closed her eyes, wishing she could disappear. Her mother had to know what she'd said was so far from the truth as to be laughable.

"Where *is* Sarah?" Reverend Hopkins asked. "I hope she has fully recovered from her ordeal."

Mama's smile faded. "I have no idea," she said frostily. "That isn't what I want—"

The door opened again. Sarah stood framed in the doorway, as if Reverend Hopkins's words had conjured her.

She looked awful, Crystal thought. Her pale face was set in tense lines and dark rings circled her eyes.

Sarah glanced from one to the other of the people in the room. "I'm sorry I'm late." Her voice trembled.

A rush of compassion mixed with guilt filled Crystal. If it wasn't for Mama, Sarah would still be teacher. And she wouldn't be losing this job either.

Was there any way she could prevent that? Crystal glanced at Angela, to find the older woman's glance on her. Angela smiled.

Surprised, Crystal felt some of her tension ease.

"You're not late. We're early." Crystal said warmly, smiling at Sarah. She wouldn't blame Sarah a bit if she refused to speak to her.

"It really doesn't make any difference whether

you're late or not, Sarah," Mama said, "because you—"

Angela stepped forward and gave Sarah a warm hug. "No, it doesn't, Sarah dear. We're so glad to see you here. We were wondering where to start today. Now you can tell us."

Sarah hugged her back. "Oh, I'm sure you don't need me that much."

"Yes, we do," Angela said emphatically.

She dropped her arms from around Sarah and turned to the others in the room. Her bright blue glance settled on Crystal's mother.

"Enid was just telling us what a fine job you've done all these years directing the pageant. Weren't you, Enid dear?"

Mama stared at Angela for a long moment. Finally, she nodded. "Why, uh, yes, I believe I was," she said slowly.

Astonishment and relief filled Crystal. She smiled at Sarah again. "No one could handle the pageant as well as you do."

"Sarah, it's good to see you," Reverend Hopkins said heartily. "I hope you have no lingering bad effects from the fire."

"I'm fine," she said. She pulled herself up taller and straighter.

Her voice sounded stronger than it had a moment ago, too, Crystal realized. And she didn't look as pale either.

Mama's reassurance that Sarah was still in charge of the pageant seemed to have revitalized Sarah.

Crystal didn't understand why her mother had suddenly changed her mind and decided not to force Sarah to give up the pageant, but she was certainly glad.

Crystal stepped forward. "I have the rest of the day and evening free, Sarah, so I can help with anything that needs doing."

Her satchel held a mound of papers that needed grading. But she'd do that later, even if she had to stay up until midnight. It didn't make much difference anyway, since she'd given the papers a cursory glance and seen the children hadn't even tried to do the work correctly.

"Well, ladies, I must be going. If you need anything, let me know," Reverend Hopkins said.

He gave the women his warmest smile.

His glance met Crystal's and seemed to linger for a moment.

Crystal felt her heart thump in her chest, then begin beating faster.

Oh, David was such a handsome man. She watched him leave, his muscular body moving across the room with not a wasted motion.

She'd thought of him as David again.

And she didn't care. She would think of him as David anytime she felt like it.

After all, no one could read her mind.

CHAPTER ELEVEN

Hunter's mother glanced up from the breakfast table as he entered the kitchen. She gave his heavy old pants and corduroy shirt a surprised look.

"What are you up to today?"

"Since I'm still waiting for Dudley's answer on the loan, I can't do anything about my cannery right now. So I'm hauling wood."

He gave her and Angela, across the table, a smile he didn't feel, then sat down and helped himself to eggs and biscuits.

"Are we out already?" his mother asked.

"No. But maybe Sarah's woodpile is getting low."

His mother's smile widened. "We wouldn't want that to happen."

"No," Hunter agreed. He sipped his coffee, trying to convince himself he was doing the right thing. Sarah might come out and demand he take the wood back to their woodlot before he had it unloaded.

"Just go ahead and do it," Angela said. "Sarah won't cause a scene in front of her neighbors."

Hunter, his fork halfway to his mouth, gave her a surprised look.

Angela smiled widely. "You'll see. It will be all right."

"Yes, it will," his mother agreed. "Sarah's a sensible woman."

"But a prideful one," Hunter said.

Naturally, he hadn't told his mother or Angela about what had happened at Sarah's house a few days ago. But somehow, they seemed to know. It was in the way they looked at him.

When he'd left Sarah's house he'd been determined to wait for her to make the next move. Despite her denials, he thought she still loved him. But she was a long way from forgiving him.

After the first time he'd tried to talk to her a few days ago, he'd known she still felt deep anger toward him, but he'd expected that to lessen when he finally told her everything.

What a fool he'd been to believe that.

And if he waited for her to make the next move, he might wait for a long time. Too long for his impatient nature.

Sarah hadn't been at church Sunday. He'd counted on that—her sitting next to him, sharing a hymn book. It would have been a good chance to soften her.

His mother, concerned, asked Angela to go see if she was all right. Angela returned saying Sarah was as good as could be expected and to send Nicholas over as usual for his studying on Monday.

Today was Tuesday. Hunter had waited long enough.

"Sarah has a lot of pride," his mother agreed. "I

admire that, but sometimes I could shake her. She's always willing to help other people, but she hates to accept help from anyone herself.''

"When you're at rock-bottom, pride is often all you have left,'' Angela said.

His mother frowned. "Surely Sarah doesn't feel that bad. If she does, we have to do something to help.''

Hunter hoped to God she didn't, but he feared Angela might be right. "That's just what I'm planning today, Mama.''

He finished his coffee and rose. "Will you walk Nicholas to school, Angela? I'd like to get an early start.''

"Of course. You just go ahead.''

In the hall, he met Nicholas, who was dressed for school.

"Where are you going, Daddy?''

"To haul some wood for Sarah,'' he said. He liked the sound of that. Not only haul it but chop it and bring some in her house, too.

And after that, talk to her.

He headed out to the big woodlot in back of the house.

An hour later, Hunter pulled the wagon to a stop in the lane behind Sarah's house. He didn't see a sign of her. Good. He'd like to be well into the unloading before she spotted him.

Her woodpile *was* low. Not more than enough to see her through another week.

Hunter guided the horse into the big backyard and quickly began. The sun shone and the snow had nearly melted. Only a few small patches remained here and there.

The wood was well-seasoned hardwood, some of it

apple from a couple of old trees he'd felled last year. That would smell good burning.

He'd just gotten started when he heard the back door open. His arms full of wood, he glanced toward the house.

His heart gave a leap. Sarah stood on the back porch. She was frowning, her arms folded across her chest. Not a good sign.

"Good morning, Sarah," he called.

Instead of answering, she unfolded her arms and walked down the steps.

Hunter carefully stacked the wood he carried, then straightened up. Sarah was halfway across the yard, her face unsmiling, her stride determined. He grabbed another armload, and when he had finished stacking it, she was standing beside him.

"Nice day," he offered, smiling.

Sarah didn't smile back. She refolded her arms. "What do you think you're doing?"

Hunter kept his smile in place. He gestured at the wagon. "Bringing you some wood."

"I don't need any wood," she said, her voice crisp.

Hunter shrugged. "You may not today or tomorrow, but you will pretty soon."

"I'll worry about that when the time comes. I can buy wood when I need to."

Hunter was beginning to share his mother's sentiments. He felt like shaking Sarah himself. Imagining his hands on her shoulders, he revised his thoughts.

No, what he wanted to do was pull her into his arms and kiss the stubborn look off her face.

If he thought that would work, he'd do it, too. Unfortunately, he didn't. At this point, it would only make things between them worse.

He'd try another tack. "Mama wants to pay you back for helping her so much these last few months."

His mother hadn't exactly *said* that, but he knew she felt that way.

Sarah's frown lessened just a bit.

"Faith doesn't owe me anything," she said. "I wanted to help her."

Hunter felt a surge of satisfaction. She'd just given him a perfect response.

"And now she wants to help you. Surely, you wouldn't deny her that."

Sarah looked confused. She bit her lower lip.

Hunter imagined himself giving her tiny love bites on that full pink lower lip. Then deepening the kiss . . .

He felt his body heating and reluctantly pushed the images aside, concentrating on what he had to do.

Which was get himself inside her house to talk to her.

And maybe more.

There was still a spark between them. He had to fan it . . . but not too much or it would go completely out . . . .

"Mama doesn't like to be beholden to anyone," he said, pressing his advantage. Sarah couldn't balk at that, since she was much the same way.

The seconds ticked by, while he watched her struggling with her conscience and herself.

Finally, she heaved a sigh. "Go ahead and unload the wood. And thank Faith for me."

Hunter nodded, turning to the wagon again, concealing his satisfied smile.

"And thank you, Hunter, for bringing it," Sarah said from behind him.

He glanced at her. "You're very welcome, Sarah," he answered, his voice and words as politely formal as hers.

She quickly turned and walked up the yard to the house, her back straight, her head high.

Hunter continued with his work. He had to admire her spunk even while exasperation surged through him.

But if she thought he'd finish his task, then quietly leave, she was sadly wrong. He'd be tired and thirsty by that time. Even if Sarah was still angry with him, she couldn't refuse him a glass of water.

He set to work with a will. After he finished unloading the wood, he saw she didn't have much split for the kitchen range. Had she been doing that herself, too? No doubt.

He tugged loose the ax sunk in the scarred cutting stump and laid down a chunk of apple wood.

Half an hour later, Hunter stuck the ax back in its place and straightened his aching back. Sarah wouldn't have to split any wood for a good long while.

He was a little out of shape. Too many years of doing indoor work and living in the city. It wouldn't take long for him to get back into shape though, now that he was home again.

Home. He savored that word in his mind. Home in Little Bethlehem, where he belonged.

Where his true love lived.

Hunter's pulse began to race at that thought. He glanced toward Sarah's house. He hadn't seen or heard a peep from her since she'd gone back inside.

He was truly thirsty now. Asking Sarah for a drink of water wouldn't be just an excuse to go inside. He picked up a huge armload of the split wood and headed purposefully toward the house.

Through the window in the back door he saw Sarah sitting at the kitchen table, knitting. Her head was bent, her fingers flashed among strands of brown yarn.

A stray sunbeam hit her hair, making the light strands stand out in the brown.

She raised her head, and their glances met. For a moment, her face was vulnerable, open. She looked like the young girl he'd grown up with and suddenly fallen in love with one day.

Guilt and grief struck Hunter's heart.

Why hadn't he been strong enough to wait for her?

Sarah's face closed. The vulnerable look faded. She laid her knitting down on the tabletop and rose.

She was no young girl now. She was a strong, determined woman.

Sarah opened the kitchen door.

Even on this wintry day, she smelled of violets. Her fair skin was a bit flushed; her hazel eyes showed glints of green. He burned to sweep her into his arms and kiss her until nothing mattered except their feelings for each other.

But he wouldn't. Besides his arms were full of wood that was getting heavy.

"Come inside and put that wood down," she said, her voice polite and colorless.

But you don't feel like that, Sarah, my girl, he told her silently as he entered the cheerful, warm room and dumped his load into the woodbox behind the stove.

If you'd lost all your love for me, you couldn't have kissed me like you did a few days ago.

Now he had to figure out how to stay long enough to thaw her some. To fan those flames just the right amount . . .

Over her protests he made several more trips and filled the kitchen woodbox, then the parlor's.

After depositing his last load he went to the kitchen range. Her head turned away, Sarah stirred cocoa in the blue-speckled pan.

He stripped off his gloves and held his hands out to the stove's warmth. "Chilly out there," he said.

"Yes, but the sun's shining. It should warm up soon."

"Could a thirsty man get a drink of water?"

She gave him a quick look. "Of course. And thanks again for carrying all that wood in."

"You're welcome."

At least she was talking to him.

Hunter watched as Sarah walked to the washstand, where a pail of water sat, a dipper inside it. She moved so gracefully, her lissome curves not hidden by the green-and-brown-checked cotton dress she wore.

He tore his glance away. *Go slowly,* he reminded himself.

His gaze fell on the pan of cocoa.

"Mmm, that smells good," he said.

That was subtle, Hunter, he told himself. Never mind subtlety. He'd do whatever worked.

Sarah brought the glass of water and held it out to him. He took it, trying not to touch her fingers as he so badly wanted to do. He wanted to touch a lot more than her fingers if he was going to be honest.

"Sit down, and I'll bring you a cup," she said.

A flash of satisfaction went through him. He dampened it.

He'd realized another thing these last few days. He'd have to start all over again with Sarah. Court her as he'd done when they were so young. One step at a time, no matter how he burned to hold her and love her.

Hunter seated himself. Sarah brought him a steaming cup and refilled her own.

She sat down, giving him a quick glance; then she hastily bundled up her knitting and placed it on another chair, as if she didn't want him to see.

He puzzled over that for a moment; then a light dawned. He'd bet she was making him a Christmas present.

A pleased feeling went through him, until he realized that didn't mean anything. She always gave his mother a homemade gift. Naturally, this year she'd include the others now in Mama's household.

He hadn't thought about giving Sarah a Christmas gift, but of course he'd have to. *Wanted* to, he amended.

He glanced across the table. Sarah's slim fingers curved around her cup, her head was downcast as if she didn't want to look at him.

No use talking further about the past that still stood between them like a brick wall. He didn't want to start an argument.

Nicholas. Sarah would talk about him, discuss his learning problems.

Hunter sipped his cocoa and put the cup down. "Thanks for finding time to help Nicholas with his reading and writing."

Sarah glanced up, her mouth tightening. "Time is something I have plenty of."

Hunter mentally kicked himself for reminding her she'd lost her teaching position.

"It's still very generous of you," he said. "What with Christmas coming, you no doubt have a lot of things to do."

Come into my arms, he told her silently, despite his resolutions of only a few moments ago. He willed her to feel the strength of his desire. *Let me hold you, love you.*

She shrugged, her glance sliding to the pile of knitting on the chair beside her. "Some."

What else could he say about Nicholas? He couldn't say his son's skills had improved a lot in just a few days.

He glanced out the window. His horse was getting restless despite its buckets of grain and water. He couldn't stay much longer.

He saw something else.

"It's snowing again! If it lasts, I'll take Nicholas sledding this afternoon."

Sarah also glanced out the window, and when she turned back to him, a tiny smile curved her lips.

Those delectable lips he wanted so much to kiss.

How he'd love to pull her out into this snow, laugh with her as they played like children. There was no chance she'd go along with that.

"Good," she said. "Nicholas will enjoy that."

How he'd like for Sarah to be snuggled up against him in the old sleigh, blankets piled on their laps . . . snow crunching under the sleigh runners, a moon overhead . . .

His smile widened. "Remember the fun we used to have in the winter?"

Still smiling, she nodded. "Yes."

Keep on fanning the spark.

"How long's it been since you've made a snowman?"

Her smile died. "Last winter, at the schoolhouse. I helped the children make a huge one."

He'd put his foot in it again. Wasn't there anything

he could say that wouldn't remind her of losing her school?

"What about a snowball fight?"

At her tight-lipped look, he shook his head. "Another thing you did at the school. Sarah, I did all I could to prevent what happened, but I failed."

She looked at him a moment. "I know. I—I don't think I even thanked you for what you tried to do. But I appreciate it."

He yearned to pull her into his arms and tell her it didn't matter about the school. Beg her to marry him. Make her see they could have a full, happy life.

But it was too soon for that.

Twice she'd kissed him with passion since his return, proving beyond doubt her physical feelings for him still lived. He thought her love did, too.

But that wasn't enough. She had to be willing to give her heart and soul to him again.

Her mouth firmed. Her look became direct. "There isn't anything you can do. I'll manage. In the spring, I'll try to find another teaching job away from here."

Alarm ran through him. He *had* to keep her here in Little Bethlehem until she realized they still belonged to each other.

"Maybe it won't come to that. Wouldn't you miss the town?"

Wouldn't you miss me and Nicholas?

She stared at him. "*You* left. You were gone for eight years."

Her voice held a challenge.

He didn't want to pick it up.

"Yes, and I missed it every day of those years. I'm so glad to be back I feel like shouting with joy each morning when I wake up. I never want to leave here again."

But you may have to, his mind said. *If you don't get things straightened out with Enid. If you don't get backing for your cannery.*

"It's a good town to bring up children in," Hunter said. "Nicholas is happy here."

"Yes," Sarah agreed. "I have a lot of good childhood memories."

"So do I," Hunter said, his spirits lifting again. "Daddy and Mama enjoyed the winters as much as I did."

"Yes," Sarah said again, her face softening. "I remember all three of you on that big sled. Faith didn't care if the neighbors were scandalized."

"Nope, she didn't. I don't think it would take much to have her out on it again."

"You still have that sled?" Sarah asked.

"Yep. Saw it in the barn the other day."

"Daddy used to take me sledding," Sarah said in a moment. "Mama never felt up to those things." She gave him a quick glance. "But you know all that."

"Yes." He held her gaze steadily. "Your father used to take *both* of us sledding," he reminded her.

"That's right," Sarah said, her eyes taking on a faraway look, as if she was lost in the past.

Fan the spark, Hunter told himself. This was a past Hunter wanted her to be lost in. One which could bring them closer together again.

"Do you ever ice-skate now?" he asked, hoping this wouldn't bring back another memory of activities she'd shared with her schoolchildren.

Sarah's eyes refocused. "Oh, yes. When Brinkman's Pond freezes solid, half the town turns out to skate."

A picture of them, arms linked, gliding smoothly down the length of the pond, filled his mind.

Right after he'd managed the sleigh ride, he'd pray for the snow to melt and a good, hard freeze to come.

"Good. I'm glad that hasn't changed. Remember how we raced each other?"

"Yes, and you didn't always win."

The ghost of a smile still lingering at the corners of her mouth widened into a small grin.

His breath caught. A *grin*. A real grin.

"What if I told you I *let* you win those few times?" he asked.

"I'd say your memory was faulty," she shot back, her hazel eyes sparkling. "Neither of us *let* the other win anything."

No, not even a kiss, he told her silently, remembering the first one they'd shared. He hadn't stolen it from her. She was as eager and ready as he. That kiss had been so sweetly, innocently passionate . . . .

It was all he could do to keep from asking her if she remembered that experience, too.

If he did she'd have him out of here in ten seconds.

"Are you still a good skater?" he asked instead. "Wonder who'd win now?"

Couldn't she hear the other meaning in his voice, in his words? Didn't she know he wanted them both to win in this game of love?

Her eyes flickered, the color darkening a little.

He tensed, half expecting her to push back her chair and rise, signaling his wangled visit was ended.

"Yes," she said, her voice steady. "I'm better. Since I've had so much more practice."

Eight years more practice. The words hung in the air. But she didn't say them.

Hunter's tension eased a bit.

"I've let my skating skills rust. But I'll get them back. Then I'll challenge you to another race."

"No," she said lightly, "Leave that to the young ones. I'm just an old-maid school—"

The sparkle in her eyes faded. And the softness of old memories shared. Sarah rose, pushing back her chair.

She picked up her cup and saucer in one hand and held out the other for his. "I didn't realize how late it's getting. I won't keep you any longer."

Hunter's jaw tightened. He had to leave now. And much too soon. He hadn't accomplished his mission.

He also rose, handing her his dishes.

Sarah walked across the room and put them in the pan sitting on the back of the stove.

"I remember that pan," he said, looking at the galvanized tin. "It belonged to your grandmother. She'd fill it full of popcorn for Christmas Eve and put a big red bow on the side."

Sarah turned. "Yes," she said casually, as if it were of no importance.

It was though, and she knew it. There were too many memories between them, too many ties for her not to be aware of them.

She followed him to the back door. His hand on the knob, he turned to her one last time. "Good-bye, Sarah. I'll be waiting for the pond to freeze."

He wouldn't wait that long. If this snow stayed, he'd ask Angela to invite Sarah for the sleigh ride.

Sarah gave him a small smile, her glance cool. "Thanks again for bringing the wood. And please thank Faith, too."

His smile was wider. "I will. You know Mama's still in your debt, so this won't be the only thing she offers."

"She's not in my debt and I don't want her to feel like that," Sarah protested.

"Mama has a lot of pride, too," he reminded her.

He wanted to kiss her. Just a simple good-bye kiss. His gaze traveled up to her eyes again and held.

Sarah's lips parted a tiny bit. She moved forward a fraction of an inch. If he hadn't been looking so intently at her he wouldn't have caught it.

Yes, the spark was still alive.

She still loved him. The smoldering embers would burst into flames again. But it would take work, lots of it. He had to make her see the bonds between them had never broken.

"Good-bye, Sarah," he said again.

Did she know how much he wanted her?

When Hunter turned and opened the door, he heard a tiny gasp from behind him. He hoped it was a frustrated gasp. He hoped she'd expected him to kiss her and was disappointed.

But he wasn't sure.

He wasn't sure at all.

CHAPTER TWELVE

"Walter, please stop that," Crystal said, trying to put authority into her voice and knowing she'd failed.

Walter didn't even glance in her direction. He just pulled back on the leather of his slingshot again and let it whack against Roger's shoulder.

One of the girls giggled. Out of the corner of her eye, Crystal saw Lorna Miller's anxious, half-pitying frown.

She felt her face warming. She blushed so many times a day it was a wonder her face hadn't turned permanently red.

The noon meal hours, like now, were the worst. Since there was no schoolyard, the building being surrounded by weeds and bushes, the children had to stay indoors all the time, except for trips to the outhouse, which the boys took full advantage of.

Today, they'd finished eating and there was still

half an hour before school started again. Walter and Roger were, as usual, acting up.

The day after they'd walked out of school to join the other two hooky-playing boys, four irate mothers had descended on Crystal, demanding she keep better order. Saying they wouldn't even have known their sons weren't at school if George Randolph hadn't seen them sneaking around in town.

Crystal hadn't known what to say or do. Finally, the women had left, and at once the children had begun their tricks again.

Walter tired of teasing Roger and climbed on a desk. He puffed out his chest and started beating it. "Look at me. I'm an ape!" He made a warbling sound that made some of the children giggle and some look disgusted.

Nicholas gave Walter a wide-eyed, admiring glance.

"You sound more like a monkey to me," Lorna said. "Get down from there, Walter Darby."

He gave her a scornful look. "I don't have to mind you. You're not my teacher."

He glanced at Crystal, grinned and beat his chest and warbled again.

"Hey, you're not a good ape. Look at me." Roger got up on another desk and began beating and warbling himself.

Crystal wrung her hands, tears coming to her eyes.

Hearing the creak of the rusty old door hinges, she glanced toward it. Angela, dressed in a blue cape and carrying a covered pail with a red bow tied around it, entered.

Crystal closed her eyes, her mortification complete. If things weren't bad enough, Angela had to come in now.

But instead of looking shocked, Angela beamed at everyone.

"Hello," she said, her merry voice rising above the noise. She raised the pail and shook it. "I've brought some cookies."

To Crystal's amazement, the room instantly quieted. Walter got down from the desk, followed by Roger. The children crowded around Angela, but in an orderly way, respect in their faces.

"Christmas sugar cookies," Angela said, taking off the pail's lid. She removed a large napkin from the pail, spread it across an empty desk top, then laid the cookies, sparkling with sugar and cut into Christmas shapes, on it.

Five minutes later, the children were settled in small groups, quietly talking as they ate. Crystal sat in her desk chair, Angela beside her in a chair she'd pulled over.

Crystal looked at Angela in wonder. "How did you do that? Are you a teacher?"

Angela gave her merry laugh that sounded like bells tinkling. "Not at the moment, child. But, yes, in my time, I've done some schoolmarming."

Crystal sighed, feeling tears coming to her eyes again. She blinked them back, hoping Angela hadn't seen. But one escaped and rolled down her cheek.

Angela wiped the tear away with a gentle finger. "What's the matter? Are you having trouble?"

Crystal tried to laugh, but what came out was a strangled sound. "I'm just no good at this. I *hate* teaching."

"Then why are you doing it? You don't have to teach to earn your living."

Crystal was surprised Angela didn't know. Everyone

else in town seemed to. "Because my mother wants me to."

Angela smiled. "Crystal dear, you're past the age when you're required to do what your parents want. I don't mean you should show them disrespect, but if you're not suited for this job, and it's making you so miserable, why don't you give it up?"

Put like that, so clear and simple, it did sound absurd. What was she afraid of? Did she think Mama would turn her out of the house? No, of course not. Even if Mama wanted to, Daddy wouldn't let her.

Did she think they'd lock her in her room? Feed her bread and water? Both ideas were so ridiculous that despite her misery Crystal felt a smile tugging at her lips.

The truth was, her parents wouldn't *do* anything to her.

What she feared was her mother's tongue. If she quit, Mama would be at her all the time, haranguing.

Crystal's incipient smile died.

Angela shook her head. "Your mama loves you dearly, and she thinks she knows what's best for you, but that isn't always the case."

Crystal's eyes widened. How had Angela gotten right to the heart of the matter? Known just what the problem was?

Angela patted Crystal's shoulder. "You're a grown woman. You know yourself better than anyone else ever can. And you're very fortunate that you don't have to take any job that comes your way to survive."

"The only thing I'm really good at is overseeing a household. I've helped Mama with that since I was twelve."

Angela beamed, clasping her hands together in front of her. "Domestic tasks are still most women's domain. Can you actually perform household chores, or do you just make sure other people do them properly?"

"I love to cook, and I don't mind cleaning. I can do a lot of things." Crystal glanced at the stove and made a face. "Except build fires."

Angela smiled and nodded, as if she didn't find this lack shocking. "Have you thought of marriage? A pretty girl like you should have all the bachelors in town fighting over her."

David Hopkins's handsome face filled Crystal's mind's eye. She could feel herself blushing again.

"Two or three years ago, I had some suitors. Mama didn't like any of them. And I didn't much either."

And David Hopkins wouldn't please Mama.

"So none of the suitors suit?" Angela's blue eyes twinkled merrily. Crystal had to smile back.

Angela patted her shoulder again. "You're old enough to know your own heart, dear. I must be getting back. I guess we'll see you at the church?"

Crystal's blush deepened. Had Angela discovered she had a secret yen for their minister?

"You'll be there to work on the pageant preparations won't you," Angela went on.

"Oh, yes, of course," Crystal answered, relieved.

"Good-bye until then." Angela picked up her now empty pail, folded the napkin, and put it inside. She poked at the red bow until it stood up jauntily again. "Children have bottomless stomachs, don't they?"

Crystal didn't want to think about this particular bunch of children that she must try to discipline and teach for several more long hours today.

"Thanks for bringing the cookies, Angela. It gave me a few minutes of peace."

"Peace is one of the most wonderful things in the

world," Angela said. "It's what Christmas is all about."

Crystal closed her eyes. Yes, it was, and since she'd taken this job, she'd had neither peace nor Christmas spirit.

Angela turned to the room. "Good-bye, children."

All the children said good-bye back. She waved and left.

Crystal took a deep breath and turned to face her charges again. They still stood looking toward the door Angela had just gone out.

Why, their expressions were almost pleasant, Crystal saw, amazed. Her spirits lifted a bit. Maybe they'd just needed a treat. Maybe they'd behave this afternoon and listen to what she said.

Crystal cleared her throat and stood up. She forced a smile. "It's time to get back to our lessons, children," she said, hating the wobble in her last words.

Walter grinned at her. "But I didn't finish showing everyone my ape imitation." He climbed up on a desk again and started pounding his chest and yodeling.

"Neither did I," Roger said, climbing on another desk.

Crystal's spirits once more sank. Whatever magic Angela had possessed had obviously left with her.

Nicholas climbed up on a desk next to Roger's and began beating his chest and imitating the ape noises.

Crystal sucked in her breath, her humiliation complete. Her own nephew was openly defying her! Two other boys joined in and most of the other children cheered them on, clapping their hands and laughing.

She clenched her hands into fists at her sides and closed her eyes. She couldn't stand another day of this. Not even the rest of this afternoon.

She heard the door open on its creaking hinges again and slam against the wall.

Crystal jerked her head around. A bunch of women, some carrying babies in their arms with toddlers at their feet, and a few men stood in the open doorway.

They looked angry and all of them gaped at Walter and Roger and Nicholas, still standing on the desks.

For the second time in an hour, Crystal wished the floor would open up and swallow her.

Rosie Darby's outraged voice rose above the melee. "Walter, you get down off that desk this minute. Do you hear me?"

Walter turned a startled face toward his mother. "Yessum," he said and quickly scrambled down.

"Roger, you do the same," Joanne Kane barked. Her son hastily obeyed. "I never saw such a shameful spectacle in my life. Nicholas Winslow, you get down, too. You just wait until your Daddy hears about this!"

Crystal swallowed. And Hunter would go straight to Mama. She'd never hear the end of it.

Other parents chided their offspring, and in a few moments, all the children sat meekly at their desks.

Acting like butter wouldn't melt in their mouths, Crystal thought, her amazement mixed with growing anger.

Mrs. Kane turned to Crystal, her dark eyes shooting sparks. "Miss Cunningham, after the boys played hooky the other day, I went to the other parents, and we're here to talk to you. We don't have a lot of time to waste either. We need to get back to work."

She glanced around. "We can't believe you have no more control of the younguns than this."

"That's right," Rosie Darby said, her voice indignant.

Annoyed agreement came from the other parents.

Crystal swallowed, trying to think of some way to defend herself, to explain why she'd let her classroom get so completely out of hand.

Her classroom?

No, this wasn't her classroom. Everything suddenly became clear in her mind.

It had never been her school or her children. It never would be.

This was *Sarah's* classroom. These were *Sarah's* schoolchildren.

Crystal raised her head and looked the other woman in the eye. "I'm not cut out to be a teacher, Mrs. Kane. I don't like the job and I don't want to do it."

Mrs. Kane gaped at her. "Then why in tarnation did you take it?" she demanded.

"Yes, why?" a chorus of voices rose all around her.

Crystal took a deep breath and let it out. "Because my mother wanted me to," she said for the second time in a few minutes.

"That's not a good enough reason," another woman said.

"No!" others joined in.

Crystal took another deep breath. "You're right. It isn't. Would all of you like to have Sarah Calder back?"

This time the children joined in the chorus of yesses that arose, Nicholas's voice louder than the others, a wide smile on his face.

Crystal didn't care. She smiled and nodded. For the first time since she'd started this horrible job, she felt lighthearted and happy.

"Then come with me."

She didn't know where Hunter was, but she'd find him. He'd help her get this mess straightened out.

* * *

An hour later, Crystal, flanked by Joanne and Rosie, walked up the front steps of her parents' house and opened the ornate front door.

Mattie Randolph, hurrying down the hall, stopped in surprise. "Why, Miss Crystal, what are you doing home at this time of day?"

The girl's glance took in Rosie and Joanne, then went over their heads to the group of people crowding the driveway, to the buggies and carriages, even a wagon, behind them.

Crystal tilted her chin up and firmed her mouth. "We're here for a meeting, Mattie. Go tell Mama. I know she's here. The carriage is out back."

Mattie blinked and retreated a step. "Yessum, she's here, but she's not gonna like all these folks barging in on her."

Crystal firmed her mouth a little more. "Move aside, Mattie."

Mattie did, her astonished gaze leaving the crowd and settling on Crystal with new respect.

That made Crystal feel better. She must look determined and sure of herself, even if inside she quaked.

She hadn't minded everything she and Hunter had done this afternoon nearly as much as she dreaded facing her own mother.

Crystal went inside, Joanne and Rosie and the rest following closely.

"What in the world is all the commotion out here?"

Mama came briskly down the hall from the direction of the kitchen, wearing a big white apron.

Her eyes widened as she saw the throng, and she frowned at Crystal. "Why are you here instead of teaching your school? And what are these people doing here?"

Crystal drew a deep breath and held it for a moment before releasing it.

"It's not my school, Mama—it's Sarah's. She shouldn't have lost it. These people are here to see that she gets it back."

Her mother's mouth dropped open. She looked at Crystal as if she'd never seen her before. "What is the matter with you? Is your head addled?"

Crystal took another deep breath. "No. I finally got it on straight, thanks to some things Angela said."

Her mother closed her mouth with a snap. "What does Angela have to do with any of this?"

"That's not important."

To Crystal's relief, her nervousness ebbed by the second. Those first words, when she'd talked back to her mother, had been the worst.

"Now, if you'll please step aside, we'll go to the parlor, where there's more room. Mattie, will you show everyone in there?"

Her eyes still fixed on Crystal as if she were a stranger, Mama opened and closed her mouth again, then moved to the side.

The group of people nodded respectfully. Led by Mattie, they headed for the parlor.

Crystal stayed behind. "Hunter is bringing Dr. Lawson and Daddy up with him for the meeting."

"What meeting?"

"The emergency school board meeting. Hunter and Joanne and Rosie and I got everyone together."

Enid was backed against the hall settee. She sat down with a plop. "You . . . *you* arranged all this?"

Her voice was so incredulous, Crystal had to smile.

"I helped. Everyone wants Sarah back as teacher."

Her mother stared. "I can't believe that."

"It's true. I never should have tried to teach. I'm no good at it."

"That's just because it's so new to you. Naturally, it will take a while to get used to it."

Crystal sighed. "I don't *want* to teach. This was your idea, not mine."

"Fiddlesticks," her mother said briskly, getting up and removing her apron. She folded it and handed it to Mattie, who was now back in the hallway, her eyes avid with interest.

Crystal knew she had to finish this. Her newfound courage might not last.

"That's not all, Mama. You have to stop pushing me at Hunter. We could never care for each other in that way. Besides, everyone in Little Bethlehem knows Hunter's in love with Sarah."

Her mother glared. "I don't know what's come over you, but I won't listen to this nonsense."

Crystal tried to summon a return glare, but settled for a frown. "It's not nonsense. I mean every word. If you won't let me live my own life, I—I'll go to Spring Grove and be Aunt Belle's companion. She's wanted me to do that since Uncle Isaac died."

The two women had never gotten along. It would humiliate her mother if she did this. Crystal stood her ground, head up.

Mama's glare faded into a frosty look. "What do you plan to do with your life? Become an old maid?"

Crystal's cheeks burned. Mama had given in, but not gracefully. "No, I hope to marry and have a family of my own."

"I didn't know anyone had offered for your hand. Or is this another surprise you've kept from your father and me?"

"No. But that doesn't mean no one ever will."

Behind her mother, Mattie grinned, silently clapping her hands in support.

Crystal heard another buggy pull up. Mattie hurried to the door and let in her father and Dr. Lawson, and behind them Hunter and David. Her father looked flustered, Dr. Lawson and Hunter determined and David concerned. His dark hair was tousled endearingly.

Crystal's fingers itched to run her hands through it and smooth the locks down.

He smiled at Crystal.

She smiled back, her heart fluttering. "The others are in the parlor."

Hunter gave her an encouraging smile, which she returned.

"This is most irregular, Dudley," her mother snapped.

Unsmiling, her father looked at her mother. "Enid, everything about this mess has been irregular and should never have happened. I don't mind bending some rules to try to make things right."

All the men headed for the parlor.

Mama opened her mouth again, but nothing came out. She sat down on the settee.

Crystal brushed by her, following the men.

Every seat in the big room was filled. Mattie brought in some dining room chairs and put them in any empty spaces.

Joanne Kane made room on the settee she occupied with Rosie Darby and motioned for Crystal to join them.

David settled into a chair right in front of Crystal. Her heart did a happy little skip.

Hunter, Dr. Lawson, and her father made their way

to the area where the official members of the school board were seated.

David shifted in his seat, making Crystal newly aware of his tall, strong body. She suddenly wondered if her hair was mussed, and she wished she'd worn something more flattering than her gray bombazine gown.

Her father, still looking determined but flustered, quickly brought the impromptu meeting to order.

"As far as I know this kind of meeting isn't actually illegal. Does everyone agree to go ahead with it?"

A loud chorus of ayes answered.

"We have only one thing to deal with," her father continued. "Whether to reinstall Sarah Calder as the teacher in Little Bethlehem's school."

Crystal saw Hunter frown and his mouth tighten as if he was worried about the outcome.

David shifted in his seat again. Resolutely, Crystal kept her eyes off him.

"Before we vote, does anyone want to take the floor?"

"I would," Burt Williams said.

Wearing old work clothes, he looked at her father. "Dudley, we've known each other twenty years. I've come to you more than once to borrow crop money."

Her father nodded. "Yes, of course, Burt."

"Have I ever not paid you back on time?"

"No."

"I've been ashamed of myself since I voted to fire Sarah. I'm votin' to put her back. In the spring, I'm goin' to need a loan. If you can't see your way clear to give me one, I'll try that new bank in Spring Grove."

Her father's florid face was redder than usual. He looked embarrassed, ashamed, and angry.

"Burt, have I ever given you reason to believe my

loans have anything to do with how you vote on school board business?"

The parlor door opened, then closed. Crystal glanced back. Mama stood just inside the room, her face set and angry.

"Nothin' like this has come up before. And we all know how your wife feels about Sarah."

Crystal saw her father's mouth thin and tighten.

"Sarah's been wronged," he said heavily. "This meeting is to try to rectify that wrong."

A satisfied look on his weathered face, Burt sat back down.

Crystal darted another glance at Hunter. His frown had smoothed out some, his mouth relaxed a bit.

"Does anyone else want to speak?" her father asked. He glanced across the room and his face tightened more as he saw her mother.

"Yes, I do." Oliver Madison, owner of the biggest mercantile in town, rose.

Oliver looked uncomfortable, Crystal thought, watching him run his finger around the edge of his tight-fitting collar. Unlike most of the others here, he wore a suit with a white shirt and tie.

"What Burt said also applies to me. We've talked about a loan to expand my store. I'd like to do business with you, but as Burt says, there's a new bank in Spring Grove now."

Her father's face darkened. "I've never given loans with any other consideration than if the borrower can repay them. I never will."

"That's all *I* need to hear, too." Oliver quickly sat down.

Crystal frowned. Her father suddenly looked old and tired. Was he all right?

He took in a breath and let it out. "Does anyone else have a piece to speak before we vote?"

"Yes!" Her mother's voice, shrill with anger, came from the back. "Sarah Calder was fired for carelessness with the children's lives. I can't believe all you parents want to put her back in as teacher."

Crystal sighed. Mama wouldn't give in gracefully on this either.

She glanced at Hunter again, wondering if he'd speak up for Sarah.

His frown was back, his mouth tight again. He rose from his seat. "Dudley, may I have the floor?"

Her father turned and looked at him. "Hunter, you defended Sarah right nobly at the other meeting. And if necessary, you can do it today. But I want you to wait a minute."

Not looking satisfied, Hunter sat down again.

Her father glanced around the crowded room. "Would any of you parents care to comment on what my wife said?"

"I would." Rosie Darby heaved herself to her feet and turned toward the other woman.

"Most people didn't believe that hogwash about Sarah—*I* never did. But I couldn't do much about it since Morse ain't on the school board. Walter ain't learned a thing since your girl took over. Half the time I don't even know if he's in school. Crystal's a nice, sweet girl. She just ain't a good teacher. She said so herself. We need Sarah back right now."

Beside Crystal, Joanne clapped her hands in approval. "Rosie's right!"

Voices raised in agreement came from all around the room.

Crystal glanced at Hunter again. His arms were folded across his chest and he wore a satisfied smile.

Her father pounded on a table with his fist since he didn't have his gavel.

Gradually, the room quieted.

"It seems pointless to take a vote," he said. "But I guess we should try to maintain some kind of order."

Crystal heard her mother's sniff all the way from the back of the room. "I am resigning as a member of this school board," she said frostily, then left the room, banging the door behind her.

The remaining board unanimously voted to rehire Sarah as Little Bethlehem's schoolteacher.

Afterward, the room erupted with happy cheers, people shaking hands and clapping each other on the back.

Hunter quickly left the room. Crystal was sure he was going to tell Sarah the good news.

David moved around, talking to everyone. When he reached Crystal, his smile broadened.

"A wonderful thing was done here today."

Crystal's heart fluttered again. She felt warm inside just looking at him. "Yes," she agreed. She wished he'd stay and talk to her, but how would that look?

She suddenly didn't care, but of course she couldn't tell him that.

But to her surprise, he lingered, as if he *wanted* to stay. Finally, he moved off. Crystal looked after him, a yearning expression on her face.

She should feel sorry for Mama's humiliation, but she didn't. Mama had brought it on herself by treating Sarah as she had.

One of her mother's favorite expressions was if you make your bed you have to lie in it.

She guessed Mama had a pretty miserable night ahead of her.

CHAPTER THIRTEEN

Slowing his rapid pace down the street, Hunter opened Sarah's gate and looked toward the house. The curtains in her front room were pushed aside to let in the wintry sun, but he didn't see any movement inside.

His pleased excitement dimmed a bit. He hoped she was home. He badly wanted to be the first to tell her she had her school back, to see the happy look on her face.

He should have waited for the other school board members. This wasn't proper procedure, but after all the rules that had been broken today, one more shouldn't matter.

He hurried up the walk and across the porch and knocked on the door. He heard no movement and disappointment grew inside him. Sarah must not be home.

Then he saw a flash of green skirt, saw her coming from the kitchen, and his heart lifted.

He hadn't seen her since he'd brought the wood. Only two days ago. It seemed as if weeks had passed. He wondered if she felt like that, too. He still hadn't gotten the sleigh ride arranged because most of the new snow had already melted, like the earlier falls.

She swung the door open, her hazel eyes widening in surprise, mixed with caution.

How long would it be before delight sprang into her eyes when she saw him? The joy she made him feel with every sight of her?

Hunter smiled. "May I come in, Sarah? I have some wonderful news for you."

She looked even more surprised and didn't move aside. "What are you talking about?"

"I don't want to discuss it standing on your doorstep."

She moved back, but reluctantly.

Hunter came inside and paused. "Can we sit down?"

Sarah frowned, then shrugged. "Of course." She led the way to the kitchen, Hunter following, enjoying the back view of her as he did.

He drew in an appreciative breath. The big, cheerful room smelled of spices and sugar, reminding him it wouldn't be long until Christmas.

And with the news he had to tell Sarah, her Christmas would certainly be brighter than she'd expected.

"Been doing some baking?"

Sarah nodded at the table. On one end, rows of cookies, cut out into various Christmas shapes, dotted with raisins and nuts, were laid out. "These are for Nicholas and the schoolchildren."

Her voice softened when she said his son's name, Hunter noticed. That was a good sign. Her love for Nicholas would have to eventually grow to include him, wouldn't it?

"They look delicious." Without waiting for her to invite him, afraid she wouldn't, Hunter sat down at the table.

In a moment, Sarah did, too, across from him.

"Now," she said, clasping her hands in front of her on the tabletop, her expression still guarded, "what is this wonderful news you have to tell me?"

He gave her another smile. "The others will be here to see you soon. I just couldn't wait."

Sarah frowned again. "*What* others? Hunter, will you please get to the point?"

"The school board voted to rehire you as Little Bethlehem's teacher." He felt a rush of warmth just saying the words and waited for her exclamations of delight.

Instead, she stared at him, her face settling in lines of disbelief and shock. "Rehire me?"

Of course she'd be stunned, Hunter told himself. She hadn't expected anything like this to happen. But once she understood, she'd be overjoyed.

He beamed. "Crystal got all the parents and school board members together for a special meeting at the Cunninghams."

"Why would Crystal do that?"

Hunter gave her a perplexed stare.

"Because she hates to teach. And because she and a lot of others thought you weren't treated fairly."

Sarah abruptly pushed back her chair and stood, her hands on the table edge, grasping it tightly. The muscles of her face were as tight as her white knuckles.

"Where were all my champions when Enid demanded that I be fired?"

Hunter's puzzlement at Sarah's attitude grew. "They were afraid of the Cunninghams. Some of them need loans from the bank."

"And now they don't?"

"Oliver and Burt said they'd try the new bank in Spring Grove," Hunter said, frowning. "Sarah, aren't you happy about this? Don't you want your job back?"

He saw her breasts move as she drew in a breath, then expelled it.

A rush of desire went through him. He pushed it down. As much as he wanted her, loved her, this wasn't the time for showing her how he felt or even thinking about it.

"Of course I do," she said tightly.

"Then what's wrong?"

"It's the *way* it's being offered."

"The way? What do you mean?"

"They're only hiring me back out of desperation," Sarah said, her voice quavering on the last words. "Crystal doesn't want the job and there's no one else available."

Hunter pushed his chair back and rose, too. "Sarah, you've got things all wrong. It isn't like that."

"Isn't it? Are you telling me those aren't the facts?"

"Those are some of the facts, yes," he admitted. "But . . . that's not the way it happened. Sarah, everyone wants you back. Even if there *was* another qualified teacher available, they'd still choose you."

Her face stayed tight. "You can't say that for sure. I won't go back with this blot on my record. I won't be remembered as Sarah Calder, the teacher who got fired for negligence and then was hired back out of desperation."

This wasn't going at all as he'd expected. But he could understand the way she felt. In her circumstances, he'd probably feel the same.

They stood there staring at each other.

"Are you saying you're going to refuse to teach here again?"

The sounds of horses' hooves came from outside.

"Here's the rest of the school board," Hunter said. "Will you talk to them?"

Sarah glanced toward the window. "Yes, I'll talk to them," she finally said.

Hunter felt a bit easier. "Good. Do you want me to go to the door?"

He suddenly realized this situation was a bit awkward. He was alone here with Sarah. Both of them going to the door together would set tongues to wagging, but he didn't see any way out of it. He couldn't sneak out the back door and pretend he'd never been here.

He walked with her to the door and stood behind her when she opened it. Dudley and the rest of the board members stood on the porch, Joanne and Rosie behind them.

As he'd expected a few eyebrows were raised at him standing there with Sarah.

Dudley didn't look good, Hunter noticed. His naturally florid complexion was darker than usual, his face set in lines of strain.

"Sarah, we'd like to talk to you," Dudley said. He glanced over her shoulder at Hunter. "I guess the reason we're here won't be a surprise."

"No," Sarah said, moving aside. "Come in."

She gestured toward the parlor, its door standing open. Everyone followed her into the room. There weren't enough seats, and Hunter went to the kitchen for more.

"I'll help," Burt Williams said.

In the kitchen, Burt picked up a chair then glanced at Hunter.

"After the way I voted against her before, I hate to face up to Sarah."

Hunter guessed most of the board members felt that way. He picked up a chair, too. "That can't be undone," he finally said.

He thought about telling Burt how upset Sarah was, but decided against it. They'd all find out soon enough, and maybe she'd calmed down by now.

In a few minutes everyone had a seat. Dudley sat beside Sarah on a small settee.

Sarah's face was set.

Dudley's smile was strained. "You know why we're here. Everyone in Little Bethlehem wants you to take your job back."

Sarah gave Dudley a direct look. "I can't believe Enid does after the accusations she hurled at me. I see she's not here."

To Dudley's credit, he didn't flinch or look away. "Enid resigned from the board."

Surprise rippled across Sarah's features.

"We don't deserve gettin' you back after the way you've been treated," Rosie Darby said. "Wouldn't blame you if you never spoke to any of us again. But, Sarah, we need you bad."

"Sarah, all my children are grown and gone," Dr. Lawson said. "But in my opinion, you're the best teacher Little Bethlehem has had in a long time."

Relief filling him, Hunter saw Sarah's set features had softened. Her eyes looked oddly shiny as if she fought back a tear or two.

"Then none of you believe I was careless with the children's lives?" she asked.

A loud no resounded through the room.

Dudley cleared his throat. "That, of course, goes for me, too. Sarah, I'm ashamed of my part in this whole sorry mess. I'm resigning my position as board president. I'd like Hunter to take over. It's high time we had some new, younger blood."

Hunter jerked his head around to stare at the older man. Dudley's face was darker than before. He tugged at his collar. It had taken a lot of courage for him to admit he'd been wrong.

Dudley turned to Sarah. "Can you forgive us and be Little Bethlehem's teacher again?"

Dudley's voice sounded shaky, Hunter thought, his concern for the older man growing. He hoped it was just from emotion.

Hunter glanced at Sarah. Her eyes were glistening now, her features softened completely. She looked at Dudley for a long moment, then turned her head and smiled at the other people crowding the room.

"Yes, I will," she said, her own voice shaking a little.

Joanne Kane stood up and clapped. In a moment, everyone else was doing the same.

Hunter applauded along with the others. But his mood was far less jubilant than theirs. These last few minutes had brought home to him just how much of herself Sarah had invested in her teaching job.

It meant the world to her.

And if they married, she'd have to give it up.

His work was cut out for him. It was going to be hard enough to persuade Sarah to marry him. He also must convince her she'd never regret making that decision.

An odd, strangled sound drew his head sharply around.

Dudley clutched his chest, his face almost purple. Hunter jumped up but before he could reach him the older man had toppled to the floor.

CHAPTER FOURTEEN

Sarah hurried down Main Street, preoccupied with the list of things she must do today. It felt wonderful to have that sense of urgency back, she thought—trying to get all her errands finished on the only day she would have until next Saturday.

Yesterday, her first day back as Little Bethlehem's teacher, had gone well. All the students, even Walter and Roger, had seemed glad to see her.

Of course, some of them had had to test her first to see if they'd be able to get away with the undisciplined behavior Crystal had put up with. Even Nicholas had thrown a spitball at one of the girls, she remembered, her lips curving in amusement.

She'd been amazed, but all it took was a quelling look from her to settle him down. Maybe it was even good for him to loosen up a bit.

After the first hour, she'd had her classroom under control again, just as it had been before.

Oh, what a relief it was not to worry about trying to find another teaching position. To know the blot on her reputation was expunged.

Dudley had behaved in so honorable a fashion that day. Her forehead puckered.

She hoped he was better. He'd been taken home unconscious from a heart spell. Enid was beside herself, everyone said. Staying by his bedside day and night, letting no one else but Dr. Lawson near him, and accepting no neighborly help.

Sarah lifted her head in time to see two figures standing before the door of Madison's Mercantile. Her heart leaped.

Hunter had his head bent toward Nicholas, a smile curving his mouth as he listened to something his son said.

Nicholas smiled back, the sweet smile that always turned her to mush. It was obvious he loved his father very much.

Just as you do, a taunting inner voice said.

No, she didn't, she denied, her lips tightening. Hunter drew her physically—she couldn't deny that. Probably he always would.

But she didn't love him. How could she after he'd told her the whole story of what had happened eight years ago with Beryl?

Love had to be accompanied by trust, or it wasn't real love. She could never trust him again. That just wasn't possible.

And why was she worrying about that now? When Hunter had come to her house a few days ago to tell her what the school board had decided, he'd shown no signs of wanting to sweep her into his arms. Nor had he the day he'd brought her the wood and cut it.

Had he decided to give up on her?

I made the mistake eight years ago, Sarah. But you're the one making it now.

No! She wasn't. She was protecting her heart from being broken again.

Hunter and Nicholas went inside the building without looking her way. Sarah stood for a moment, undecided, then tilted her chin and followed them. She needed some things from here. She wouldn't let the fact Hunter was in the store stop her from getting them.

They stood in the middle of the big front room, looking at a brightly painted fire engine suspended from the ceiling, swaying enticingly. Nicholas's small face held a yearning expression.

The sight of the toy brought back memories of the day the schoolhouse had burned and made Sarah's stomach tighten uncomfortably. It surprised her that Nicholas wouldn't feel the same way. But she guessed children got over things faster than adults.

The household section was in the back of the store. She had to go past them to get there. Taking a deep breath, Sarah approached.

Hunter glanced up as she stopped. A spark seemed to appear in his dark eyes for a moment. Or had it? The next instant he nodded and smiled in a merely friendly fashion.

Absurdly, she felt disappointment snake through her and pushed it down. She smiled back. "Hello, Hunter, Nicholas."

"Good morning, Sarah," Hunter said.

"Miss Sarah!" Nicholas tore his absorbed gaze from the fire engine to give her a wide smile. "Isn't that a keen engine?"

Sarah's glance met Hunter's and she saw in his eyes

the same mixture of emotions she felt. Amusement and a little surprise at the boy's interest in this particular toy.

She and Hunter were in tune with each other, just as they'd always been . . . .

She pushed that errant thought down. It didn't matter. They could never go back to those times.

"Yes, it is, Nicholas," she made herself agree.

"I hope I get this for Christmas," he told her, his dark eyes sparkling.

"Perhaps you will," she said, then started to go around them.

"Wait, Sarah," Hunter said. "I'd like your opinion about something if you don't mind."

She *did* mind. She wanted to finish her errands and get out of here.

How you lie. You're afraid to be around Hunter because all you can think about when you're near him is how much you'd like to be in his arms again.

She ignored that, concentrating on her dilemma. She couldn't be rude and refuse him. Not in front of Nicholas. "Of course," she said politely.

"We'll be back in a minute," Hunter told Nicholas.

The boy, absorbed once more in the fire engine, nodded.

Sarah followed Hunter across the store, both of them speaking to an occasional acquaintance. Sarah was glad neither Gladys nor Irene were here to give them interested, speculative looks.

Hunter stopped before a sewing machine set up in a place of honor and turned to her. "What do you think of that? Do you think Mama would like one of these?"

Looking at the gleaming black metal machine, Sarah considered his question carefully.

Finally, she nodded. "Yes, I'm sure she would. Faith loves to sew, but she's finding it hard nowadays with rheumatism making her hands so stiff and sore."

Hunter nodded, too, his expression pleased. "That's just what I thought. This would make it easier for her."

"Oh, yes, a lot easier," Sarah agreed.

They were standing too close together. She could feel his closeness, his warmth, in every part of her body. She took a step away from him.

Hunter's mouth tightened a bit, as if he'd noticed her slight withdrawal. "Good. I'm going to get her this for Christmas."

"That will be a lovely gift. Well, I'd better be about my errands. I've a lot to do today."

She managed another smile and turned to leave, then felt his hand on her cloak sleeve.

"Don't go yet."

His hand was warm . . . so warm. Just as it had been that evening in her hallway when he'd kissed her. When she'd kissed him back so shamelessly.

What did he want? She stopped and turned toward him again, hoping her face didn't show her inner turmoil.

His hand stayed on her sleeve another moment; then he lowered it. "How are things going at school?"

"Fine," she answered quickly.

"Teaching means more to you than just about anything, doesn't it?"

Surprise went through her. Both at his question and the controlled intensity in his tone. As if her answer was very important to him.

"I love teaching, yes."

Love. Why had she used that word? It made her think of another kind of love. That she'd never have now.

"Could you give it up?"

Suddenly, she realized why he'd asked her this. Hunter *hadn't* abandoned his campaign to try to win her back. If she married, she could no longer teach.

A rush of warmth went through her, dismaying her. She fought the feelings. She wouldn't give in to this. Not again. Not after all the years of pain he'd caused her. Might cause her again if she gave him the chance.

"No," she told him, forcing herself to look him straight in the eye. "I couldn't."

Something hopeful in his dark gaze seemed to be blotted out at her words. He stared at her for a moment longer.

A hand tugged at her cloak. "Miss Sarah! Will you come with us to get a Christmas tree?"

She glanced at Nicholas's eager face. That was the last thing in the world she wanted to do.

"I'm sorry, honey, but I have so many errands today. I don't think I can."

The eagerness left his eyes.

Guilt went through Sarah. Just as she'd killed Hunter's hopefulness a few moments ago, now she'd done the same to his son.

She found she couldn't refuse this little boy she cared for so much.

"Maybe I can hurry up and finish."

A smile bright as the sun spread over Nicholas's face.

"Oh, goody!"

Behind her, Hunter cleared his throat.

Sudden embarrassment swept over Sarah as she realized only Nicholas had extended the invitation. His father hadn't said a word.

"That's wonderful, Sarah," Hunter said heartily.

Something else was in his voice, too.

In a moment, she figured out what it was. She'd unwittingly given him new ammunition in his campaign by letting him see she had a hard time refusing Nicholas.

It was done now. She'd just have to make the best of it. Stay with Nicholas during this excursion, not get close to Hunter. In any case, there'd be no chance for romantic overtures from Hunter with his son present.

Sarah turned to Hunter again, a casual smile fixed on her mouth. "What time are you going?"

His expression held the blend of emotions that had been in his voice. With just a trace of smugness added.

Her smile tightened.

He obviously saw that too, and his expression changed. Lost the smugness, became something else that disturbed her even more.

"Right after dinner. With these short days, we don't have a lot of time. Of course, it's too early to put up the tree—it will dry out. But you know Mama. Nothing would do her but to get it up today."

Yes, she knew Faith and her resolve to be the first person in Little Bethlehem to get her Christmas tree up and decorated.

"I do," Sarah agreed. "All right."

Up until a couple of weeks ago, she would have been at Faith's house today, helping her with dinner and chores. Now, with Angela there, she wasn't needed. Hadn't she told herself that was what she wanted? To stay away from Hunter was her avowed desire.

"Come on over for dinner. Mama told me to ask you if I saw you."

Nicholas tugged at her hand, his eyes shining. "Will you, Miss Sarah?"

She couldn't refuse that offer either without appearing hopelessly rude. "All right," she said again, smiling down at Nicholas. "Now I'd better do the rest of my errands."

Two hours later, Sarah sat beside Hunter at Faith's kitchen table, all too aware of their chairs being so close together their sleeves almost brushed when they moved their arms.

Faith had neatly maneuvered that seating arrangement.

Sarah glanced across the table at her. The older woman looked pleased with herself. When their glances met, Faith's smile was pleased, too. Almost smug, as her son's had been not long ago.

Sarah returned the smile, then quickly lowered her head to her plate. Angela had cooked a delicious dinner, but Sarah couldn't give it the appreciation it deserved.

Sarah knew Faith would be happy if she and Hunter got back together. But now it seemed a new dimension had been added. Faith wasn't above aiding and abetting her son's cause.

Looking back, Sarah realized this had started when she stayed here after the fire. Some of Faith's—and probably Angela's, too—insistence she stay longer had been based on trying to keep Sarah and Hunter closer together as long as possible.

As if to confirm her thoughts, Faith sighed. "I've missed you coming over on Saturdays, Sarah."

"It's only been a couple of weeks," Sarah protested.

"It seems longer."

"I've missed you, too, Miss Sarah," Nicholas put in, talking around the mouthful of fried chicken he was chewing.

"Nicholas, don't talk with your mouth full," Faith

said, but her voice was indulgent. Obviously, she didn't mind that Nicholas had added to Sarah's dilemma.

"Of course, I've missed all of you," Sarah finally answered, her glance sweeping the table to include everyone. "But you don't really need me now with Angela here."

Sarah hoped that remark would be as hard for Faith to get around as her own statement a minute ago had been for Sarah.

"We miss your *company*," Faith said. "Did you think the only reason I liked having you here was for the work you did? Not that it wasn't deeply appreciated, of course."

She turned to Angela with a smile. "Just as yours is, too, dear. And *your* delightful company."

Hunter reached for the bowl of mashed potatoes and his shirtsleeve brushed against Sarah's bodice sleeve. Even that tiny a contact sent a shiver through her, which she hoped no one noticed.

Faith was a lot more adept at this verbal sparring than Sarah had expected. Sarah was again in the position of trying to think of something to say that wouldn't make it seem she agreed with Faith's feelings.

Oh, but you do agree with them. That's why it's so hard for you to get ahead of her, her mind said. *You feel as if you belong with this family as much as Faith does. You've told her and Hunter, too, that she's like a mother to you.*

But that didn't mean she could ever live here, or anywhere else, with Hunter and Nicholas as a family, as Faith obviously wanted and hoped would happen.

She wondered if Faith knew the whole story of what had happened that long ago night. And if so, would it make a difference to her?

She probably knew, Sarah decided. And it wouldn't make a difference. She loved her son so much she could forgive him anything. And she thought Sarah should be able to, also.

If only things were that simple.

"It's a lovely day to go for the Christmas tree," Angela said cheerfully. "Not too cold, but brisk enough to remind everyone it will soon be Christmas."

Sarah felt some of the tension leave her. Angela always seemed to have that effect.

"Yes, it is," Faith said. "I can't wait to get it in the parlor and start putting the decorations on."

"You'll have to be sure and keep the trunk in water," Hunter said. "Or it will dry out long before Christmas gets here."

Faith made a tsking sound. "Do you think you need to remind me of that? I've been putting up my tree this early since before you were born."

Hunter laughed, the deep, pleasant sound sending new shivers down Sarah's spine.

"How well I know that, Mama. I think Gladys and George went after theirs this morning."

Faith's head shot up. "I didn't see them going anywhere."

Sarah had to hide a smile at the agitation in Faith's voice.

"I was only joking, Mama," Hunter said, relenting. "No one tries to beat you out in having the first tree up in town."

Faith frowned at her son. "Why should they? I guess a poor old lady like me deserves to have a few pleasures."

"You're not a poor old lady, Grandma," Nicholas said. "You told me we're rich because we have one another."

Faith's face softened into a fond smile for her grandson. "And so we are, child. So we are."

"We are indeed," Angela echoed.

"I know what Daddy is getting you for Christmas," Nicholas said, giving his grandmother a mischievous smile, then grinning at his father. "So does Miss Sarah."

Hunter gave Nicholas a mock frown. "And that's our little secret, remember?"

He turned to Sarah and smiled, as if they were all one happy family, sharing everything.

Sarah felt tears behind her eyelids. How she wished she could fully share in the love this family wanted to offer her. That she had once, years ago, thought would be hers one day.

It still could, her mind said. *It's only your own stubbornness preventing it.*

No, she answered, blinking back the tears. *It isn't only that. I can't grab at happiness now, years too late, and expect it to work out. How could I trust Hunter not to hurt me again?*

You could try. If you weren't such a coward, you could at least try.

I'm not a coward, she protested. *I'm only being sensible. And keeping my heart from being broken again. I couldn't stand that. I simply couldn't.*

But, as always, her relentless mind had the last word.

Don't you know your heart will be broken anyway if you give up this second chance?

CHAPTER FIFTEEN

"You three go on ahead and get the tree," Angela said as soon as dinner was over.

"Yes, do," Faith echoed, pushing back her chair. "Angela and I can clean up in here in no time."

Sarah knew they were right, and the short winter afternoon would soon be over, but didn't they realize their eagerness for her to be off with Hunter was obvious? Probably, and they didn't care, she decided, getting up herself.

"We shouldn't be long," she said, trying to think of some way to let them know she understood their all too transparent aim and that it wouldn't work.

"Oh, take your time," Faith said. "You know how particular I am about my Christmas trees."

Sarah sighed inwardly, wondering if Faith's words were meant to signal Hunter that he should dawdle, be with Sarah all the rest of the afternoon.

"Yes, I know, Mama. We'll find a good one."

His words and tone sounded innocent, and maybe they were. Faith was only saying what everyone in town knew. She did expect to get a beautiful tree each year. All the time that Hunter had been living in St. Louis, he'd come home for Christmas, cut down and put up the tree for his mother.

He'd always been a good son to Faith.

Yes, of course he had. Why was she thinking of this now? She wondered. She didn't need to be reminded of his admirable qualities. He had many.

But steadfastness and faithfulness were two that he was lacking in or he could have waited for her as he'd promised.

She pushed those thoughts and the pain they brought to the back of her mind. She was doing this for Nicholas and she'd be cheerful and see that he enjoyed the outing as much as he expected to.

A few minutes later, Sarah walked toward the woodlot at the back of the property. She was beside Hunter as he pulled the big sled, with the ax on it, behind him over the thin layer of snow on the ground.

Nicholas ran on ahead, his excitement making it impossible for him to keep to their slower pace.

If anyone saw them, they'd look exactly like a father, mother, and child out together on this happy holiday excursion.

What do you mean—if anyone saw you? her mind asked. *Surely you don't think you could do anything in Little Bethlehem without someone taking note?*

And everyone in town also knew they *weren't* a happy, complete family.

She moved a little away from Hunter, as if that could make a difference. The air was brisk, cold enough for the season, but still pleasant since they were bundled up.

"Daddy! Come look at this tree!" Nicholas yelled.

"Guess we'd better," Hunter said, grinning at her. "Maybe he's found the perfect one on his first try."

"Could be," Sarah answered, not able to keep from smiling back.

Hunter didn't sound unhappy at the idea that he might not spend much more time with her this afternoon, Sarah noticed and quickly pushed down the disappointment that thought brought.

"See?" Nicholas said when they reached him, proudly pointing at a towering, dark green cedar easily twelve feet tall.

Hunter cleared his throat. "That's a beauty," he said gently, "but I'm afraid it's way too big."

Sarah's heart softened as she listened to and watched the father and son. Hunter was so good with Nicholas. He seemed to truly enjoy being with his son whenever he could. So many fathers didn't pay that much attention to their children, unless they were scolding them for some transgression.

Nicholas looked a bit crestfallen; then he brightened. "Yeah, I guess so, Daddy. They don't look as big out here as they would inside, do they?"

"No, that's why it's hard to figure out which one is the right size," Hunter agreed, giving Nicholas an approving nod.

Nicholas nodded gravely back. "I'll go look for a littler one."

With that he was off again.

Hunter turned to Sarah, the fond smile he'd given Nicholas still lingering. "He may have some trouble with book learning, but he's a smart boy."

"Of course he is," Sarah hastened to agree. "And his reading and writing problems will only take time to overcome."

"I'm glad you have so much faith in him. It means a lot to both of us."

Sarah felt her heart softening even more. "Naturally, I do, but it's not just a matter of faith. Anyone can see he's a very intelligent little boy."

Hunter shook his head. "No, not everyone. Enid doesn't think so. That's one reason she wants to get her hands on him. She believes he needs to go to a special boarding school she's got picked out in another state."

Sarah drew her breath in sharply. "He's far too young to be away from his family. And I don't think he needs it anyway."

Hunter's mouth tightened. "Exactly my feelings. Especially since the school is primarily for children who have real handicaps—ones they'll have all their lives. She told me of this plan when I went over to see Dudley yesterday. Knocked me for a loop. Of course, she was upset, anyway, about Dudley and . . ."

His voice trailed off, but Sarah knew what he'd almost said. "About the school board's decision to rehire me," she finished. "I'm sorry if that's made trouble for you."

His face relaxed a little. He took a step nearer to her. "Don't worry about that. I'm sure Enid's had this idea all along and just now sprung it on me."

And she has other plans, too, Hunter, Sarah told him silently. *She'd still like to see you and Crystal married. If one idea to get control of Nicholas doesn't work, she'll try another.*

She kept her thoughts to herself though. Somehow, she didn't want to bring up anything that would start an argument. Not now.

Hunter took another step closer to her. "Sarah,"

he said, his voice soft, almost a whisper. "I've missed you so much these last few days."

That was a strange thing for him to say, as if they'd been together and then recently apart. She knew what he meant though. Until he'd finally told her what had happened between him and Beryl, there *had* been a kind of closeness between them, flawed though it was, since his return to Little Bethlehem from St. Louis.

Their glances met and lingered. "Sarah . . . " Hunter said again, even more softly.

"I've missed you, too," she heard herself saying and knew it was true, no matter how much she denied it. She felt a yearning toward him, a need to be closer . . . .

Her feet seemed to have a will of their own. She stepped toward him.

The move brought them so close they were almost touching.

Hunter reached out a glove-clad hand and touched her face, smoothed down it. His glove was cold and slightly rough on her cheek. She had a sudden urge to pull the glove from his hand, to feel the warmth of his flesh against her own.

As if he'd read her mind, Hunter drew back his hand and did just that, then removed the other glove.

When he cupped her face, she drew in her breath at the heat of his hand against the winter coolness of her skin.

"Oh, God, you feel so good," Hunter said, his voice tight and roughened.

As if he were fighting hard to keep hold of his emotions, Sarah thought. As if he were afraid if he didn't, he'd lose control . . . .

Against all reason, excitement flooded her. She

fought it, fought admitting, even to herself, how much she wanted him to kiss her as he'd done before. Do more than kiss her . . .

They stayed that way as the seconds ticked by, their faces almost touching, dark gaze locked with hazel, tension slowly building inside them until Sarah felt she might explode.

"Kiss me," she heard herself saying. "Oh, Hunter, please kiss me!"

His dark eyes, so close to hers, widened. His hands stilled on her face. She heard him draw in a ragged breath.

Then his big hands and his strong, muscled arms went around her, drawing her close to his hard body.

Sarah's arms slid around his waist as she strained to get closer still. She rested her head on his chest while more moments passed. She felt the pulsing of his heart against her face and was comforted by that steady beat.

Finally, she raised her head to find Hunter gazing down at her as if he'd been waiting for that lift of her head, an expression of infinite tenderness on his face.

That was her undoing. Her heart constricted with pain and desire. She wanted him. Oh, how she wanted him . . . .

"Kiss me," she whispered again, marveling at her own boldness. She parted her lips in anticipation.

Hunter groaned deep in his throat. "I told myself I wouldn't let this happen for a while. I was going to court you properly . . . all over again. But I can't stop now."

A thrill whispered through her. Sarah closed her eyes, ignoring what he'd said about courting her,

ignoring everything except that he wanted her as
much as she wanted him. "I don't want you to stop."

She gasped as his lips found her own, covered them,
heated her, heated him, until it could have been
midsummer sunlight they stood in, lost in passion.

Despite their layers of clothing, she felt as if her
body was dissolving into his. They were becoming
one with each other, just as it had been meant for
them to do from the beginning of time . . . .

Hunter's hand was at her throat, fumbling with the
ties of her cloak's hood, releasing them, until her
hood fell back on her neck. He buried his hands in
her hair, released the pins that held it in its prim
bun, and it tumbled down around her shoulders.

"I love your hair," he murmured against her lips.
"It's so full of life, just like you are. I've dreamed of
it spread across a white pillow, and I'm bending over
you. You're lying there, waiting for me to claim
you. . . ."

His evocative words poured into her, making a
trembling start in her knees and spread upward until
her whole body was shaking in his clasp.

"Yes," Sarah said, her voice a whisper. "Yes, oh,
yes!"

Hunter's warm mouth left hers, lowered to her
throat, kissed the pulse that throbbed there, made
more tremors go through her.

"Daddy . . . Miss Sarah . . . come see! I've found
another tree. And it's just the right size."

Nicholas's voice, carried on the slight breeze that
had sprung up, froze them. Hunter's mouth stayed
on Sarah's throat for a moment longer. Reluctantly,
he lifted his head and started to draw away.

Sarah stared at him with heavy eyelids. "Don't go.

Don't leave me," she said, hearing the slow huskiness in her voice.

"I have to. Nicholas . . ."

"Daddy! Miss Sarah! Come on."

Hunter pulled completely away, gently steadying Sarah until she stopped swaying.

Sarah abruptly came to herself, gasping with shock. She stared at Hunter with dazed, shocked eyes, then jerked frantically at her hair, pulling it back, twisting it into its accustomed bun.

But the pins were gone, scattered on the ground. She'd never find them! And her lips were kiss swollen. Nicholas couldn't see her like this!

"I can't . . . Help me find my hairpins," she whispered.

Hunter dropped to his knees, scrambled for the scattered pins, finally dropped some in her palm. Gave her a slow, sweet smile. "Here."

She steeled herself against reacting to that smile.

He hadn't found all the pins, but these would have to do. Quickly, Sarah pushed them into the bun, then retied her hood.

Hunter still stood, looking at her, an expression on his face she couldn't define.

"We'd better go to Nicholas," she finally said.

Hunter nodded. Again, that melting smile pulled his lips upward. "I was going to wait until you came to me, but I didn't think I could stand it. But you did, Sarah. You did. You came into my arms. You asked me to kiss you."

Sarah drew in her breath, trying to deny his words. But she couldn't. He told the truth. She *had* come to him. She *had* asked, almost begged, him to kiss her.

Oh, where had all her sturdy vows gone? They'd

melted at the first touch of Hunter's hands. Melted easily and swiftly, just as all the snowfalls had these last two weeks.

She should never, ever have come out here today.

"Come on. Let's go to Nicholas." Hunter, still smiling, picked up the sled ropes and went ahead.

If she had any sense, she'd go home right now. If she had any sense, she'd never agree to anything like this ever again.

Anything where there was the remotest possibility of them being alone together.

Hunter paused and looked back at her. "Coming?"

Sarah drew herself up. She wouldn't run home like a silly schoolgirl. She couldn't leave now. Nicholas would be upset and with good reason. None of this was his fault.

The responsibility for most of what had just happened rested squarely on her shoulders.

"Of course," she said, forcing her voice to steadiness, and caught up with him.

Nicholas was once more standing by a shapely cedar tree, a slightly worried smile on his face.

"See? This one isn't too big, is it?"

Hunter let go of the sled ropes and, cocking his head, considered the tree from all angles. Finally, he nodded. "Looks like it might be just the one."

Nicholas's smile widened. "Can we take it home?"

"I don't see why not." Hunter got the ax from the sled and approached the tree.

A few minutes later, with the fragrant cedar tied to the sled, they all three headed back toward the house.

"I picked a good one, didn't I, Miss Sarah?" Nicholas asked, his voice happy and possessive. He slipped his mittened hand into hers.

Instinctively, Sarah's gloved hand tightened around Nicholas's, bittersweet feelings swirling inside her.

Yes, they were too much like a real family. She had to refuse any more such invitations. Nicholas would be hurt, wouldn't understand, but it had to be that way.

Because no matter how much her body wanted Hunter, her heart and mind knew she'd done a reckless, foolish thing a few minutes ago when she'd kissed him.

Now Hunter would be encouraged, would think that she was weakening . . . that all it would take to win her back was the courting he'd mentioned . . . .

He was wrong! How could he think she'd be able to trust him now, believe nothing like what had happened before could happen again?

It had taken too long, given her too much anguish to get over the first time.

She wouldn't—*couldn't*—risk breaking her heart over Hunter a second time.

As they walked out of the woodlot and into the back yard, George Randolph opened his back door and came out into his yard. He waved when he saw them.

"Got your Mama's tree already, I see," he called, grinning.

"Yep," Hunter called back. "She couldn't wait another day."

"Didn't figure she could," George said.

"Nicholas picked it out," Hunter said, smiling down at his son. "Isn't it a beauty?"

George tilted his head, looked the tree over, then nodded. "Sure is."

Nicholas beamed.

Sarah's heart squeezed painfully.

George's glance took in their little group. Sarah was sure she saw a gleam in his eyes. And a kitchen curtain twitched as if Gladys had looked out.

Naturally, Gladys and George would think that she and Hunter were courting again, since they were out here together like this. By tomorrow, half the town would know.

It was already too late to keep Nicholas from being hurt. He wouldn't understand why she refused future invitations.

She shouldn't have come!

Without warning, another memory assailed her. That last Christmas before Hunter left, he'd cut the tree for her and her mother, put it up, and helped her decorate it. Her mother had enjoyed that tree so much . . . .

She and Hunter had shared so many, many things. Everything she did reminded her of something they'd done together.

Out on the road, a carriage passed, an expensive one. It looked like the Cunninghams' although she knew it wasn't.

The Cunninghams. Crystal. Pretty Crystal, who looked so much like her sister, Beryl . . . who'd been Hunter's wife. Who'd been Nicholas's mother. Crystal, who Enid wanted to become Hunter's new wife . . .

How *could* she forget what had happened, when so many things in this town reminded her of it? Reminded her that she didn't know what lay in the depths of Hunter's heart.

Just as she and Hunter shared the good memories, so, too, did they share the bad, the unforgettable ones.

If only she could forget!

But she *had* almost fallen into Hunter's arms. She

had asked him to kiss her, and when he had, she'd shamelessly kissed him back. Would probably still be kissing him if Nicholas hadn't called.

A picture slipped into her mind's eye. She and Hunter, lying on their cloaks spread under one of the fragrant cedars in the wood lot.

Kissing, caressing . . . going on to that ultimate joining that they'd never known, although she had dreamed of it many a night. It had been in her mind in many a waking dream, too.

She couldn't deny she wanted that joining.

Yes, she did.

CHAPTER SIXTEEN

Faith pushed her dishtowel inside the newly washed lamp chimney—a regular Saturday chore—and carefully twisted it around to dry the glass.

"Wouldn't it be nice to have those newfangled electric lights like they do in some of the cities?"

Angela put another clean chimney down on the cloth spread across the kitchen table. She glanced up at Faith and gave her what could only be called a mischievous smile.

"You will have it in time."

Faith fitted the gleaming chimney onto a lamp, which also had a newly trimmed wick; then she stood back to admire the results.

"That does look nice, if I do say so myself. I guess there's some satisfaction in household chores, even if they are tedious."

She glanced over at Angela. "You sound very positive about the electric lights."

Angela nodded, serenely. "Haven't you noticed how all the new inventions start in the cities, then later come to the small towns and the countryside?"

Faith considered a moment, then nodded. "Of course, you're right. I can wait, but I would like to have a sewing machine. Gladys says hers saves so much time she can't believe it."

"Mercy, yes. I would think so." Angela's merry smile had a different element to it now, Faith thought—almost secretive. As if she knew something Faith didn't.

"Did you water the Christmas cactus?" Faith asked in a moment. "I was going to earlier, but I forgot."

"Yes," Angela said. "And it's starting to bud out. Looks like it may be in full bloom by Christmas day."

Faith felt excitement sweep through her. "Oh, do you really think so? It hasn't bloomed on Christmas for years now. That would be so wonderful."

Angela nodded. "I believe it will. Just have faith." She laughed merrily. "That shouldn't be hard to do, should it, dear?"

Faith sighed and shook her head. "You don't know how many times I wish Mama hadn't given me that name. It's been a sore trial for me to live up to."

"But it's a wonderful name, just the same," Angela insisted.

"I guess so. But my faith has been tried so much over the years. Especially these last eight. It was such a shock when Hunter married Beryl. I'd had my heart set on having Sarah for a daughter-in-law. As much as I love Hunter, I still have a hard time accepting what he did."

Faith paused, surprised at herself for being so open with a woman she'd known such a short time. But it seemed as if she'd known Angela all her life. And could trust her completely.

Angela's face sobered. She patted Faith on the shoulder. "I know, dear. But you have to believe things will work out for the best."

Faith nodded. "I try to. And we do have Nicholas. A sweeter child doesn't live on God's green earth than that one."

"He is a good boy," Angela agreed. "Handsome and intelligent. And maybe you will have Sarah for a daughter-in-law after all."

Faith drew in her breath at the finally voiced hope she'd had since Hunter had returned to Little Bethlehem. She dried the last chimney and put it on its lamp.

"I was encouraged that Sarah went with Hunter and Nicholas to get the tree. Although she did seem a mite reluctant."

"Naturally. She's afraid of getting hurt again," Angela said. "We need to think of other ways we can get them together. That can only help."

"You're right," Faith said, brightening at the suggestion.

"I was wondering about a sleigh ride," Angela said in a moment.

"A sleigh ride?" Faith asked doubtfully. "Do you think Sarah would agree to that."

"She would if you and I and Nicholas were going along, too."

Faith shot her a quizzical look. "But if we're all along, there wouldn't be much chance of any sparks flying between Sarah and Hunter."

Angela gave her another mischievous grin. "I think we could all be too tired at the last minute. Or maybe afraid we were coming down with a cold or something."

"Why, Angela, you sly thing!" Faith's grin was full of mischief, too. "Do you really think that would work?"

"Yes, Mama, I think it's an excellent idea," Hunter said, coming into the room.

Faith whirled, a little embarrassed. "How did you sneak up on us like that? I didn't even hear the front door open."

Hunter smiled. "No wonder. You two were so busy plotting and planning you wouldn't have heard the last trumpet."

"Hunter!" Faith said reprovingly, feeling her face redden. "How you run on."

"Not that I object to anything you can concoct. I've been thinking about a sleigh ride myself. Of course, we'll need snow and that's beyond our control."

"We must all pray for snow," Angela said. "Pray very hard."

Faith sighed. "Yes, I guess that's all we can do, but I'm not sure God pays attention to such things as that."

"Have you forgotten not a sparrow falls but He takes notice?"

Faith smiled at her friend. "Angela, you always manage to make me feel better about everything. And you're right, of course."

Angela gave the other two a merry smile. "I hope so."

"Where's Nicholas?" Faith asked, glancing around.

"He went home with Sarah for his lesson," Hunter said. "Since he's missed some lately, Sarah offered to do one today to catch up."

"Is Sarah coming over this evening to help us decorate the tree?"

"No." His smile faded.

Something nice must have happened between him and Sarah while they were getting the tree. But then afterward things hadn't gone well, Faith decided.

"I was counting on her spending the evening here."

"So was I, but I couldn't persuade her."

Faith realized they were all three talking openly about their hopes for Hunter and Sarah to marry. It was a big relief not to have to sneak around.

"If we want Sarah in this family for keeps, we're going to have to do a lot of plotting and planning," she said forthrightly. "She's running scared and no wonder."

Faith gave Hunter a straight look.

His face turned serious. "And it's my fault."

"Yes," Faith agreed. "But that's in the past. You've paid for that mistake. We've got to make her see that everything will be all right in the future."

"Don't you think I've been trying to convince her of that?"

"But she's not convinced. Maybe she's afraid that the same thing might happen again the way Enid is throwing Crystal at you. You need to have a talk with Crystal. Tell her once and for all you've no intention of marrying her."

Hunter huffed out a sigh. "I've been racking my brain for some way to do that which wouldn't embarrass the girl. I think Crystal has other interests anyway."

Faith's eyes lit up. "Oh? Who?"

Hunter tilted his head and gave his mother a wry grin. "Mama, I know you're not a gossip like some people in this town. But just the same, keep this to yourself. I believe she's setting her cap for Reverend Hopkins."

Faith's mouth rounded into a surprised O. "Well, I never. Do you really think so?"

Hunter shrugged. "Just a hunch from a few things she said and how she said them. Now, remember," he cautioned again, "don't tell Gladys."

Faith's eyes danced. "I wouldn't dream of such a thing. Now go ahead and bring that tree in so we can get it set up. We'll have plenty of time to talk while we decorate after supper."

"All right." Hunter left and Faith turned to Angela. "Crystal and David Hopkins! Would you ever have thought such a thing?"

Angela didn't look surprised. "Why not? Crystal's a sweet, pretty young girl and David is a handsome young man. No reason on earth why they shouldn't be attracted."

Faith bit her lip. "Hunter didn't say anything about David being interested in Crystal. Just the other way around. But tomorrow at church I'm going to notice everything I can about those two."

Angela picked up a lamp to take it back to the parlor. "I can't wait for tomorrow."

"Neither can I. Life just keeps on getting more interesting by the minute, doesn't it?"

"That's the way it should be," Angela said, passing by Faith, carefully holding the lamp aloft. "Life is meant to be lived with joy and love and of course some other things to keep it from being dull."

"I can't imagine life being dull in Little Bethlehem."

Faith picked up another of the lamps. "And now

I'm going to check on that Christmas cactus to see
how its buds are doing.''

Hunter carefully adjusted the heavy wool blanket
around Sarah's knees. "There," he said at last, smiling down at her. "You should be warm enough now."

"I'll be fine." Sarah gave him a tight smile in return.

Why had she let herself be maneuvered into this
outing where she and Hunter were alone together?

And only the day after she'd vowed anew not to let
it happen again!

Hunter walked around to his side of the sleigh, slid
onto the seat, and picked up the reins, clucking to
the patient horse. They started up again, the sleigh
runners hissing smoothly over the fresh snow.

Oh, she was certainly warm enough. Even without
the blanket.

And Hunter knew it of course. He was well aware
how his touch, his nearness affected her.

So why in heaven's name had she accepted the
invitation for this sleigh ride when Faith, Angela, and
Nicholas had decided not to go?

Because I have no willpower where Hunter is concerned,
she answered herself. *No matter what my better judgment
tells me I should do, I ignore it.*

The last-minute reneging of the other three was
suspicious. That all of them should suddenly be so
"tired" and worried about maybe coming down with
a cold didn't ring true.

Faith's glance hadn't quite met hers, and Nicholas
had a merry look in his eyes, as if he had a secret.
Only Angela had seemed her usual friendly, cheerful
self.

"Wonderful afternoon," Hunter said. "I couldn't

believe it when I woke up this morning and it had snowed all night. Just the right kind, too. Packed tight enough so that the runners whiz along.''

The front seat was wide enough for three people and she was sitting well over on her side, so why did it seem as if they were very close together?

And that she felt his warmth when that was impossible in this open vehicle.

"Yes, the ride is very smooth," Sarah finally answered.

"Do you remember the last time we did this?" Hunter asked.

Sarah tensed. She wouldn't let him start the kind of reminiscing they'd done at her house the day he brought the wood. Not *any* kind. That would only serve to soften her toward him. And her foolish body was already too soft, too willing to fall into his arms.

She couldn't allow that when she had no intention of marrying him.

She closed her mind to everything that had happened between them in those happy past days, willing herself not to remember.

"No," she answered, "I don't."

"*I* do. I don't guess I'll ever forget that day."

It was obvious he was going to continue whether she contributed anything or not, and despite her vows of a moment ago, her curiosity stirred.

She peeked over to find him glancing her way, an expectant look on his face.

"I can't believe you could forget."

He paused.

A premonition came to her that she should stop him . . . but she didn't.

"It was the last year . . . I was here. About this time of year, too. We'd gotten a couple of miles out of town when the sleigh hit a big rock and broke a runner.''

She sucked in her breath, memories assaulting her.

''Do you remember now?'' he asked, still in that slow voice.

Sarah swallowed. ''Yes. But I don't want to talk about it.''

She'd told him that so often since his return. It made her sound stubborn and closed minded.

But she wasn't! She was just afraid to let him get behind her defenses because her physical desire for him was so strong it overruled her sensible side.

The side she must listen to or risk heartbreak again.

''We need to talk, Sarah, no matter what you feel now.''

His slow, gentle words and his steady gaze were almost hypnotic. She couldn't summon a protest.

''We started to walk back to town to get help. You rolled a snowball and hit me in the back with it and then I got you and . . . one thing led to another.''

Pain pierced her heart as the memories now came thick and fast.

Oh, yes, one thing had certainly led to another. Laughing, she'd turned to run from him and had stumbled, fallen in the snow on her back. Hunter had bent down to lift her up . . . .

''Your cheeks were like roses,'' Hunter said in those soft, intimate tones, as if he'd read her mind. ''Your eyes were shining. You looked so beautiful I couldn't stand it. I picked you up and carried you back to the sleigh. . . .''

And there he'd kissed her until she was breathless, until nothing existed except their desire for each other. It was only when he began unbuttoning her dress, when his hot mouth found her breast, that she'd come to her senses.

"We nearly became one that day, Sarah," Hunter said, his voice still soft with memory. "We should have. We'd have belonged to each other then, and nothing would have ever separated us."

His last words broke the spell he was weaving around them, brought protests up from her heart. "You're trying to blame me for what happened with Beryl, aren't you? Saying that if I'd let you make love to me that day, you'd never have left me."

"No, I'm not blaming you. I got over that foolishness a long time ago." His dark gaze bored into hers with an unwavering steadiness.

Her feelings started that roiling inside her that so confused her she couldn't think straight. "And what if I'd gotten with child? Then where would we have been?"

A sense of déjà vu came over her. She'd asked him this same thing that evening when he'd told her the full story. Why had she asked him again?

"Married," he said simply, his voice firm and sure. Just as it had been that evening.

She fought to keep a level head, answer him with reason, not let emotion cloud her thoughts.

"You knew I *couldn't* marry you. I had obligations to my mother. Promises I had to keep. We already talked about this."

"I know, but I've always believed we could have worked things out."

"And I've always believed we couldn't." She'd been so sure of that before. Was she now?

For long moments, their gazes stayed locked. Hunter's dark and steady, hers hot with confusion and anger.

Finally, she took a deep breath and wrenched her gaze away from his, looked down at her gloved hands in her lap.

"Why are you doing this? Why are you bringing up things that are over and done with and can never be changed?"

He gave her a slow, sweet smile. "I'm trying to put a chink in your armor. Open the way to where you might be able to forgive me and believe we could be happy together now."

She jerked her head up again, knowing the pain she felt must show on her face. He was still in the same position. His gaze was still as steady and firm as before. But pain was in his eyes, too.

Her confusion grew. She desperately tried to marshal arguments to counter his reasoned attack, but failed. What he said made sense to her. She didn't know why when only a few days ago it hadn't, but it did.

She'd always considered herself a reasonable person. One who could listen to both sides of an argument and be able to decide in a fair manner which person was right.

"Maybe I *was* partly at fault for what happened," she said at last, her words slow, each one hard to speak.

Surprise came into his face. He shook his head. "I already said I'm not trying to fix blame. That's not what I meant."

"Maybe so. But . . . you did leave me. You married Beryl and lived with her for seven years. You can't erase that."

"I'm not trying to. I only want to make you see we can talk about it, then lay the past to rest."

Pain shot through her again. "What if that isn't possible?" she cried.

She saw him swallow, but he didn't speak.

Seconds ticked away before she answered. "I . . . think I can forgive you," she finally said.

His whole face leaped to life. He tugged on the reins, brought the horse to a halt on the deserted back road, then hooked the reins on the door handle. He moved closer to her on the seat.

"I'd begun to despair of ever hearing you say those words."

Sarah shrank back, shaking her head. "No. Stop. You don't understand. Forgiving is one thing. There's more than that involved."

He checked his advance. Sat very still. "Then suppose you tell me."

"It's the *forgetting* that's hard," she burst out. "Stopping the pictures my mind keeps giving me of you with Beryl. Of her giving birth to Nicholas. To the son that should have been ours! How can I ever get those images out of my mind?"

He looked at her as the silence drew out. The light in his eyes was dimmed, but not completely gone.

"I don't know," he finally said. "I had to try to be a good husband to Beryl, to try to forget she wasn't you every minute of those years."

His unexpected words took her aback. She hadn't been looking at it from his viewpoint. And she didn't want to now. She wanted to hug her feelings of being wrongly treated to her, keep them undisturbed.

The realization shocked her. Made her feel petty and selfish, even as she tried to convince herself this was only another way of trying to protect her heart from being broken again.

Her sense of fairness won. She drew in a deep

breath, then let it out. "I—I'd never even tried to understand how you felt," she said honestly. "All those years I thought you were in love with Beryl."

Her admission was hard to make and left her feeling raw inside. "But it was your own fault it happened. You brought it on yourself."

Hunter reached for her glove-encased hand. "I know that," he said gently. "I've never tried to pretend otherwise. I'm . . . happy you can at least understand some of my own feelings."

As always, his touch felt so good, so right.

Yes, his touch is wonderful, her sensible part said. *But that doesn't mean it's right. Or that you should give in to your physical cravings. You didn't eight years ago. Where is the strength you had then?*

Gone. Dissolved in all those nights she'd spent alone in her cold bed. Wondering what making love with Hunter would have been like. Living it in her fantasies.

Sarah moved closer to him at the same time he moved closer to her.

She lifted her face to his as naturally as a flower seeks the sun. When their lips met and clung she thirstily drew in the kiss, opened her mouth beneath his to deepen it.

She stripped the gloves from her hands, slipped her bare hands around his neck, shivered at the shock of pleasure the feel of his skin and silky black hair against her fingers gave her.

She felt his answering shiver and that increased her pleasure and burgeoning desire, made her press herself against him.

"Sarah," he whispered against her mouth. "Oh, Sarah, you are so sweet. I want you so much. I need you so much."

His words thrilled her. They were just what she wanted to hear. What she *must* hear. "I want you, too," she whispered back.

With a groan, he devoured her mouth, tried to bring her even closer to him.

A jingle of bells and a clattering of horses' hooves came from nearby. Merry calls and laughter rang out; then came a hiss of runners as another sleigh passed them.

Hunter's body tensed. He held on to Sarah for a moment longer, then let his arms drop and moved away.

Dazed, Sarah sat back against the seat. She had no idea who was in that other sleigh, but she knew they must have seen her and Hunter locked in each other's arms.

"I hope George Randolph wasn't driving that sleigh," Hunter said ruefully.

Her lips still felt warm and tingly from Hunter's kisses. Her body still longed for his touch. She *wouldn't* let this end here. Not this time.

And to satisfy that physical yearning, you'll forget everything else? Forget your doubts are a long way from being resolved?

Yes, she would. She had wanted him so long and had thought that aching desire could never be satisfied.

She gave him a straight look.

"I don't give a hoot who saw us," she said, amazed at her boldness.

Hunter looked startled, then grinned. "I don't think this is the right place to ... continue with what ... we've started."

There was an unspoken question in his voice. He was asking her if she wanted to continue what they'd begun.

And she did. Oh, yes, she did.

She took a deep breath for courage. "No," she agreed. "But my house would be."

The words hung between them in the chilly air.

Hunter reached for her hand again, twined his fingers into hers. "Are you sure about this?"

"As sure as I've ever been in my life."

Forget her doubts. She would at least have this night of passion no matter what came after.

The short winter afternoon was waning. A huge red sun hung in the western sky, low on the horizon. Soon it would be dark.

"I'll drop you off at your house and take the sleigh home."

He paused; then his eyes darkened and his fingers tightened on hers.

"Then I'll be back."

Excitement raced through her at his words, his meaning.

"And I'll be waiting for you."

CHAPTER SEVENTEEN

Tamping down the excitement building within him, Hunter unhitched the horse, then rubbed the animal down and gave it hay and grain. He'd have George help him put the sleigh away in the barn in the morning. George would be sure to give him sly looks and try to find out what had happened between him and Sarah on the ride.

That thought gave rise to others. How beautiful Sarah had looked when he walked her to her door a few minutes ago. The excitement he saw in her eyes matched his own. It was all he could do to leave her there without even a kiss.

He knew better than to kiss her. He couldn't have stopped at a kiss. And he certainly couldn't have left the horses and sleigh sitting in front of her house all night.

All night ... He felt his body hardening at the

thought of being with Sarah tonight. Making love to her.

"Stop that. First you have to eat supper with your family and keep them from finding out what's really going on. Or what will be later on tonight. You hope."

He still couldn't believe Sarah had been as eager to continue their lovemaking as he. That she'd suggested he come to her house tonight.

And maybe when he got there, she'd have reconsidered, become horrified at her rash decision, and when he knocked on her door, she wouldn't let him put a foot inside.

"That's just a chance you'll have to take," he advised himself, closing the barn door behind him and heading for the house.

A welcoming plume of smoke came from the chimney, hanging in the still, clear night air as he crunched through the snow. He wasn't looking forward to the next few minutes.

He smelled chicken and dressing as soon as he opened the front door and his mouth started watering. Leftovers from dinner and just as good as then.

"Is that you, Hunter?" his mother's voice called from the kitchen, an eager note in its tones.

"Yes, Mama," he called back, hanging his coat and cap on the hall tree and walking to the kitchen, bracing himself for three sets of equally eager eyes and faces.

Angela was putting food into serving dishes at the big kitchen range and gave him a warm smile and nod.

His mother glanced up from the table, where she was setting down plates and cutlery. "You're early," she said. "We didn't expect you back this soon."

There was disappointment in her voice and he knew why.

You expected me and Sarah to still be spooning in some deserted by road, didn't you, Mama? he asked her silently.

"Oh, it's not so early." He hoped his smile let her know he was well satisfied with what he'd accomplished during the sleigh ride.

She cocked her head, then smiled back in a way that told him she got his message.

Hunter heard a clatter on the stairs and a few moments later Nicholas hurried into the room. "I had a good rest, Daddy," he said. "Did you and Sarah have a nice ride in the sleigh?"

"Yes, we did."

Hunter reached for his son and hugged him, and as always, he felt a rush of tenderness and love. Nicholas deserved a complete, happy family. And maybe, just maybe, he was going to get one.

"I'm glad to hear that," his mother said, her voice a trifle arch. "You couldn't have had a prettier afternoon."

Angela brought the food to the table and they all sat down. After Angela said the blessing, they started passing the bowls around.

How was he going to sneak out of the house after everyone had gone to bed without his mother's still sharp ears hearing him?

Sneak out?

He grimaced at that thought. He was a man of thirty, and this was his family home. He shouldn't have to sneak around to do anything.

On the other hand, he couldn't announce he planned to spend perhaps all night at Sarah's. As much as Angela and his mother were trying to promote the possibility of a match between him and

Sarah, they wouldn't approve of that. No, they'd be shocked.

He raised his head and looked at both women.

Or would they?

Had his mother perhaps anticipated her wedding vows and stolen some hours with his father? He felt a little startled to be thinking such thoughts, but on further consideration, he decided he wouldn't be surprised. He'd been told his mother was a pretty lively young woman, given to impulsiveness.

As for Angela, he felt sure she'd been an attractive woman in her younger days, too. Surely, she'd had beaux. He wondered why she'd never married.

He smiled at the way his thoughts were wandering. "Mama, please pass the potatoes," he said, and when she did, he grinned at her.

She grinned back. "You're in a peppy mood tonight."

He suddenly realized he wasn't doing his later plans any good, so he patted a feigned yawn with his hand.

"I'm tired. Nothing like a sleigh ride to get you to bed early. How about you, Nicholas? Are you ready to hit the hay?"

Nicholas frowned. "I rested this afternoon, Daddy. I even went to sleep."

"Tomorrow's a school day," Hunter reminded him. "You want to be rested for Sarah."

His choice of words made desire sweep through him.

He wanted to be rested for Sarah, too, because he hoped they wouldn't get too much sleep tonight. Both of them would be stifling true yawns tomorrow.

You're building yourself up to what may be a big disappointment, his mind warned. *What if Sarah's lamps are off and her door is locked when you go over later on?*

He quickly turned aside that dismal prospect and finished his supper while keeping up a conversation with his family.

He'd cross that bridge if he had to.

Sarah built a fire in the kitchen stove, hurried through supper, then quickly cleaned up the kitchen. The supper fire had heated the water in the reservoir. There would be plenty for a bath.

She was halfway through the bath before she allowed herself to think about why she was bathing. And why she was going to rub glycerine and rosewater into her skin afterward, until her body was fragrant with its aroma.

Sometime tonight Hunter would knock on her front door and she'd let him in. They'd go to her bedroom and they'd make love.

Her heart thudded against her chest wall as she pictured them together. Hunter would slowly undress her until she lay naked before him. Then he would undress himself and slide under the covers and take her into his arms. Their heated, bare bodies would touch and cling.

She felt herself warming just thinking about it, although this wasn't the first time this daydream had been in her mind. Nor the dozenth either.

But this time it would be real.

And are you sure you're ready for it? her mind asked. *It's not too late to back out.*

Yes! She was ready. And it *was* too late to back out. She didn't *want* to.

She finished bathing, dried herself, and got into a new, lace-trimmed nightgown that Faith had given her for a Christmas gift last year. Then she put on her robe and slippers.

After dragging the tub to the back porch steps she tipped it so the water ran into the yard; then she stored it in its accustomed place.

In the kitchen again, she closed the door, then stood with her back against it for several moments, trying to calm her racing heart as once again doubts assailed her.

How could she have asked Hunter to come here tonight? Asking him to come and make love to her was what it amounted to. Her mother would turn over in her grave if she could have witnessed Sarah's bold behavior.

Or would she?

Sarah thought back to photographs of her parents when they'd first married. Her mother was very pretty, her father handsome. She was sure there had been strong passion between them until her mother's health became so delicate.

Maybe her mother would have done this very thing under the same circumstances.

The thought was startling, but it was enough to get her moving again. She sped to her bedroom and removed the sheets from the bed, then made it up with fresh ones, the scent of lavender sachet wafting out from their folds as she smoothed them into place.

Unlike your mother, you're not planning to marry. What would she think of you?

That didn't matter tonight. She wouldn't listen to that nagging voice.

She looked at the bed for long moments, biting her lip, trying to decide whether to turn back the covers. Would that look too daring—almost indecent—to Hunter? Should she remake the bed as if she had no idea what she expected to happen between those sheets tonight?

"Oh, for heaven's sake!" she scolded herself. "Stop this silly dithering. Hunter already knows how bold you are. After all, he's coming here at your invitation."

She pulled back the covers with a swoop, then moved away a little. The bed looked inviting, and it smelled delightful.

On an impulse, she slipped off her robe and slippers and slid between the sheets, then lifted her arms to an imaginary Hunter.

Embarrassed again, she quickly got up.

She sat down at her dressing table and brushed her hair out. Crackling with electricity, it clung to the brush, and with difficulty, she tamed it until it lay waving down her back, halfway to her waist.

She stared at herself in the mirror, seeing a woman past her first youth. Her hazel eyes were wide, their expression a mixture of anticipation and apprehension. Her virginal white nightgown looked too girlish for her age, but that couldn't be helped. It was the only new one she had.

It was getting late, she realized. Why wasn't Hunter here?

What if he'd decided not to come?

That sudden dismaying thought took the breath out of her. Oh, no, he couldn't do that to her. He *wouldn't* do that to her.

But what if he did? What if he'd thought better of it, realized what a rash decision they'd made?

Sarah pushed back her chair, got up, and began pacing the floor. Oh, what a fool she was! Why had she done this? Which would be worse: Hunter knocking on her door or not coming at all?

A knock sounded on the front door.

Sarah jerked to a stop, her heart hammering against her ribs. She couldn't answer the door. She just couldn't.

The knock came again. Louder. Oh, Lord, what if it wasn't Hunter at all?

"You nitwit," she scolded herself.

She hurried across the hall and swung open the door.

Hunter stood there, his coat hanging open, his head bare, moisture sparkling in the dark waves of his hair. A tentative smile curved his mouth.

"Hello, Sarah. It's snowing again," he said, gesturing to the yard behind him, where Sarah saw lazy snowflakes slowly fluttering down.

"So I see." She stood there, just looking at him.

"May I come in? You're shivering and your feet are bare."

Sarah suddenly realized she was not only barefoot, but she had forgotten to put her robe back on and she wore only her thin nightgown. She hoped none of her neighbors were watching.

She wrapped her arms across her shivering chest and moved back hastily. "Of course."

Hunter entered, closed the door behind him, and turned toward her. He frowned. "You're freezing. You need to get more clothes on."

She gaped at him, startled at his words.

Oh, I thought you were here to help me get out of the ones I already have on. Or was I mistaken about that?

At the look on his face, she feared for a horrible moment she'd spoken the words aloud.

Her mouth dropped open and she knew her face was bright red. She couldn't seem to do anything but stand there staring at him like an idiot.

Hunter smiled at her. A radiant smile. He shrugged out of his coat and gloves and flung them at the coat rack, where they slid off and fell in a heap onto the floor.

He stepped forward and wrapped his arms around her. His body heat came through the material of his shirt, enveloped her in warmth.

"Sarah, Sarah, Sarah," he said. "You smell so good I could eat you up. Put your arms around me. I'll have you warm in no time."

She did as he asked and slipped her arms around his neck. Then to her amazement, Hunter reached down and picked up her icy feet, slid her legs up his trousers.

From some instinct she didn't even know she had, Sarah wrapped her legs around his waist, clung to him.

"That's right," he said approvingly. One hand on her bottom, the other gripping her shoulders, he held her tightly against him and headed for her bedroom.

One lamp burned, turned down low so that only a soft glow filled the room.

At the bed, he gently slid her between the sheets. He stood there over her, smiling down.

Sarah found her agonizing embarrassment had gone. She smiled up at him. This was Hunter. The boy and man she'd loved most of her life.

You're forgetting those eight years when everything was wrong, when he was with Beryl, her mind nudged her. *Even now, you're not sure of his love. Maybe you never will be.*

Resolutely, she turned it off. She'd gone too far to retreat now. Much too far for second thoughts.

She didn't know when it had happened, but she

knew she loved him. Had never stopped loving him
no matter what she'd told herself.

She wanted and needed him.

She couldn't send him away now. She *wouldn't*.

She would have this night and let tomorrow take
care of itself.

Sarah reached her arms up to him.

His smile faded as he looked down at her. "You
don't know how many times I've dreamed of this
moment. Despaired of its ever coming to pass."

"So have I. But it's here," she said simply.

His eyes had darkened until they seemed black. He
fumbled with the buttons of his shirt, jerked it off,
his trousers soon following, then the remainder of
his clothing.

Sarah watched the dreams she'd had blending with
reality until she felt as if she were floating in a waking
dream . . . .

Hunter slid under the sheets, pulling her against
his nude body. She gasped with delighted shock at
the contact.

In a few moments he'd slid her gown off, and this
time she pushed herself against him before he could
move her.

Waves of sensation swept over her as she savored
the feel of bare flesh touching bare flesh in a dozen
different places—a dozen different and wonderful
ways.

Her dreams had been only a shadow of the reality.
How could anyone truly imagine this sheer delight
until they had experienced it?

She felt Hunter's body hardening against her. Especially that part of him she'd never seen until a few
moments ago. It had looked . . . big. Now it felt that

way, pushing against her stomach, throbbing with urgency.

"I didn't mean for this to happen so fast," Hunter said, his mouth against her ear. "I planned for us to sit in the parlor for a while, kiss each other, lead up to this gradually."

"I guess that's the way I thought about it, too," Sarah admitted.

Suddenly, a mischievous imp took hold of her.

"We could get dressed and start all over again," she said, her voice demure.

He jerked his head up and stared down into her eyes, his expression astonished. "What?"

The imp still had her. She shrugged, still demurely. "I wouldn't want to change any of your plans."

"If you think for one moment I'll let you out of this bed now, woman, you're crazy," he growled.

He suddenly lowered his head, nipped at her earlobe, then slid his tongue into her ear, twirling it around.

Sarah gasped, her body, so close to his, bucking upward. All her mischief fled, replaced by passion.

He chuckled into the ear he still so expertly teased. "That's more like it," he approved.

Sliding one of his hands under her bottom, he brought her against his lower regions again. That big, hard part of him pressed against her urgently, hotly.

"Stop it," she gasped. "Oh please stop."

"All right." He removed his tongue from her ear, moved away, and lay beside her.

Sarah felt bereft and lonely. But she'd asked him to stop. "I didn't mean for you to completely stop," she said. "I just meant to slow down a little."

She felt him shrug.

"Sorry. You said stop, so I stopped."

That same little imp must have hold of him, too. Would she have to beg him to continue?

Sarah bit her lip. She was so new to this lovemaking business. He was probably lying there laughing at her greenhorn ways.

She couldn't stand it any longer. If she had to beg, then beg she would. But maybe words wouldn't be necessary. She turned on her side, facing him. Tentatively, she reached out a hand, encountered his flat, hard-ridged male stomach. She stroked her fingers down it until she came to his navel.

He lay there, not moving a muscle. Inspiration came, and she circled a finger around it, much as he'd done to her ear. Then she lowered her head and twirled her tongue in the indentation.

She heard a faint groan and lifted her head, leaving her hand across his stomach. Instantly, his big hand clamped down on her smaller one. "Don't stop now, Sarah."

"Oh, so you want me to keep on?" she asked innocently.

"Yes," he said tersely. His hand guided hers back to his navel, then lower . . . folding her fingers over that most male part of him that throbbed with need and desire.

He felt very hard, yet velvety soft at the same time, she marveled. And stroking him seemed the most natural thing in the world, although she'd never done it before. Hadn't even dreamed of doing this . . .

Her fingers stroked and squeezed, enjoying the new sensations . . . .

"Stop!" he said, his voice strangled sounding. His hand clamped down on hers again. "Or I won't be responsible for what happens."

The imp seemed to be back again. In all her daydreams, she'd never once thought that lovemaking could be fun, could make a person want to tease the other, to laugh and enjoy the shared laughter.

Sarah wiggled her hand out from under his and moved away a little, settled down on her back again. "All right," she said as he'd said to her.

"You minx." So swiftly she gasped, he moved over her, loomed above her, his dark eyes burning into hers.

Her amusement fled as she gazed upward at him. This was Hunter, she reminded herself again, almost desperately. The boy she'd grown up with, learned to love at an early age, then lost.

Now she had him back again.

But you don't know if you want him back except for this one night, her mind whispered.

Impatiently, she pushed the voice away. She'd listen to no more cautions, no more warnings.

Tonight was hers and Hunter's. She would savor it, draw every iota of passion and fire from it.

But who was this taut-faced, black-eyed man staring down at her with such burning intensity he frightened her? She was suddenly aware of how big he was, how hard muscled.

He could do anything he wanted to her and she couldn't stop him.

She drew in her breath. A small whimper escaped her.

Instantly, his face relaxed. His eyes became Hunter's velvety brown eyes once more. "What's wrong? Did I hurt you?" he asked, his voice concerned.

She smiled tremulously up at him. "No. Just for a moment you looked like a stranger. You scared me."

But wasn't he a stranger now? This wasn't the same man she'd loved eight years ago.

His face softened even more. "I never want to scare you, Sarah. Please forgive me. It's just that I've waited so long, so very long for this to happen between us."

Her fears evaporated. She smiled back at him. "I've waited, too, Hunter."

Slowly, slowly, he lowered himself so that his body was fully against hers, in the age-old way man has touched woman since time's beginning. His seeking mouth found hers, his lips brushing hers at first, then moving over them in a maddening caress that made her part her lips, seek his tongue with her own.

While their tongues met and retreated, Hunter's lower body began moving slowly against her own in the same kind of mating dance. Instinctively, she moved her thighs apart and heard him draw in his breath against her mouth.

His lips left hers, moved to her throat, where they kissed the throbbing pulse in her neck before moving lower to where her aching breasts waited.

His first touch on her engorged nipple made her groan. She squirmed beneath him, making little moaning noises.

"Don't ask me to stop now. I can't," he said hoarsely.

"I don't want you to stop. I *never* want you to stop," she assured him.

His lips were so soft, yet they brought forth from somewhere inside her feelings she'd never known were there, hidden, waiting for his touch, this moment . . . .

He lifted himself from her, loomed above her again. "Forgive me, Sarah, but is this the first time for you?"

She stared at him. "Wh—what?"

"You're so beautiful. And it's been eight years. It's

hard for me to believe that no man has ever possessed you."

At last she understood what he meant. "Of course it's the first time," she said, surprise in her voice.

An expression she could only describe as joy filled his face. "Thank you, Sarah," he whispered. "I'll be as gentle as I can."

Gently, he nudged her thighs apart; then she felt him at her most private place, touching, still gently, yet hot and seeking. And she knew the gentleness couldn't last. She didn't want it to last.

She wanted more than gentleness. She wanted all there was to know, to feel, to savor.

She moved her legs wider apart. "Go ahead," she whispered. "I'm ready."

Still gently, Hunter moved one finger inside her, finding her sweet moistness. He felt himself harden more. Yes, she was ready. More than ready.

He withdrew his finger, moved himself against her portal, pushed just a little, then a bit more, until he encountered the obstacle he'd been waiting for.

"This may hurt," he said again and pushed harder until the barrier was breached and he was fully inside her.

Sarah gasped.

He gathered her tenderly against him, his mouth finding hers again. "I'm sorry if I hurt you," he said breathing the words into her open mouth.

"You didn't," she whispered back.

She moved against him, restlessly urging him to continue. He thrust inside her again, glorying in her instant response, then again and yet again.

Slowly as the snowflakes drifting down outside, they moved together; then their bodies gathered momentum, as the snowfall changes into a raging blizzard, until they reached their peak together.

Then, slowly again, they spiraled down and drifted off to sleep, still tenderly holding each other.

During the night they woke and shared their passion again.

Later, Hunter came suddenly awake, some sixth sense telling him morning wasn't long off.

He had to go, he realized reluctantly, and before daylight. It would never do for any of the neighbors to see him leaving Sarah's house early in the morning.

He'd let nothing sully Sarah's good name and reputation. Especially not after what she'd already gone through these last few weeks with her teaching job.

The lamp was still lit, lending enough light to the room so he could see Sarah's hair spread across her pillow, just as he'd imagined it many a time. She was asleep, her lashes dark on her fair skin, a look of peace and contentment on her face.

Pain and regret hit him as he looked at her.

How he wished she were eighteen again and he twenty. That none of the events of the intervening years had happened.

As soon as the thought entered his mind, he denied it. No, he couldn't wish that. Because of those events he had Nicholas.

And soon, soon now, they would be a family.

Gently, he lifted Sarah's hair from her neck and kissed her vulnerable-looking white nape. She stirred sleepily and murmured something.

He hated to wake her, but he couldn't leave without a word. "Sarah," he whispered close to her ear. "I have to go now. Before it gets light out."

Instantly, she awoke. She turned to him, her hazel

eyes gazing into his as if she were waiting for something from him.

He smiled at her, tenderly.

"And I have to get ready for school," she finally
said, her voice oddly flat.

Maybe she was tired. They hadn't done a lot of
sleeping during the night just past. He sighed. "Lucky
you. This uncertainty about my business is driving me
crazy. I'm not used to inaction. I don't like it."

He glanced down at her with amusement. "Here
we are talking like an old married couple, not two
people who just spent their first night together."

Her face tightened. She looked down at her hands.

Uneasiness went through him. What was wrong?
Was she having an attack of shyness? Was she remembering their wild abandon? After all, she'd never
made love before. Yes, that must be it.

Exultation filled him. Sarah was truly his now.

"Are you so disappointed you don't want to talk
about last night?" he asked, not able to keep a teasing
note out of his voice. Her eager response had been
real—he was sure of that.

She lifted her head and gave him a wan smile. "Do
you think I'd tell you if I were?"

He smiled back. "Yes, you probably would. Or the
Sarah I knew years ago would have anyway."

Her smile faded. Her face paled. She gave him a
serious look. "I'm not the same Sarah I was eight
years ago."

His uneasiness returned at her words, her intonation. He reached for her hand, brought it to his lips,
kissed the smooth back. "No. There was very little
girlish hesitation in you last night."

He saw her swallow.

"I do have to go . . . and right away," he finally

said, not able to push aside the disquiet that was creeping over him. He rushed on, trying to dispel the feelings.

"Soon, Sarah, I won't have to go. Soon we'll be a family and I'll sleep beside you every night."

He felt her sudden tenseness and drew back a little to look at her. "What's wrong?"

Her face had tightened again, as it had before. "Last night I . . . wasn't thinking about . . . the future. I was only thinking about how much I wanted you."

Wanted him. Not loved him. He stared at her. "I wanted you, too, of course. But not just for one night. For always. Surely you know that."

She looked away from him. "I told you I'm not ready to even think about that."

Surprised shock hit him. "But last night changes everything. We have to marry soon. What if you're already with child?"

Suddenly, she rolled away from him and sat up, pulling the covers up around her. Her face had paled; the lines of tension were more pronounced.

"Just like you and Beryl married as soon as you'd made love to her?"

His shock deepened. "No, not like that at all. Why are you saying these things?"

She gave him a straight look. "We said nothing about marriage when . . . we agreed to this."

"I didn't think we needed to. I thought you felt the same way I did."

"And how is that?" she demanded. "How *do* you feel? As if you have to do your duty and marry me because you took my virginity and I may possibly be carrying your child?"

He felt frustration and anger growing inside him.

He nodded. "Some of that, of course. I'm a responsible man. Do you think I'd bed you, then desert you?"

Her eyes were bleak. "No. Of course not. No more than you deserted Beryl. Although you told me not long ago that you never loved her."

He jerked himself out of the bed, found his clothes, and began dressing, his anger growing. "What happened between us is nothing like what happened with Beryl."

"Oh, isn't it? What's so different? You wanted her so badly you couldn't wait to take her. You can't deny lust is a big part of what you feel for me, too."

Hunter felt as if he were in the middle of a nightmare from which he'd never awaken. He'd thought that, after their embrace and conversation in the sleigh, Sarah had managed to come to some kind of terms with what he'd done. With the entire situation.

Why did you think that? his mind asked. *She only said she wanted you.*

She never said she loved you. Or wanted to marry you.

This time he had to listen . . . and agree.

Sarah had let that want and need override her still present doubts and anger. If he hadn't been so eager to make love to her, he'd have seen that.

He'd have realized how unlike Sarah it was for her to be so bold. To invite him to her house. Her bed.

He buttoned his shirt with shaky fingers, then looked at her again.

She still sat in the bed, still held the covers close to her neck.

He had to hear her say it though. "You haven't forgiven me at all, have you? Nothing has changed in your feelings."

He saw her swallow. She glanced down and picked

at a loose thread in the sheet. She said nothing for seconds, then finally looked up at him again.

"I think I've managed to forgive you. But I don't know if I can ever forget."

His misery eased a little. This was Sarah, he reminded himself, who was honest to a fault.

He tucked the shirt into his trousers. "That's a start, I guess. But we can't let this ride. We have to talk about our future."

Her face was closing up again. "No, we don't. Not right this minute. Or even this week or next. We can worry about the future if we have to. I . . . need more time. And there's one thing we haven't discussed at all. I'd have to stop teaching if we were to marry."

Tension seized him again. He'd known this was coming, but not this soon. "No, we haven't. But I've thought about it a lot. I know you love teaching and would hate to give it up. But surely marriage and having a family could make up for that loss."

"Yes. If the woman could be sure she'd made the right choice. That the man would never give her reason to regret it."

He felt as if she'd slapped him. "You don't trust me, do you? Even now after what happened between us last night."

"Satisfying our desire didn't resolve anything else," she pointed out.

He started to deny that, insist that for him it been a lot more than just satisfying his desire. Then decided against it.

She wasn't listening or believing him.

Had she believed *anything* he'd told her since his return to Little Bethlehem?

"I guess you're right about that," he finally said.

Their gazes locked and held.

Finally, Hunter sat down in a chair and found his shoes and socks. "I thought you knew how I felt. How could a decent man feel different? Want to do anything else?"

She shook her head, turned away from him. "You'd better go."

Hunter stood up so suddenly the chair he sat on swayed and almost tipped over. He righted it again, willing himself to stay calm. Losing his temper now might make him lose the only woman he'd ever truly loved.

He turned to face her again. "All right. I'll come over this afternoon after school and we'll talk."

"No!" she shook her head vehemently. "Not so soon. I need time, I said. To . . . think."

"All right," he said again. "I'll leave the next move up to you. But, Sarah, remember, we can't wait too long."

"We've waited eight years."

Hunter clenched his hands into fists at his sides. Without trying to touch her again, he turned and left the room, closing the door quietly behind him. Another hour and it would be light outside. He had to hurry. Some townspeople were up and about already.

He picked up his coat from the floor, where he'd dropped it by the hall tree. His mouth tightened as he remembered with what high hopes he'd entered this house last night.

He'd thought that, once they'd made love, Sarah would know, as he did, they must always be together. That the way before them stretched wide and relatively trouble free.

How wrong he'd been.

CHAPTER EIGHTEEN

Crystal paused outside the church, wondering if David was inside. Since she hadn't gone to church Sunday, she hadn't seen him since last Thursday, when Sarah's job had been rightfully returned to her.

Oh, what a relief it was not to have to wake up every morning to face another day of trying to teach.

Life wasn't completely wonderful though. She missed living at home. Especially since her father was sick. Of course she went to see him every day, but her mother wouldn't let her stay long. She didn't want anybody with him but herself.

Mama had told her last Thursday, her voice so cold and sharp it had sent shivers through Crystal, that she thought it would be best if Crystal stayed with her cousin Sally for a while. Mama was angry at her defiance, and although she couldn't stand the idea of Crystal staying with Aunt Belle, she didn't want her at home either.

Maybe it was time she left home for good. Got married, like most of the girls in town her age. All Sally could talk about was her fiancé and their wedding planned for next summer. It made Crystal feel left out.

Thoughts of marriage made her think of David. There was no man in Little Bethlehem she could even consider marrying except David.

And she had no idea how he felt about her.

She wondered if he was in the parsonage. Smoke came from the chimney, but this time of year he'd keep a fire banked whether he was home or not. She stood there a few moments trying to think of an excuse to knock on the parsonage door.

Nothing came to mind except telling him how much she liked him. And of course she couldn't do that.

Sighing, she gave up and went inside the church. To her disappointment, she didn't see David there either. She might as well see if Sarah needed help with the pageant. She was a little early, but she could wait if no one was there yet. She went to the back room and opened the door.

But someone *was* there. Hunter stood facing the side window, still wearing his wraps. He quickly turned and seemed disappointed to see her, as if he'd been hoping for someone else. He gave her a strained-looking nod and smile.

"Hello, Crystal," he said. "How's your father today?"

Worry hit Crystal again at the mention of her father. "About the same. He doesn't act like he recognizes us most of the time, but every once in a while he seems to."

"I went to see him this morning, but Enid wouldn't

let me. She said he was sleeping. Every time I've gone there, she's said that. I'm worried about him."

"So am I. Dr. Lawson comes every day, but he says nothing can be done. We just have to wait and see if he gets better. And that's so hard to do! Just wait."

"Yes, it is. Will you let me and my mother know if we can do anything?"

"Of course," Crystal agreed. "Everyone has tried to help, but Mama won't let anyone do anything— even me. She just sits by his bedside all day and sleeps on a cot in his room at night."

"She'll make herself sick," Hunter said.

Crystal sighed. "That's what I keep telling her. I try to talk her into letting me sit with Daddy, but she refuses."

Through the concern for her father, a thought came to her. This was a chance to tell Hunter she wouldn't be chasing after him in that humiliating way any longer. She'd better hurry. Soon other people would be here to work on the pageant.

Crystal cleared her throat. "I'd like to say something to you."

Hunter nodded. "All right."

"I . . . just want you to know that I—I never was interested in you . . . as a prospective husband," she said, finding the words hard to say. And they weren't coming out right either.

"Not that I don't *like* you," she hurried on. "I do. I always have. I think you're a very nice man and that Beryl was lucky to get you. But . . ."

Hunter's handsome face was easing into a relieved smile.

"That was Enid's idea," he finished. "I thought so all along. Your heart didn't seem to be in it."

She let out her breath in relief. "You're right! I

was so embarrassed, but Mama said that we needed to—''

Crystal broke off, feeling her face reddening. But she had to finish now. ''That we needed to keep you in the family. Because of Nicholas.''

His smile faded, the tight lines coming back. ''I've never tried to keep Nicholas away from your parents. All of you are his family, too.''

''I know that, and so does Daddy.'' She paused and swallowed. ''Or at least Daddy did before he got sick. I think Mama does too. But she's got to have everything just the way she wants it.''

Crystal drew a deep breath. ''It isn't good for people to always get their way. I finally realized that a few days ago. I'm going to live my own life from now on.''

Hunter's face relaxed again, into another smile. ''Good for you. You're a pretty girl and smart, too. You can do whatever you want to do.''

His encouraging words didn't make her feel better. They made her realize anew her inadequacies. ''I'm not so sure about that, but I'm going to try.''

She felt tears pricking her eyelids and blinked. Worry about her father mixed with other worries. ''Thanks for being so understanding. I dreaded having to tell you all this. It's so embarrassing.''

She felt a tear fall to her cheek and reached up a hand to wipe it away. ''Oh, why does life have to be so complicated?'' she asked, her voice trembling.

Hunter crossed the room until he was beside her. ''I often wonder that myself. Here.'' He handed her his big white handkerchief.

Gratefully, she took it and wiped her eyes, then looked up at him. ''It's not that I don't want you in our family. That wasn't what I meant. I could easily love you like a brother, Hunter, if that's all right with you."

He gave her another, more tender smile. "That's fine with me, Crystal. I could love you like a sister, too."

For the first time in days, since her father's sudden illness, Crystal felt as if she were with someone who truly cared about her.

Mama was mad at her, Daddy was very sick and might not ever get any better . . . and as far as she knew, David looked upon her only as a little girl, the daughter of one of his parishioners.

She felt tears coming again. She took a step closer to Hunter and flung her arms around his neck. "Oh, everything is so awful right now. I just don't know what to do."

Hunter put his arms around her and patted her on the shoulder. She rested her head on his broad chest, feeling comforted by the warm, caring human contact. From the feeling of sharing her burdens with another person.

She didn't know the door had opened and someone had entered until she heard an indrawn breath from across the room and felt Hunter stiffen.

Oh, Lord, was that Mama? She'd think Crystal had changed her mind and that she and Hunter . . .

Crystal hastily dropped her arms from around Hunter's neck, drew back, and glanced across the room to the door.

But it wasn't her mother.

It was Sarah, with an awful expression on her face. She looked as if she'd just seen her best friend die before her eyes.

And that wasn't the worst of it.

David stood beside Sarah. He looked shocked and

startled and something else, too—something she couldn't interpret.

Sarah stood there for a few more seconds while everyone kept on staring at one another and not saying a word.

Then she whirled and ran from the room.

David gave one last look at Hunter and Crystal; then he, too, hurriedly left.

He didn't close the door and Crystal heard him saying, "Sarah, wait. Please wait."

The front door of the church opened, then closed with a decisive thud.

Just as she had last week at the school when the mothers had come in and found the boys behaving so outrageously, Crystal wished the floor would open up and swallow her.

She'd thought her life was a complicated mess a few minutes ago!

How could she explain to Sarah that what she'd seen wasn't what it looked like?

As for David.

A pain pierced Crystal's heart.

She couldn't explain to David without giving away how she felt about him.

And what if he didn't return her feelings?

Sarah heard Reverend Hopkins's urgent call, but ignored it as she hurried out of the church. She knew he meant well and only wanted to help, but she couldn't bear to talk to anyone right now, even her own minister.

She listened, but to her relief, he didn't follow.

She crunched through the snow still on the sidewalks as she hastened home. Halfway there, she remembered why she'd been at the church.

For the pageant rehearsal this afternoon.

But she couldn't go back there! Not after what she'd just seen.

Angela, as well as several others who could handle the rehearsal, would be there. They wouldn't mind taking over this one time for her.

A picture flashed into her mind. She and Hunter talking that evening when he'd told her what truly happened between him and Beryl. Still in shock over his revelations, Sarah had accused him of being interested in Crystal. He'd vehemently denied that.

"You liar!" she said aloud. Fortunately, there was no one else on the street at the moment.

"Why were you holding her in your arms? Why was she holding on to you like she never wanted to let you go?"

Pain surged through Sarah again, blending with her anger. No wonder her doubts had stayed, despite her realization that she loved Hunter, had never stopped loving him.

Those hours with him two nights ago had been wonderful, satisfying the physical longings she'd had for years. She'd felt closer to Hunter than ever before . . . wanted to stay in her bed with him forever. She even thought most of her doubts were resolved, that Hunter's tender lovemaking proved he truly loved her. And that she would be able to trust him.

She was ready to tell him she loved him.

But afterward, when he woke her . . . something was wrong. He talked about immediate marriage, about them being a family . . . about the possibility of her being pregnant . . . .

Everything but about how much he loved her. She

didn't know why it was so important for her to hear him say those words, but it was.

Her dreamy, romantic mood had been shattered. The doubts had come surging back. Along with the painful memories of what had happened eight years ago.

The vision of him and Crystal locked in each other's arms flashed into her mind again. If he truly loved Sarah, he couldn't go from her bed into Crystal's arms two days later.

This was too much like what had happened eight years ago. Then he'd gone straight from Sarah's arms into Beryl's bed . . . and into marriage with Beryl.

Was Hunter just incapable of being faithful to one woman?

The thought chilled her to her marrow. But maybe it was true.

Her mouth tightened. "Your intuition knows more than you do," she told herself, hurrying even faster, eager to reach the sanctuary of her little house.

Still, she couldn't help listening for sounds of Hunter following, calling to her to wait for him.

But he didn't.

Sarah's hurt and anger grew. That must mean he didn't want to talk to her, that he knew he couldn't explain what she'd seen in the church.

Finally, her house was in view. She almost ran the last half block, relieved that none of her neighbors were on the street.

She hastened up the steps and turned the handle of the unlocked front door, went inside, and closed the door behind her, relief going through her.

Her glance fell on the hall tree, where Hunter's gloves hung. The sight of them, bringing back memories of the night they'd spent together, intensified her pain and confusion.

Pull yourself together, she told herself. *You can't let this destroy you.*

Resolutely, she took off her cloak and hung it up, then headed for the kitchen, determined to push aside her personal problems.

She'd have a cup of tea and get to work on the remaining Christmas gifts. Nicholas's mittens were finished, as was Faith's knitted tea cosy.

And Hunter's muffler, which was a good thing, because she didn't think she could face having to finish it.

All that was left was Angela's gift, which was partly finished. She'd finally decided to make her a tapestry traveling bag since the one she'd arrived with was old and shabby, obviously having seen long, hard use.

She'd finished making up the fire when a knock sounded on the door.

Her hand froze on the kettle she'd just filled with water.

Hunter.

Gladness sprang up in her heart. He *had* come after her! That feeling was followed by another rush of pain and anger. What could he say that would help? How could she believe what he said?

If you don't talk to him now, you never will, her mind told her. *You can't let it end like this.*

Leaden footed, she walked back to the front hall, then stood there, twisting her hands together, looking at the solid wood of the door.

The knock came again. Louder and impatient sounding this time.

Her thoughts did another flip-flop. Maybe that was a good sign. Maybe Hunter *did* have some kind of a

believable explanation for what she'd seen and was
in a hurry to give it to her.

She wouldn't smile, nor would she frown. She fixed
a calm, yet stern, look on her face to show she was
willing to listen and then make up her mind.

Sarah turned the knob and swung the door open.

Enid Cunningham stood there, her sharp-featured
face tight with anger.

CHAPTER NINETEEN

Her first instinct was to slam the door in Enid's face. Then lock it for good measure. The other woman looked angry enough to push her way in if Sarah denied her access.

But before the thought was completely formed, Enid had her foot in the door and was halfway through.

"I have something to say to you," Enid said sharply, closing the door behind her.

The older woman's cloak was carelessly tied at the neck. She had dark circles under her eyes, and her face was haggard, as if she'd not been sleeping or eating well.

Of course she hadn't, Sarah thought, with Dudley as ill as he was. Sympathy welled up in her despite all that had happened and all the ill will Enid bore her.

"How is Dudley?" Sarah asked.

Enid didn't answer. She stood there, her burning eyes fixed on Sarah.

Sarah shrank back, away from the waves of enmity that seemed to hang in the air around Enid.

"Dr. Lawson just told me Dudley may never get better," Enid said, her voice bitter and accusing. "He may die."

"I'm so sorry," Sarah managed to get out. "Is there anything I can do?"

Enid laughed, a harsh croak. "You've done enough already!

Sarah moved back a bit farther. "What are you talking about?"

Enid leaned closer. "As if you didn't know! As if all this mess wasn't your doing!"

Had Dudley's illness unhinged Enid's mind? She had to talk calmly, try to calm Enid down.

"I don't know what you mean," Sarah said in low tones. "Give me your cloak. We'll sit in the parlor and talk."

She reached out a hand.

Enid slapped at it. "Get away from me, you viper. Do you think I'll let you get your clutches on me after what you did to Dudley?"

"What do you think I did to Dudley?" Sarah asked, hoping her voice didn't show her alarm.

Enid laughed again. "Oh, aren't you the innocent one? Setting up all that nonsense last week. Getting all the parents so riled up they didn't know what they were doing. Why, that was the most disgraceful excuse for a school board meeting I ever hope to see."

Sarah's mouth dropped open as she finally understood what Enid was getting at. "Are you blaming *me* for what happened at that meeting? I didn't know anything about it until it was over."

Enid's lips curled in a mirthless smile. "That's what *you* say. But of course anyone with any sense knows better. *You* got my Crystal stirred up, made her think she couldn't be a good teacher, got her to do all those things."

Sarah drew herself up and looked Enid in the eye. "I did no such thing. I haven't talked to Crystal alone since she took the teaching job."

The awful smile stayed on Enid's mouth. "Go ahead. Lie yourself blind. Do you think I'd believe anything you say? Crystal has always been a sweet, biddable girl. She'd never have done what she did unless someone put her up to it."

"It wasn't me," Sarah protested, sickened. She *had* to make Enid see how wrong she was.

"You were the one who stood to gain. You certainly can't deny how much you wanted your job back."

Sarah swallowed. "No, I can't deny that," she admitted. "But that doesn't mean I did what you're accusing me of."

Enid leaned forward, the venom in her face, her gaze deepening. "Of course you did. And now my Dudley may die because he got so upset that day. And it's all your fault!"

Sarah sucked in her breath. She had to convince Enid how wrong her suspicions were, how warped her thinking was. But Enid was beyond listening to reason.

Still, she *had* to do something. They couldn't keep standing here in the hall with Enid spewing accusations, getting more worked up all the time.

Another knock sounded on Sarah's door. Her nerves tightened to the breaking point, she jumped and let out a little cry.

The knock distracted Enid, too. She moved back a step and glared at the door.

Sarah moved around Enid and opened it.

Hunter stood there.

Sarah's heart thumped. She'd been so caught up in Enid's nightmare attack, she'd blotted out all her personal worries and fears.

Now everything came flooding back.

Hunter's face was tense, his jaw clenched. He looked angry, concerned, and as confused as she felt.

Somehow, she had to give him a signal that their own affairs had to wait. That a more urgent situation must be dealt with now.

She stepped back. "Why, Hunter, come on in," she said pleasantly.

Surprise joined the other emotions on his face. No wonder. Whatever he'd expected, it wasn't for her to welcome him inside in such cordial, unconcerned tones.

She jerked her head a tiny bit to one side, trying to make him understand what she needed him to know.

Hunter stepped past her, still frowning in confusion. When he saw Enid, he stopped short.

"I didn't expect to see you here, Enid."

Enid turned her ravaged face on him. "I can't say the same," she snapped. "Naturally, you'd be here— *now*."

Hunter looked from her to Sarah, his frown deepening. "What do you mean *now*?"

Enid sneered. "Why, now that Crystal has decided she wants nothing to do with you."

Sarah stared at the other woman, then at Hunter. The scene she'd witnessed at the church a little while ago certainly didn't fit with what Enid had just said.

But at the moment Enid was irrational, Sarah reminded herself. She might say anything.

To Sarah's amazement, what looked like a relieved smile curved Hunter's mouth.

"Crystal and I just had a talk about that very thing. She told me she felt only a sister's love for me."

He turned toward Sarah. "Then she gave me a sisterly hug. And I gave her a brotherly one in return."

Sarah drew a sharp breath as she stared at Hunter. *Sisterly and brotherly hugs?* Was he telling her that was all she and David had witnessed?

That what she'd seen wasn't a betrayal by the man she'd made glorious love with only two nights ago? Had she leaped to the wrong conclusions because she hadn't trusted Hunter? Because she hadn't believed he truly loved her?

"No, I'm not surprised to see you here," Enid said again, still in that hateful, sneering tone. "Sarah's your only hope now, isn't she?"

She turned to Sarah and looked her up and down as if finding her beneath her notice.

Sarah felt a sense of foreboding, although she wasn't sure why. What was Enid rambling on about now? And why was she believing anything the woman said?

Hunter's face closed again. "Enid, I'd advise you not to say things you'll be sorry for later."

Enid jerked her head around to glare at him.

"Why should I be sorry for telling the truth?" she demanded harshly, then turned back to Sarah.

"He really wanted Crystal, you know. He was crazy about her. When she turned him down, he had no

other choice but you since he needs a wife if he wants
to keep Nicholas with him.''

Sarah raised her head, Enid's words swirling inside
her like a viper's venom.

Don't listen. This is only more of Enid's ravings.

"That's not true,'' she said, but the tremble in her
voice belied the words.

Enid smirked. "Oh, isn't it? Why don't you ask
Hunter if he doesn't feel it would be to his advantage
to get married soon?''

Shock washed over Sarah, as she remembered
Hunter's words early this morning.

We need to get married very soon.

He'd said that was because he feared she might be
carrying his child. She'd had trouble with that reason,
because it was why he'd married Beryl. And if Hunter
hadn't loved Beryl, maybe he didn't love her either.
Maybe he was driven only by a sense of duty.

That had been bad enough.

But what if even that wasn't the real reason? What
if the true one was completely self-serving?

She turned her stricken face to Hunter and her
heart grew colder at the equally stricken look on his
face.

He took a step nearer to her. "Sarah, it wasn't like
that. I know you love Nicholas as if he were your own
child. We could be a happy family.''

All that was true, but it wasn't what she needed to
hear now. She needed him to say he loved her more
than anything in the world. And that was the reason
he was desperate to marry her.

Maybe then, she could trust him with her life.

Enid laughed harshly. "You'd better hurry up with
your schemes, Hunter. Judge Wilson is a good friend

of ours. I've talked to him more than once about Nicholas's learning problems. He agrees with me that the boarding school is an excellent solution."

She drew herself up. "I must get back. I left that flighty Mattie with Dudley. If he wakes and calls for me, she won't know how to comfort him."

She walked past Hunter and Sarah, opened the door, and let herself out.

Sarah listened to Enid's footsteps as they gradually died away. Enid had walked instead of taking her carriage, which wasn't like her and proved how disturbed the woman was.

So why was she paying any attention to what Enid had said?

Because Hunter hasn't convinced you she was lying, her mind told her. *Because you can't bring yourself to believe him either.*

Finally, Sarah glanced at Hunter. Nothing had changed. He still looked troubled; he still frowned.

"Sarah, can I talk to you?" he asked. "This is a muddle, all right, but not as big a one as you think."

Anger flared through her. "How could it be any worse?"

"A lot. If I didn't love you, if I'd just tried to talk you into marriage as a convenience for me."

"Why should I believe you didn't do just that?"

His dark brows drew together. "Because I'm not a liar and I'm telling you so."

"And just like that, I'm supposed to believe you. Enid says Crystal broke off with you—and you just admitted that, too. I imagine you had a pretty good idea she was going to do that before today."

"She didn't break off with me! There was never anything between us."

Sarah glared at him. "Make up your mind. That's not what you said a few moments ago."

He glared back at her. "I didn't say that. If you'd listened to me instead of Enid, you wouldn't be so confused."

Her anger flared higher. "Oh, so now I'm just a silly woman who got confused—is that it?"

"No! Yes! I don't know." He raked long fingers through his dark hair.

"If you don't know, I'm sure no one else can," she said primly, crossing her arms over her chest. Deep inside, she hurt so fiercely she didn't know how she was still standing.

And her confusion kept on growing.

"I was *right* not to trust you," she burst out. "Here you were courting Crystal and me at the same time. If one of us didn't work out, the other one would. Was that it, Hunter?"

He looked tired, suddenly, and older than his years.

"No, that wasn't it," he said, his voice dead. "You told me you could forgive me, but you were afraid you could never forget. Or ever trust me."

"Yes. Or believe you truly love me. I still feel that way."

Did she? Did she know how she felt?

"I couldn't live that kind of life. Always wondering if you doubted everything I told you."

She struggled to get words past her dry throat. "I didn't ask you to live any kind of life with me."

They stared at each other like mortal adversaries for long moments. Finally, Hunter sighed and shook his head.

"I wanted you to marry me for all the reasons that were brought up today. I love you, but I also love my son and I *won't* lose him! I don't want to run away from Enid's threats either. Take Nicholas and Mama to St. Louis, where we'd all be miserable."

Pain went through her. He hurt, too—she knew that.

But not as much as she.

"I don't want to lose you either, Sarah. But it looks like I've never had you. Only your body—not your heart and soul."

"You had those eight years ago. It's not my fault you destroyed my trust."

His jaw tightened. "No, it's not. I've already said that more than once. If you can't give me everything, we should say good-bye right now."

"How can we say good-bye when we'll see each other every day, Hunter Winslow? One or the other of us *would* have to move away from Little Bethlehem."

"It's not going to be me," Hunter declared. "I've been away from here too long. I'm never leaving again. I'll figure out some way to stop Enid."

"Neither am I. It's my home as much as yours."

They looked at each for a few minutes more. Finally Hunter huffed out a sigh.

"I guess we're two of the most stubborn people who ever walked the earth. I promised you time to sort things out, decide how you feel. Do you still want that, Sarah? Or shall we forget everything that's been between us and treat each other as friends?"

"What about your worries I might be with child?" she blurted out before she could stop herself.

A muscle tensed in his jaw. "You wouldn't talk to me about that, remember? Have you changed your mind?"

"No," she said quickly, stung that he was taking that attitude, then instantly realizing how inconsistent she was. He was doing what she'd told him to do, and that didn't satisfy her either.

"All right then. Do you want more time? I love you and want to marry you, but only if you believe in my love and can trust me."

His voice was so calm and rational it made her furious. As if he were discussing some minor concern that didn't matter much to either of them.

Instead of perhaps the most important decision they'd make in their lives.

Go ahead and finish things now, one part of her mind told her. *No,* another part urged. *Don't rashly do something you'll regret the rest of your life.*

"Yes," she finally said, her tones as measured as his own had been. "I want more time."

Hunter nodded. "And do you want to keep on helping Nicholas with his lessons?"

The pain inside her deepened. He wasn't going to forget that, was he? No, having Sarah for a wife would help him in so many ways.

"Of course."

"I was thinking, since it's so close to Christmas, we might stop for a couple of weeks."

"That's fine," she managed.

Hunter stood there for a moment longer. "Good-bye, Sarah."

"Good-bye," she answered.

Hunter turned and walked away, and it was all Sarah could do to keep from calling after him to come back, that they would talk this out.

Sarah shut the door, wanting badly to slam it so hard every neighbor she had would hear and poke his head out to see what was going on.

Talking wouldn't help. Either she believed Hunter

loved her or she didn't. Either she trusted him or she didn't.

Despair hit her.

She didn't know if she'd ever be able to do either of those things.

And that was no basis for a marriage.

CHAPTER TWENTY

Hunter hurried down Sarah's steps and set off down the sidewalk, anger lending speed to his already rapid strides.

He was getting very tired of leaving Sarah's house in anger. Leaving *Sarah* in anger.

But his fair nature made him admit he couldn't blame Sarah for this latest debacle.

What would he have thought if he'd seen Sarah in some other man's embrace? If someone had told him the things Enid had?

What if he found Crystal, brought her to Sarah's house, and had her confirm he'd told the truth? Would that convince Sarah she could trust him?

No. Even if she believed Crystal, it wouldn't solve the problem. That had to come from within Sarah.

He smacked one fist into the other palm in frustration. He'd promised to give Sarah time—but that had been two days ago. Since he didn't know if she'd let him in her house, he'd gone to the church hoping to find her there alone so they could talk.

It was just a twist of malicious fate that Crystal had arrived before Sarah. That had caused Sarah to come in and find him with his arms about Crystal.

But he'd have been able to convince Sarah of the innocence of that scene if Enid hadn't spouted her vicious lies about him wanting to marry Crystal and turning to Sarah out of desperation when Crystal spurned him.

Getting married again *would* keep Nicholas safe from Enid's schemes. Would stop his worries about having to move away from here.

But he wouldn't have asked Sarah to marry him if he didn't love her.

And the only way he could prove that was by marrying her and living with love and trust between them every day . . . every hour.

It was a vicious circle. He had to be married to her to prove his trust and love and she wouldn't marry him until he proved both those things.

Lost in his gloomy thoughts, he didn't realize he'd reached his family house. He stared up at it, at the Christmas wreath on the door, the evergreen garlands twined around the porch railing, like most of the other houses in town, and he thought darkly he'd never felt less festive.

As it had been all this month, the inside of the house was filled with a spicy, delicious aroma. He walked to the kitchen and found Angela taking a pan of gingerbread men out of the oven. His mother sat at the table, laboriously sewing up a ripped seam in one of Nicholas's shirts.

Angela glanced up and smiled. His mother frowned at him.

"There you are," she said. "We waited, but Angela finally had to take Nicholas to the church for the pageant rehearsal."

Hunter smacked his head. "I'm sorry. I forgot all about that."

His mother put down her sewing. She flexed and extended her fingers, grimacing as if they hurt, making Hunter glad he'd bought the sewing machine, which was safely hidden in the attic until Christmas.

"What's wrong?" she asked. "You look upset."

"Oh, nothing." He couldn't tell either of these women his problems.

But why couldn't he? Why not talk about his troubles with his family? Maybe they'd be able to give him a few new insights.

"Everything's a mess," he said, pulling out a chair and sitting down across from his mother.

"Everything?" Angela asked, cheerfully as always. She brought a plate of the fresh-baked gingerbread men to the table.

He managed a smile for her. "No, I guess not. But the two most important things in my life are."

Angela seated herself, too, then picked up one of the cookies and bit into it. "Not bad, if I do say so myself." She tilted her head and smiled at him. "Why don't you tell us."

"All right, I will," he said, glad of the invitation.

Hunter paused, not knowing exactly where to start or how much to say. He couldn't discuss his night with Sarah.

And how could he tell them Sarah didn't love and trust him even after their night of passion?

But he *could* talk about his business problems. "I can't do anything about getting the cannery set up until Dudley recovers. He made it clear he'll be the one to decide on my loan. There's no telling how long he'll be sick. I don't intend to sound callous," he apologized. "I like Dudley and hope he gets over this completely."

His mother nodded, biting her lip. "It does sound bad, from what I've heard. Everyone says Enid is acting like she's half out of her head."

Yes, he could vouch for that.

"She wouldn't let Angela and me and Gladys past the front door yesterday. She won't allow anyone except herself to take care of Dudley or even help with him. She stays with him night and day. Of course she can't keep that up forever."

"No," Hunter agreed, remembering Crystal had said much the same thing earlier today.

No wonder Enid had looked so wild and haggard and had acted so outlandishly. To her credit, he knew she genuinely loved Dudley. That was proved with her devotion to him now.

"If I had any sense, I'd go to the new bank at Spring Grove and ask for a loan," Hunter went on. "I know my proposal is sound. I have enough of the local farmers interested, too, to make it a solid investment for the bank. I plan to provide seeds for the vegetable growers and grain for the meat producers."

"Yes, we know it's a good plan," Faith agreed.

"Did you ever think about taking in partners in this enterprise?" Angela asked.

Hunter shot her a surprised glance. Angela was so much the epitome of cheerful domesticity, he'd never have thought she'd have a head for business.

"No. I've always wanted to own my own business, run it myself. I got enough of working for other people in St. Louis."

"You wouldn't be working for someone just

because you had a partner. Dr. Lawson strikes me as a shrewd, thrifty man," Angela went on. "And he'd make a fine, trustworthy colleague."

So he would, Hunter thought, more surprise running through him, as he considered what Angela had said. Having a partner *wouldn't* be the same as working for a company owner. And he and the doctor had always gotten along well. He'd trust the man with his life.

That was fine as far as he was concerned, but what made him think Doc Lawson would be interested?

"He probably has enough to do to keep up with his medical practice," Hunter said.

"You'll never know unless you ask him," his mother said a little tartly. "Don't give up before you even try."

With a spark of amusement, Hunter recognized that last remark as one she'd nudged him along with during his growing-up years when he'd been reluctant to tackle some job.

He nodded. "You're right, Mama. Maybe I'll do just that."

He smiled at Angela. "Thanks for the suggestion."

"You're welcome." She smiled back and passed him the plate of cookies. "Try one."

Hunter did, savoring the blend of spices and molasses. The more he considered Angela's suggestion, the better it sounded. If he had a partner—or partners—with some capital, he wouldn't have to borrow so much.

If he had to go elsewhere for a loan, that would make a difference. A bank that was unfamiliar with him would be more inclined to go along with a loan for a smaller amount. And having someone like the respected Dr. Lawson as his partner would swing a good deal of weight with prospective lenders, too.

Some of his anxieties about getting his business off the ground eased. Maybe things would work out after all. Either with or without the help of the Little Bethlehem Bank.

Then guilt struck him. Dudley had always been decent to him, even when he'd let his wife meddle in things that were no concern of hers. Hunter sincerely hoped the older man would recover, both for Dudley's sake and because he was Nicholas's grandfather and the boy needed him.

Those thoughts led him back to his other problem. *Sarah.*

His buoyed-up feelings drained away, bleakness filling him again.

"All right, son. What else is bothering you?" his mother asked gently. "Are things not going well with you and Sarah?"

"You could say that."

The two women were giving him interested, concerned looks. Angela as well as his mother truly cared for him and Sarah. Confiding in them couldn't hurt.

It was time—past time—that he learned to do that. Ever since his marriage to Beryl, when he'd left Little Bethlehem so precipitously to live in the city, he'd kept his personal problems to himself.

He had been ashamed of his actions and regretful of the mess he'd made of three lives. He had soon realized he and Beryl had nothing in common. They hadn't even known each other. They were just two young people who'd made a mistake and had to live with it.

The only bright spot in his marriage had been Nicholas. His son made up for the things that weren't right.

That wasn't true for Beryl. She'd resented Hunter for what she considered a forced marriage, which had driven another wedge between them.

Hunter turned off these thoughts. The past was over. Now he had to try to make the most of the present and future, however difficult both might be.

But he wanted Sarah in his future!

He decided to start with what he considered the smallest problem. "She couldn't teach if we married. Sarah loves her job. What a stupid law that is!"

"It won't always be that way," Angela said, her voice confident.

His mother looked at her and shook her head. "I swear, Angela, I wish everyone had your bright outlook on everything. The world would be a better place."

Angela nodded. "The world *will* be a better place in the future in many ways. You can be sure of that."

"Maybe you can be sure of it, but lots of times I can't," his mother said.

Neither could he, Hunter thought. Especially not with things as they were between him and Sarah.

He steeled himself and quickly told Angela and his mother all that had happened this afternoon.

Once he'd said everything out loud, the problems keeping them apart seemed even more bleak and disheartening than when they were still in his head.

Silence fell after he'd finished. Angela picked up another gingerbread man and nibbled at a corner, then crumbled it in her fingers, her eyes distant as if her mind was far away.

His mother picked up Nicholas's shirt again and jabbed the material with the needle, her face somber.

Hunter hissed out a sigh, got up, and began pacing

the room. Of course there was no quick and easy solution.

Maybe there was no solution at all.

That thought made a pain jab his middle. The pain was so sharp it bent him over at the waist. He was thankful he was at the far end of the big room and the women didn't notice.

"I don't know what to tell you, son," his mother finally said, "other than just to give Sarah time. To me that's all that can help."

He heard a chair scrape and glanced over to see his mother get up, still holding Nicholas's shirt. "I need to find another spool of thread," she said, heading out of the room.

At the doorway, she paused and looked back, a troubled frown on her face. "I'm sorry I couldn't be of more help."

Hunter forced a smile. "That's all right, Mama. It was good just to share my problems with you. Thanks for listening."

"Give the girl time. Maybe things will work out." She headed upstairs, leaving him alone with Angela.

Hunter glanced toward her. She methodically crumbled another cookie. As if feeling his gaze, she looked up.

Her bright eyes seemed brighter than usual. Almost as if tears lurked, ready to fall.

Somehow, that made Hunter feel worst of all. If even Angela, who was always cheerful, always optimistic, was crying, what hope did he have of ever fixing this mess?

Hunter straightened up. Forced a smile. One thing for sure: Inaction never solved anything.

He'd promised to give Sarah time. And he would. As his mother said, that was all he could do.

In the meantime, he'd work on his business plans, try to solve those problems.

"I'm going to Doc Lawson's office. See if I can talk to him."

Angela nodded. "That's a good idea," she said.

He saw her swallow; then she got up and came over to him. She lifted one small hand and laid it against his cheek.

A curious, vibrating warmth flowed from her hand into his face, then coursed down his body. The tension and dejection he felt ebbed away.

Leaving him empty feeling, but yet curiously light and free.

"Everything will come out all right in the end," she told him. "Hang on to that. Keep on believing it."

"I will," he heard himself saying.

And, amazingly, he *did* believe it.

Crystal hurried down the sidewalk toward home, wishing the long walk was already finished. She was exhausted.

Sarah hadn't returned, and Angela had dropped Nicholas off and left, so the pageant rehearsal had been laid squarely at Crystal's feet.

She'd tried to think of some way to refuse, but she couldn't come up with anything. After all, as Little Bethlehem's former teacher, even if she'd only served for a very short while, she was the logical substitute for Sarah.

She tried to remember how Sarah handled things and did them the same way. Encouraging the younger, more timid children, and being stern with the older ones who were inclined to misbehave even at so solemn an occasion as the pageant rehearsal.

To her astonishment, the children paid attention to her. Did as she said. That built up her confidence, and she heard a new, firmer tone to her voice.

She got through the rehearsal credibly, and afterward, several of the parents complimented her on how well she'd handled things.

Crystal thanked them, wanting them to leave, so she could go home. Finally, she was the only one left.

She opened the door into the main part of the church and cautiously glanced around. David was nowhere in sight, she saw, relief filling her. She couldn't face him right now.

And when do you think you'll be able to face him? her mind had asked. *It's not going to get any easier as time passes.*

She'd ignored that and, leaving the church, had hurried toward her parents' house. It was a long walk, but she wanted to see her father again. And this time, she was going to insist that Mama let her stay longer.

Her mother had looked terrible this morning. As if she hadn't slept for days. Even if they weren't getting along now, Mama needed her and she was going to help.

Behind her, Crystal heard the sound of a buggy coming up, but she didn't turn. She didn't want to have to wave and speak to anyone right now. She needed to concentrate on making her mother listen to her.

"If I can handle the pageant, I can handle Mama," she said out loud to give herself courage.

At the sight of Crystal walking down the sidewalk, David Hopkins felt his heart skip a beat.

There she was. She hadn't gotten too far ahead of

him. He pulled on the buggy reins and let out his breath in relief. Now if she just agreed to let him drive her home.

He had to talk to her. His heart began beating faster at that prospect. What would he say? How could he let her know that in the last couple of weeks he'd grown to care for her?

He didn't understand it either. He'd vaguely known that someday he'd have to think about taking a wife, but until the day when Crystal had fallen in the church room, he'd never gotten any more specific in his thinking than that.

But since then, his mind—and other parts of him— had been returning again and again to that incident. Remembering how she'd felt when he'd lifted her up. How soft and womanly. How she'd made *him* feel. Very much a man.

And from her manner that day, he'd gotten the idea that Crystal might share those feelings.

Until this afternoon, when he and Sarah had opened the door and seen her in Hunter Winslow's arms.

Anger and jealousy surged through him again just thinking about that. He pulled harder on the reins, desperately trying to think of what to say to her.

The buggy slowed down and stopped beside Crystal.

Crystal tensed. Oh, no, who was this?

"Would you like a ride?" a male voice asked, a touch of reserve in its deep, mellow tones.

David! She couldn't talk to him. Wildly, she looked around for an escape.

Of course there wasn't any. Just the almost deserted sidewalk with patches of melting snow here and there.

The silence drew out. He wasn't going to leave. She had to say *something*.

She forced herself to turn toward him.

His hair was tousled as usual, and his coat was buttoned wrong, as if he'd been in a hurry to get it on and hadn't paid attention to what he was doing. He had a polite smile on his mouth, but it was plain he felt as tense at seeing her as she did him.

In fact, he looked as if he'd rather be anywhere but here. So she would assure him he didn't have to worry about her getting home safely.

Crystal quickly shook her head. "No, Da—Reverend Hopkins, you don't need to bother. I feel like walking."

She wondered if he'd caught her near slip and what he thought if he had.

His smile faded, a frown drawing his brows together, and she drew in her breath. He *had* caught her slip and was offended.

"It's almost dark and you still have a long walk ahead of you."

Crystal let out a breath of relief as she realized his concern was only for her safety.

"That's all right. I can see my way with the snow on the ground."

As she said the last words, a drop of rain fell on her nose. Startled, she brushed it away, hoping he hadn't noticed.

"Don't worry. I'll be fine," she repeated. "Good evening, Reverend Hopkins."

Another drop of rain fell; then it began raining in earnest.

Oh, blast it! Crystal thought. Now she'd look like a complete fool if she didn't accept his offer of a ride.

David leaned over and opened the buggy door on her side. "Come on and get in, Crystal," he said gently.

Her lips pressed tightly together, she obeyed, settling herself close to her door, then pulling it closed.

Or trying to anyway. The door refused to latch.

"That door needs something done to it," David said vaguely, as if he hadn't the foggiest notion of what that something might be.

Despite her nervousness, Crystal concealed a small smile. David's mind was always on higher matters. That was one of the things about him she found so endearing. The problems of daily life stymied him, but didn't bother him. It was a good thing his congregation gave him a handyman's services as part of his salary.

He reached across her, his coat sleeve brushing across her chest, and pulled the door forcefully closed.

Then his sleeve brushed her again as he pulled his arm back.

Crystal felt the small touches all the way through her body, all the while pretending to be completely unconcerned.

He clucked to his horse and it began walking again. A silence fell. It was so deep Crystal fancied she could feel the very air thickening around them.

She had to say something. But what? She couldn't blurt out what she desperately wanted to: What he'd seen in the church wasn't what it seemed.

Or could she?

She'd done all kinds of things these last few days she'd never dreamed she had the courage to do.

Crystal cleared her throat. Looking straight ahead, she said, "Mine and Hunter's feelings for each other are like brother and sister."

She winced at how high and strained her voice sounded.

Her side vision caught the movement of David's head. She turned her own. Their glances met. Surprise was on his face . . . and something else. Something that looked like relief.

"Is that right?" he asked.

"Yes," Crystal said, glad her voice was firmer. She cleared her throat again. "When you and Sarah came in the room earlier today, Hunter was just giving me a big-brotherly kind of hug because I'd been crying."

Again, there was silence. Finally, David said, "Why were you crying, Crystal?"

His voice had changed, too. Now it sounded gentle and concerned. And all that meant was that he was their minister, and she was one of his flock. He'd try to help her as he would the other members of his congregation.

"Because I'm unhappy and worried," she answered.

"Of course you are, with your father so ill. Would you like to pray with me?"

"Right here? Right now?" she asked, startled.

"If you like. I could pull over to the curb. Or we can wait until we arrive at your house."

The thought of them bowed in prayer with the buggy sitting by the curb and passersby giving them curious glances sent a wild urge to laugh through her. She pressed her hands to her mouth to stifle it, but she felt her shoulders shaking.

"What's wrong?" David asked, his voice alarmed. "Are you crying again?"

"No . . . no," she got out; then a laugh escaped her. More like a nervous giggle.

She turned to him to find his concerned look had deepened.

"I'm sorry, David, but what you said just struck me as funny. I didn't mean to be . . . sacrilegious."

David. This time he couldn't overlook what she'd said.

He was giving her such a peculiar look. Not concerned or upset. Interested.

"I'm sorry, Reverend Hopkins. I didn't mean any disrespect."

"I like the way you say my name, Crystal," he said.

"Wha-what?" she stammered, totally taken aback.

He smiled at her, his white teeth flashing. "I'd like for you to call me David."

Crystal wet her lips with the tip of her tongue.

David swallowed, visibly.

"Th-hen you're not upset with me?"

"Of course not. Why should I be upset with you?"

"Because I think of you as a man, not only as my minister," she blurted, then was horrified at herself. "Of course, I also think of you as my minister," she added quickly. "A very *fine* minister."

Oh, Lord, how she was rattling on. Why couldn't she keep her mouth shut?

His beautiful smile widened. "Good."

"Good?" she echoed, faintly.

"Yes. Because *I* think of you as a woman. Not only as a member of my flock. Not that you're not a very *fine* member of my flock."

He turned back around to flick the reins at his horse.

He thought of her as a woman. Chills raced up and down Crystal's spine. What other things might he . . . had he thought about her?

She quailed inside, but she'd gone this far. She had to know.

"Do you . . . do you think of me as *attractive?*"

He kept his head to the front, but he nodded decisively. "Oh, yes. You are a most fetching young woman."

Fetching? Crystal couldn't believe her ears. She would never have believed her idealistic David Hopkins had such thoughts. Would actually voice them.

Her David Hopkins?

She stared at the side of his beautifully shaped head. She liked the way his dark brown hair grew. As always, it looked made for tousling. And she'd like to be the one to do that.

"Do you . . . *like* me, David?" she asked, her low voice floating out into the chilly evening air.

His head suddenly turned toward her. The dazzling smile was gone from his face, leaving it serious, intent.

"I like you very much. I realized that today when I saw Hunter with his arms around you. I wanted to hit him."

Her mouth fell open. She felt her eyes widen. What a very unreverendly thing for him to say!

But how very manly.

"If I saw you with your arms around another woman, I'd feel the same way," Crystal said.

Their gazes met and clung. Crystal felt as if she were being pulled into the depths of him. It was a strange feeling. But wonderful.

The horse stumbled on something in the road, drawing David's attention back to guiding him.

They'd reached the outskirts of town. Where the houses were set on large plots of ground. Where her own family house waited at the top of the hill.

The road was deserted. The sun was sinking low in the sky, the short winter twilight fast descending.

"David," Crystal said, her voice trembling and breathless. "If . . . if you want to stop the buggy somewhere along the road here, I think it would be all right."

He gave her another quick, startled glance.

"Do you want me to pray with you?" he asked, surprise in his voice.

"Yes, that would be fine," she said. "But first I want you to do something else."

"What?" he asked.

Crystal pulled herself up and drew in a deep breath, then let it out.

"I would very much enjoy it if you would kiss me. That is, if that idea also appeals to you."

The words were scarcely out of her mouth before David guided the horse to the side of the road and stopped.

He hastily wrapped the reins around the post, then turned to her.

His warm brown eyes seemed darker, somehow, as they gazed deeply into hers. The expression in them made chills start chasing themselves up and down her spine again.

"I would like that more than anything in the world," he said, his voice a low rumble that vibrated through her.

He moved toward her and she moved toward him, and just before their lips met, Crystal had a moment of pure wonder.

How in the world could a day that had started out so horribly end up like this?

CHAPTER
TWENTY-ONE

Sarah—bundled in her heavy cloak, Arctics, and mittens—put one snowshoed foot in front of her, then the other. Finally, she stopped to rest, looking up the hill she still had to climb.

She was getting very tired and there was still a distance to go before she reached the top and the Cunninghams' impressive house.

It had begun snowing yesterday afternoon and hadn't stopped until a couple of hours ago. The snow lay more than a foot deep—the first big snow this winter.

"And it could have waited another few days as far as I'm concerned," she grumbled as she resumed her walk.

This quandary with Hunter had taken away her pleasure in everything, even in the snow, which she'd always loved before. At least she had snowshoes. Since she had no sleigh, this was the next best thing.

Thinking of the sleigh reminded her of the sleigh ride with Hunter. Which had made her invite him into her bed, where they'd made wonderful love . . .

Only to have the next morning end in misery. Then later the awful encounter with Enid . . . and Hunter.

She still felt torn in two different directions. One minute she believed Hunter told the truth and she yearned to go to him, to tell him she'd marry him. Once she was married, surely her feelings would change. She'd be able to trust him. Believe that he truly loved her.

Then her mood would swing to the opposite pole and she'd see Crystal with her head snugged against Hunter's chest as if that was where she belonged and wanted to stay.

If he'd lied about Crystal, then maybe he'd lied about his reasons for wanting to marry Sarah.

Finally, she'd decided she had to talk to Crystal. Ask her point-blank what was between her and Hunter.

What makes you think Crystal will tell you the truth about her feelings for Hunter? And his feelings for her?

She didn't. This was the only thing she knew to do.

How could Hunter have been involved with her? her mind persisted. *He's only been back in town a few weeks and no one has seen them together or they'd have told you.*

"There's plenty of privacy at Crystal's house, and he's been there more than once," she answered out loud.

A twinge of pain went through her as she remembered Hunter and Beryl in the Cunningham gardens all those years ago.

She passed no one on the walk. It was still early in the morning and people with any sense who didn't have to be out in this weather were snug before their fires.

Where she wished she was. And with each step, she wished that even more and wondered if she was a fool to be off on this quest.

She'd come this far though. She wouldn't turn back now.

Her snowshoes slid sideways and snow fell into the top of her boots, making her feet even colder. But if not for the snow she wouldn't have this chance. She'd be in school, teaching.

As school let out yesterday, Burt Williams had stopped by, saying the school board members had decided, since this snow looked like a big one, it would be a good idea to start the Christmas holidays. Which meant no more school until after New Year's.

The children had been ecstatic.

She wasn't glad, except for the opportunity to see Crystal. Teaching was all she had left now—and the extra things, like the Christmas pageant. She smiled wryly at that thought, since Hunter had been back in her life only a few weeks. But it was true. Teaching no longer satisfied her as it had before his return.

Stop feeling sorry for yourself. Say the word, and your days will be overflowing. You'll be Hunter's wife and a mother to Nicholas. And you might be a mother to a babe of your own.

She quickly turned the last thought off. She wouldn't even consider that possibility.

What do you hope to accomplish? her mind started in again. *Even if Crystal assures you Hunter told the truth and there's nothing between them, will that miraculously give you complete faith in him?*

"It would help," she answered, again glad the streets were deserted so no one could hear her talking to herself. "If I knew he'd told the truth about that, maybe I could believe he wouldn't run after every pretty face that came along like he did with Beryl.''

This is a foolish thing to do, her mind harped again.

Halfway up the hill she stopped and took a few deep breaths. A plume of smoke came from Dr. Lawson's chimney. And a sleigh sat in the side yard.

Sarah drew in her breath.

A very familiar sleigh.

Hunter's.

Worry hit her. What was he doing there so early in the morning? Had he come to fetch the doctor? Had Nicholas taken ill? Faith or Angela?

She stood undecided for a few moments. Maybe she should go see . . . .

No, it was none of her business. Hunter was very capable. He could handle whatever it was, she finally decided and trudged on.

Soon she was close enough to see that smoke also came from the Cunninghams' chimney. Naturally. With Dudley so ill, the house wouldn't be deserted.

The long walk to where the house sat, so far back from the road, daunted her. Again, she told herself she'd come this far and she'd see it through. The driveway was covered with snow so deep that, if not for the tall, slender poplars bordering it, she wouldn't know a drive was there.

Not that it mattered to her, Sarah thought. It was all the same when you were walking. She urged her tired body to keep going.

Halfway up the drive, she stopped and frowned. What was that at the bottom of the front steps? She was too far away to make out what it was. Maybe a stray dog?

That thought made her stop. Stray dogs that big could be dangerous if hungry—as bad as wolves. But most of them ran in packs, and she saw nothing else that could be an animal.

It didn't look like a dog anyway. It looked like a person.

Alarm shot through her. If someone had fallen and was lying out in this snow, they'd be frozen in no time.

She tried to hurry, but with snowshoes on she couldn't. She pushed along as fast as possible.

Nearing the end of the drive, she gasped. It *was* a huddled person, drawn up as if to try to keep warm. While she watched, the figure moved a little.

Relief went through her. At least the person was still conscious.

When she'd almost reached the huddled form, she recognized it.

Enid! What had happened? Why had no one inside found her?

Sarah jerked off her snowshoes and knelt beside the other woman.

Enid lay on her side, her eyes closed, at the bottom of the snow-covered steps. Thank God she wore a cloak and Arctics, but she shivered uncontrollably. Obviously, she'd been lying here for a while.

For too long to survive?

Sarah pushed aside the fearful thought and gently shook the other woman. "Enid, can you hear me? Can you get up?"

Enid moaned; then her eyelids fluttered open and she looked at Sarah. "What are you doing here?"

"Never mind that," Sarah said, tugging at her. "Come on. You have to get up and come inside."

Enid's face contorted. "I can't. I hurt myself. I think I broke my leg."

Dismay filled Sarah, but she forced her voice to

sound calm and capable. "Don't worry. I'll get Crystal or Mattie to help me take you in."

"No one's here but Dudley and me."

Sarah's dismay changed to real fear. Enid was taller and quite a bit heavier than she was. Could she get her inside by herself?

Sarah firmed her mouth. She must. She couldn't leave Enid while she went to the Lawsons. It would take too long.

"We have to get you inside," Sarah said, making her voice firm, too.

But first she'd better see how bad the break was. Carefully, she pulled up Enid's skirts, bracing herself to see a bone sticking through the flesh, but she didn't. She sighed in relief.

Looking up at the long flight of front steps, Sarah swallowed. How could they make it to the top?

"I can't . . ." Enid moaned, sinking down into the snow again.

Sarah's mouth set even tighter. "Enid Cunningham, I'm ashamed of you," she said sternly. "I always thought you were one of the strongest women I knew. I never believed you'd be a quitter."

"But my leg hurts so much," Enid wailed, tears coming to her eyes.

"I know, but you'll freeze to death if we don't get you inside. Do you want to want to do that? Do you want to leave Dudley and Crystal?"

Where *was* Crystal? And Mattie?

"N-no," Enid said. Then her eyes widened. Fear came into them. "Dudley's taken a turn for the worse. I was going to fetch Dr. Lawson when I fell on some ice on the steps. Oh, leave me and go and check on him!"

Sarah's fear increased. Dudley might well be dead

or dying. But she'd deal with that after she'd gotten Enid safely inside.

"I'll go for the doctor when I get you inside," Sarah said. "Come on now. Get up, Enid!"

She grasped the other woman around the waist and gently pulled her to a semiupright position.

Enid screamed and fell against Sarah's chest. Sarah caught her just in time to keep her from hitting the ground again and held on grimly.

"Balance on your good foot and leg," she told Enid.

"I can't! I don't have any feeling in my legs," Enid said, sobbing with pain.

New fear shot through Sarah. Had Enid been out here long enough for her legs and feet to freeze?

"Oh, just leave me," Enid begged. "Go see how Dudley is."

Sarah took a deep breath, then let it out. "I won't leave you. I'm going to get you inside. I'll have to drag you up the steps."

Enid whimpered. "No, no. I can't stand that."

"Yes, you can," Sarah said firmly. "If you think I'll let you die on me, you're sadly wrong."

Sarah grasped Enid under her arms and carefully turned so her back was to the steps. Still holding tightly to the other woman, she stepped backward, feeling for the bottom step.

Finally, she found it and gingerly put her foot down, hoping it wasn't icy. It wouldn't help any if she, too, fell and injured herself.

Sarah let out her breath in relief when her foot only sank down into deep snow. It penetrated her high-laced boots instantly with an icy chill, reminding her of how cold Enid must be.

Cautiously, she eased her other foot back so that

both were on the bottom step. The movement jostled Enid, who let out another cry.

"It's going to be all right," Sarah said. "Just hold on a little longer."

Praying the other steps were equally free of ice, Sarah eased her feet onto the next one, tightly gripping Enid's heavy, almost inert form.

It seemed to take an eternity, but finally, weak with relief, she reached the top step.

Without warning, her foot skidded and she felt herself falling.

"Hang on!" she cried to Enid, and then she fell heavily onto her back, Enid coming down on top of her.

The breath was knocked out of her by Enid's weight and pain shot through her back.

She lay there, stunned, until she could catch her breath. Thank God she'd fallen on the porch and not the steps or they'd probably be back down at the bottom again.

"Are you all right?" she asked Enid.

There was no answer.

New fear hit Sarah. She shook the other woman. "Enid! Answer me."

Enid groaned and mumbled something, but clearly she was still partly unconscious. The pain of the new fall on her injured leg must have been too much for her.

Sarah, pain stabbing her back with every movement, eased out from under Enid and hobbled to the front door.

The knob turned easily and she pushed the door open. Welcome warmth flowed out.

Leaving the door standing open, Sarah returned

to Enid and, as gently as she could, pulled her across the porch and into the spacious hall.

Enid cried out as Sarah laid her down on the floor. "It's all right," Sarah soothed her.

The other woman lapsed back into her semiconscious state.

Closing the door against the cold, Sarah looked wildly around for something to put over Enid to warm her. The big hall tree held several coats and cloaks. Sarah grabbed them all and spread some on top of Enid and, after easing up her legs and then her torso, some more under her.

Sarah tucked the coverings around Enid snugly, then stood, wincing as pain shot through her back again.

How she wished Crystal or Mattie was here.

Where was Dudley? In his bedroom, she guessed, and hurried up the curving front staircase. She'd never been upstairs in this house before, so she had no idea which room to look for.

The first was obviously a guest room, in perfect readiness for company. The second, fussily decorated and frilly looking, must be Crystal's.

Opening the third door, she gasped. This must be Enid and Dudley's room. A dressing gown lay across the back of a chair. Slippers stood by the wide bed.

But the bed was neatly made up. And empty. This wasn't the room he occupied now.

She ran back into the hall. There were two more closed doors, and Sarah jerked them both open, steeling herself for the sight of an injured, unconscious, or maybe dying or dead man, but to her immense relief, she didn't see that sight. No one was in either of the rooms.

He must be downstairs. It would be easier for Enid

to take care of him downstairs. Why hadn't she thought of that first and not wasted time up here?

Sarah hurried downstairs. Reaching the turn in the staircase, she stopped, her heart lurching.

A nightshirt-clad man bent over Enid's still inert form.

Dudley!

Holding his wife's limp hand, he glanced up at Sarah and she saw tears streaming down his face. "What happened to Enid?"

His voice was shaky and weak.

"She had a fall," Sarah called. "Stay where you are, I'll be right there."

She hurried down the rest of the stairs, trying to make sense of things. Enid had said Dudley had taken a turn for the worse. How could that be when he'd been bedfast and unconscious a lot of the time before and now he was not only out of bed, but appeared coherent?

Dudley still bent over his wife, stroking her hands and forehead, murmuring to her, tears still falling.

Sarah squatted beside them. "Let me help you get back to bed," she told Dudley, trying to make her voice come out quiet and soothing.

He shook his head. "No, no. I'm all right. You tend to Enid. What's wrong with her?"

Dudley was twice her size. She couldn't get him back to bed if he refused to go. She gave him a closer look. He had lost weight during his illness. His eyes were sunken, and he was very pale.

But his eyes were clear, his gaze steady. Instead of being worse, at death's door maybe, he appeared to be improved in health.

"She fell on the steps outside," Sarah said. "She thinks her leg's broken."

Alarm came into Dudley's eyes. "Is it?"

"I don't know. I haven't had a chance to look closely at it yet but I will now."

Sarah stood and moved to Enid's other side and knelt again. Carefully, she lifted the cloaks and coats, then Enid's heavy, sodden skirts. She touched her hand to Enid's legs, greatly relieved to feel warmth coming back to her flesh. Soon, she'd have to try to get the wet clothes off her.

A great purple bruise and swelling had formed on Enid's left ankle. Gently, Sarah pushed at the swelling, moved the ankle a little.

Enid cried out, then opened her eyes. "Oh, that hurts so much."

Her gaze fell on Dudley still crouching beside her. Her eyes widened and she struggled to rise. "Dudley, what are you doing out of bed?"

His ravaged face relaxed into a tender smile. "I heard all this commotion in the hall and then I heard you cry out. I had to come see what was wrong with you."

His hand closed over hers and squeezed.

Enid stared at him as if she couldn't believe the evidence of her eyes. "You're better," she said. "You are much better."

"I don't remember how I was, but if you say so, then I guess I am."

"You were so sick," Enid said. "And . . . you started talking out of your head. Thrashing around on the bed. I was sure you were dying."

His smile widened. "Takes a lot to kill a tough old coot like me. Now let's get you tended to."

He turned to Sarah. "I guess we'd better not move Enid until Doc Lawson looks at her. Can you go get him?"

Sarah swallowed. The thought of putting her snow-shoes back on, struggling down the long driveway, then half way down the hill to the doctor's house made her quail inside.

"Of course," she said, getting to her feet. She couldn't stop a gasp and wince of pain.

Dudley frowned. "You're hurt, too."

"Nothing serious," she assured him. "I just bruised my back a little when we fell on the steps as I was getting Enid inside."

"Snow and ice out there?" At her nod, he went on, "You shouldn't go out in it."

"There's no one else to go," Sarah said briskly.

Dudley turned to Enid. "Where are Crystal and Mattie?"

Enid didn't say anything for a moment; then she said, "Crystal's staying at Sally's. I sent Mattie home yesterday because she was coming down with grippe. I was afraid you'd get it."

Dudley's frown deepened. "I wish they were here."

Enid swallowed. "So do I," she said, her voice wobbling.

He turned to Sarah again. "I guess you'll have to go."

"Yes. Will you be all right until I come back?"

"I'll be fine."

"You need something around you. Enid has all the coats."

Dudley rose, then looked down at himself, apparently becoming conscious for the first time that he wore nothing but a nightshirt.

"I'll get some quilts from my bed."

Before she could offer, he'd gone down the hall, his gait a bit wobbly, and entered a door on the left.

Enid was looking after her husband. Tears stood

in her eyes just as they had in Dudley's eyes a little
while ago.

"It's a miracle," she whispered. "I thought he was
going to die. While I was lying out there in the snow,
I could picture him in here by himself, getting worse
and worse . . . ."

Dudley came back, carrying a couple of quilts. He
settled himself on the hall rug beside Enid and
wrapped a quilt around his legs, then spread the other
one on his wife.

"Both of you stay there," Sarah said. "I'll be back
with Dr. Lawson in a little while."

"Take care," Dudley told her.

"I walked from my house. I have snowshoes outside."

"Good, good."

"You walked all the way from your house?" Enid
asked, surprise in her voice.

"Yes."

"Why?"

"I wanted to see Crystal."

Sarah quickly turned. This was no time to explain
why her trip had seemed so urgent to her that she'd
come out in this weather.

She left the house, opening and closing the door
quickly so no cold air would blow on the two just
inside.

She'd slipped on her snowshoes and was halfway
down the drive before she realized something that
stopped her dead in her tracks for a moment.

For the last half hour she and Enid had been in
each other's presence and had talked to each other.
She'd dragged Enid up her front steps and into her
house. Physically, she had been closer to Enid than
ever before in her life.

And only two days ago, Enid had stood in *Sarah's* front hall, saying hurtful, awful things to her.

There had been no hint of that enmity today.

Sarah sighed and started walking again, her back giving her a twinge now and then.

Enid had other things to worry about now. Her own injuries had laid her low.

How would she feel later? Would she still blame Sarah for Dudley's illness? For Crystal's long-overdue independence?

"Of course," Sarah said aloud. "It would take more than what's happened today to change Enid Cunningham's ideas about anything—or anyone."

She tried to hurry her steps. Dudley seemed much better, but she didn't want to leave him alone any longer than necessary. He could have a relapse.

It was a good thing she'd come today. That she hadn't turned back. Otherwise, Enid might have frozen to death.

But her trip hadn't benefitted her at all. Crystal wasn't even here.

Never mind that. Her personal problems would have to wait.

She reached the bottom of the drive and turned right to go down the hill to Dr. Lawson's house.

Hunter's sleigh was still in the doctor's yard. Her heart began beating a little faster and relief filled her, mixed with another kind of anxiety.

The horse wasn't in sight. Hunter must have unhitched it and put it in the barn. That had to mean he'd come to see the doctor for some other reason than an ailing family member.

She didn't want to see him. Not now. Not yet. Not until her mind wasn't so muddled. Not until she knew what her decision would be. Not until she saw Crystal and talked to her.

"People have to do lots of things they'd rather not," she told herself. "So get yourself down there and stop complaining."

CHAPTER
TWENTY-TWO

By the time she reached the Lawsons' front door, Sarah felt as if she couldn't move another inch. Her feet were wet and cold, her back ached, and she trembled from exhaustion.

Millie Lawson swung open the door and her normally pleasant expression changed to concern. She stepped back, opening the door wider.

"Sarah! What are you doing here? Come on in. You look half frozen."

"I feel like it, too." Sarah forced a smile as she gratefully entered the warm hall.

Hunter's coat hung on the hall tree. His Arctics sat on a mat beneath it. A low rumble of voices came from the back of the house. One of them was Hunter's.

Sarah quickly told Millie what had happened, glossing over her reasons for going to the Cunninghams.

Millie clapped a hand over her mouth in shock when Sarah had finished.

"Oh, Lord, I'll go get Quincey. Take off those wet wraps and sit by the fire."

"I'd like nothing better, but I'll go back with the doctor. Mattie and Crystal are both gone."

Millie frowned. "Let me go."

"No, I'll be all right," Sarah said. She was younger and stronger than Millie.

"What's going on out here?"

Quincey Lawson appeared in the kitchen doorway. Sarah glimpsed Hunter behind him, looking at her. Her heart skipped a beat, but she kept her gaze from lingering on him.

Millie explained the situation, and Quincey hurried to the coat rack, jerking his battered old black coat off it.

"You'll need help. I'm coming, too, and we'll take my sleigh," Hunter said, reaching for his own outer garments. Again, he glanced toward Sarah.

Again, she evaded his eyes.

"Thanks, Hunter," Quincey said.

A few minutes later, with the horse hitched to the sleigh again and Hunter at the reins, they went up the hill.

Sarah was in the middle of the front seat, squeezed in between Hunter and Quincey. Her wet, cold feet had chilled the rest of her and she started to shiver.

Was all of it from the cold? Or was some from Hunter's nearness?

Hunter glanced down at her. "As soon as we get up there, you take off those wet boots. We should have left you at the Lawsons'."

"I'm fine. I need to get Enid out of her wet clothes," she said, feeling warmer at Hunter's concern.

Which was foolish. He would show the same concern for anyone else. He was a caring person.

Yes, and you need to take that into consideration when you're trying to decide if you want to spend your life with him, her mind told her.

"I can't believe Dudley pulled out of that apoplectic attack this soon," Quincey said. "I thought he was a goner. Or that he'd never get much better."

Glad to focus on something other than her own problems, Sarah turned to the doctor. "Do you think this improvement is only temporary? That he'll have a relapse?"

"It's hard to say for sure, but with most people I've seen who make a dramatic improvement like this, it's permanent."

Relief swept through her. "Oh, I'm so glad! Dudley's a good man."

"Yes, he is," Quincey agreed. "Too good for that wife of his, I've always thought."

He turned to Hunter. "Sorry, didn't mean to speak ill of your in-laws."

"That's all right," Hunter said after a moment. "As you know, I've had my ups and downs with Enid."

"But she's surprised me since Dudley took sick," Quincey went on. "She's been as devoted a wife as I've ever seen."

"Yes, that's what I've heard from a lot of people," Hunter agreed, but his voice was strained, his words terse.

Was he remembering what had happened the other day in her house, just as she was? And before that, the night of love they'd had together? Was he wondering how she felt, if she'd softened toward him?

No, she told herself, what was no doubt uppermost in his mind were Enid's threats, her attempts to wrest control of Nicholas from him.

Hunter's sleigh made fast work of the long drive

310   *Elizabeth Graham*

Sarah had twice struggled to traverse. He pulled up in front of the big house and stopped the horses. In a few moments all three of them were inside.

Enid still lay where Sarah had left her, well covered with the coats and cloaks and the quilt. Dudley sat close beside her, holding her hand.

Relief came over Dudley's face as he looked at Dr. Lawson. "Glad to see you!"

Dr. Lawson's keen glance quickly went over the two people. Enid seemed to be dozing, her eyes closed.

"How are you feeling?" he asked Dudley.

"I've felt better, but from what Enid's said, it appears I'm lucky to still be here."

"You are," the doctor agreed. "Well, let's see what Enid's done to herself."

While the doctor carefully examined Enid's foot and ankle, Hunter went around the house building up the fires.

Sarah went down the hall to the room from which Dudley had brought the quilts.

The room was a study, she saw, looking at the book-lined walls. Now a bed had been set up; a table alongside it held the clutter of bottles and jars a sickroom accumulates.

A small cot, its covers thrown back as if the occupant had left it in a hurry, sat alongside the bed. Obviously, Enid had been sleeping down here, too, and Dudley must have awakened her suddenly, alarmed her. And that was why she'd tried to go for help but then fallen herself.

Sarah straightened both beds, folding back the covers so they'd be easy to get into. She heard a noise behind her and turned.

Hunter stood in the doorway. "I wanted to check the fire in here."

His glance probed hers.

Sarah fought an intense longing to go to him, lose herself in his arms. She lowered her eyes.

"It's getting cold. The stove must need more wood."

"I'll tend to it," Hunter said, his voice giving no hint of how he felt.

Sarah heard him moving around the room, the sound of the stove door being opened, wood chucked inside. She kept busy tidying the table beside the bed.

"Hunter," Dr. Lawson's voice called. "I need your help."

"Coming." He hurried back to the front hall, Sarah behind him.

Enid was awake and biting her lower lip as if in pain. She gave Hunter and Sarah a quick glance, then looked away. Was she already regretting she'd had to let Sarah help her? That now both Hunter and Sarah were here to see her in need of more help and to keep on giving it?

"Is my leg broken?" Enid asked, her voice quavering.

"Not your leg. Your ankle," Dr. Lawson said. "We need to get you in bed so I can splint it."

Enid let out her breath in relief. "Oh, thank God. I was sure it was my leg."

"You still won't be able to get around too well for some weeks."

"I'll manage," she said, a trace of her old asperity in her voice. Again, her glance briefly went over Hunter and Sarah.

She turned her head and smiled at her husband.

The smile was so sweetly loving Sarah drew in her breath.

During the next half hour, Sarah got Enid into dry

312 Elizabeth Graham

clothes, and with Hunter helping Dr. Lawson, Enid and Dudley were settled in the room down the hall, and Enid's injury was tended to.

Sarah found a pair of Crystal's slippers upstairs and got out of her wet boots. Having her feet dry and warm made her feel better, and the pain in her back was easing up.

She busied herself in the kitchen, finding onions and potatoes in the pantry, and soon she had a pot of potato soup cooking.

"That smells wonderful," Hunter said from the doorway.

Sarah's hand, holding a pepper mill, jerked. "I hope it tastes good."

Annoyed with herself for reacting so strongly just to the sound of his voice, she steadied her hand and finished grinding pepper into the soup.

"I'm sure it will. You've been a good cook since you were a young girl."

His voice sounded closer. Too close. With an effort of will Sarah kept from turning around. "How are Enid and Dudley?" she asked.

"Enid's in quite a bit of pain. Doc gave her a dose of laudanum to get her to sleep. Dudley's sitting up in bed, fretting over her."

He paused, then continued. "Sarah, I'm going to go get Crystal. I know you must be exhausted, but would you mind staying here until tomorrow? I know you and Enid aren't hitting it off well right now. But Doc thinks it would be a good idea if Crystal didn't have to be here by herself with her parents."

"Of course I'll stay," Sarah said at once. "Little Bethlehem's people stick together when anyone needs help, no matter what our personal quarrels are."

She still kept her back to him, pretending the soup needed constant stirring.

"And that's one of the reasons I'm glad I moved back here. I can't imagine my city neighbors doing this much for me."

"I suppose that's true," she agreed, relieved they were managing to keep the talk away from their personal problems.

But that doesn't keep you from trembling in Hunter's presence, or stop the memories of how he held you that night . . . .

She swallowed. "Since I've never lived anywhere but here, I really couldn't say."

She congratulated herself that they were carrying on a civilized conversation. Whatever their futures held, whether they were together or apart, they'd be able to get along with each other when they met around town.

And won't you enjoy that? Thinking about those moments in his arms while you discuss the weather and town doings.

"Thank you, Sarah. I'll be back in a little while," Hunter said.

Wishing she could blank out her mind, Sarah looked up just before he disappeared out the door. A yearning went through her as her gaze traveled from the top of his dark head, down his broad shoulders and straight back. She tried to push it away, but it wouldn't go.

She loved him. Nothing was going to change that, no matter what she decided. She'd love him as long as she lived.

She pulled the soup to the back of the stove to simmer slowly, added more wood to the fire, then went back to the sickroom and glanced in.

As Hunter had said, Enid slept deeply now. Dudley,

pillows piled behind his head, also slept. Dr. Lawson
glanced up from a sheet of paper he was writing on
and smiled.

He put the paper on the bedside table, then after
another glance at his patients, tiptoed out of the
room, joining Sarah in the hall.

"They'll sleep for a while. Best thing for both of
them."

"Yes, I'm sure," she agreed, going back to the
kitchen with Dr. Lawson beside her.

"I thought I smelled potato soup," he said, sniffing
the air appreciatively. "That's always been one of my
favorite dishes."

"It's ready. Do you want a bowl?"

"Don't mind if I do." He seated himself at the big
table and Sarah placed the steaming soup in front of
him, along with thick slices of bread she'd also found
in the pantry.

He looked up. "Aren't you going to join me? I
don't like to eat alone."

She shook her head, but smiled. "I'm not very
hungry."

He took a bite, then nodded. "Excellent soup.
You've had quite a day. How's your back?"

"Better. It wasn't anything serious."

"Good. See you got rid of those wet boots."

"Yes. I didn't think Crystal would mind my bor-
rowing her slippers."

"No. Crystal's a good girl. Glad she's finally standing up to her mother. Long overdue."

His words brought back Sarah's reason for coming
here today. Crystal would soon be home and she'd
have a chance to talk to her after all. After Hunter
had left, of course.

The thought made a knot of new tension settle in her stomach.

"How are things going with you and Hunter?" Dr. Lawson asked, his voice still casual.

Startled, Sarah drew in her breath, staring at his graying head now bent over his soup. Had Hunter talked to the doctor about them?

In a moment she realized Dr. Lawson had probably just heard gossip around town. There were few secrets in Little Bethlehem.

He raised his head and gave her a level look. "Not ready to talk about it yet? All right, I'll not pry. But you won't find many men better than Hunter, despite that foolishness of years ago. This town is lucky he decided to come back to stay."

"Yes," she said in a moment. Why couldn't she look upon what had happened between him and Beryl as nothing more than youthful foolishness?

Because it had created a marriage that lasted seven years, she reminded herself. And created a child. A child she loved as her own.

And created distrust in her that she might never lose.

"I was tickled to death when he asked me if I'd consider becoming a partner in his cannery business. This town needs something like that, and if anybody can pull it off, it'll be Hunter."

Jolted, Sarah stared at him. "Hunter asked you to be his partner?"

"Yep. Yesterday. Today he came over so we could tend to the paperwork."

He gave her a surprised look. "You didn't know anything about that?"

"No." She heard the tightness in her voice and knew she was being ridiculous. She'd promised

Hunter nothing. Why should she be hurt if he hadn't confided his business plans to her? She was though, even if it didn't make sense.

Dr. Lawson had noticed. He looked uncomfortable. "This came up suddenly. I mean his decision to try to find partners."

Partners.

"Then he'll have more than just you?"

"Yes. Tomorrow he's going to talk to Burt Williams. Thinks one of the farmers would be a good balance. Burt's a levelheaded, sensible man."

She swallowed past a suddenly dry throat. "I'm sure that's true."

"Uh, oh, I guess I put my foot in it, didn't I?" Dr. Lawson asked, his voice chagrined. "No doubt Hunter wanted to surprise you with all this. Do me a favor and don't tell him I let the cat out of the bag."

"I won't," she promised, then heard the front door open again and close, and low voices from the front of the house.

"That must be Hunter and Crystal now," Dr. Lawson said. "I'll go talk to her."

Sarah stared after his retreating back, realizing a host of her assumptions weren't true.

In the back of her mind she'd thought that, if in the end she turned Hunter down, he wouldn't stay in Little Bethlehem. That he'd go back to the city because it would be too painful and awkward for them both to live here.

She'd thought this although Hunter had told her a dozen times he wouldn't leave unless he had to. What Dr. Lawson just said confirmed that. He was forging ahead with his business plans.

Did that mean he had other plans for his personal

life if he and Sarah didn't marry? That he *was* still involved with Crystal? Otherwise, would he stay here with Enid's threats hanging over him? Risk losing Nicholas?

She took Dr. Lawson's empty bowl to the dishpan and stirred the soup again, then went to stare unseeingly out the back window.

"Sarah," a voice said from behind her. Crystal's voice.

Sarah curled her fingernails into her palms. She didn't want to talk to Crystal now. But she couldn't keep on looking out this window.

She turned to see Crystal standing just inside the door. The look on the girl's face made Sarah draw in her breath, made pain surge through her.

Crystal looked radiant, luminous, as if her feet weren't quite touching the floor.

She looked like a girl in love. Requited love.

Crystal smiled at Sarah, a sweet, happy smile. "Oh, isn't it wonderful?" she asked.

Sarah gaped at her in shock. Was the girl so obtuse that she expected Sarah to congratulate her on her successful conquest of Hunter?

"I couldn't believe it when Hunter told me Daddy was much better. Mama wouldn't let me stay last night, no matter how I argued, and I couldn't sleep for worrying about him."

Relief made Sarah's knees weak as she realized Crystal's joy was due to her father's recovery.

"Yes," she managed, "we're all happy about that."

Hunter came into the room. "Any chance I could get a bowl of that soup?" His expression was merely friendly, his voice the same.

Crystal turned to him, a secret little smile turning up the corners of her mouth.

Hunter smiled back the same way. As if they were sharing a wonderful secret.

New pain hit Sarah. She'd been right the first time. No matter how much a girl loved her father, that kind of look was reserved for love between man and woman.

Don't jump to conclusions, her mind said. *Wait and talk to her.*

"Of course," Sarah said, forcing her voice to steadiness, getting down more bowls.

Somehow, she got through the next half hour, while Hunter ate, while Dr. Lawson checked on Enid and Dudley a couple more times. While Crystal kept giving everyone that luminous smile.

Crystal loved her father. She *could* just be happy about that, Sarah told herself. And the look she and Hunter exchanged could mean something innocent, too.

What? She couldn't think of a thing.

"Guess we'll be going," the doctor said finally. "I'll come back up before bedtime to see how things are."

Hunter stood beside him, his gaze carefully staying away from Sarah.

Crystal hurried across the room, threw her arms around Hunter's neck, and kissed him warmly on the cheek. "Good-bye, Hunter. Oh, I'm so happy!"

Hunter hugged her back. Then the two men were gone, leaving Sarah and Crystal alone in the big room.

Was *that* supposed to be a sisterly hug?

She couldn't keep on standing there. She turned away and began washing the supper dishes.

"I'll dry," Crystal said, still in that light, happy voice. Holding a dishtowel, she came to stand beside Sarah.

Finally, she finished the dishes and went to wipe off the table, still not looking at Crystal. But out of the corner of her eye, she saw the girl still had that dreamy look on her face.

Sarah made up her mind. She couldn't stand this any longer. She *would* talk to Crystal. Find out once and for all how she felt about Hunter.

"Oh, I'm so happy, Sarah," Crystal said. "I day-dreamed about how it would feel to fall in love like all girls do," Crystal continued. "But I never really knew what it would be like. Not until two days ago."

Two days ago. The day before yesterday. The day she and David had walked in on Hunter holding Crystal in his arms.

Blinding pain surged through Sarah. Her questions had been answered. She no longer needed to ask Crystal anything. Hunter *had* lied.

Sarah knew her heart was breaking. She could feel all the sharp pieces jabbing into her.

She *had* to get out of this room, she thought wildly, away from Crystal telling her these things as if Sarah had no feelings.

"But now I know," Crystal went on, oblivious to Sarah's rigid silence. "And he feels the same about me. He loves me and he wants to marry me. Oh, Sarah, when he kissed me, I thought I'd faint. It was a hundred times more wonderful than I'd ever imagined."

Fighting scalding tears, Sarah released a strangled sound she couldn't hold back.

"Sarah? What's wrong? Are you sick?"

Crystal was at her side, pulling Sarah's hands away from her face. "You're crying. Oh, what's the matter?"

Sarah shook her head, evading Crystal's gaze. She *wouldn't* let Crystal know how badly she hurt. "I'm just tired," she croaked. "It's been a long day."

"I'm such an idiot," Crystal said, chagrin in her voice now. She put her arm around Sarah's shoulder.

"Here I've been prattling on about David and me when you must be worn-out. And you saved my mother's life. And maybe my Daddy's. Go up to my room and lie down for a while."

Sarah stiffened. What had Crystal said?

David and me.

The only David she knew was their minister.

What on earth did he have to do with all this?

Something penetrated the haze of exhaustion and pain that enveloped Sarah.

Hunter had said once that he thought Crystal might be interested in David Hopkins as more than their family minister.

Could this be true?

Was this what Crystal meant? Wild hope began to tug at Sarah . . . but she was afraid to let it surface.

She lifted her head and swiped at her wet cheeks. "What were you saying about . . . David and you?"

Crystal's radiant smile returned. "He picked me up in his buggy the day you and he walked in and saw Hunter and me . . . " She laughed merrily.

"I know Hunter has explained to you what happened in the church and it was so silly, but I was sure David wouldn't understand."

Sarah tried to make sense of Crystal's somewhat garbled words. She didn't want to make a fool of herself. She had to be sure about this.

"You mean when you were telling Hunter you only loved him as a sister?" she asked cautiously.

Crystal laughed again. "Yes! And it was such a relief. Mama kept insisting that I try to make Hunter want to marry me, but I couldn't because I didn't feel like that about him and I knew he didn't feel like that about me either.''

Slowly, Sarah felt the broken pieces of her heart start to mend themselves. She managed a smile for Crystal.

"I'm glad you got that cleared up," she said.

Crystal let out a sigh of relief. "So am I. Now I hope you and Hunter can get everything straightened out between the two of you."

"I hope so, too," Sarah said, no longer surprised that Crystal also knew all about her and Hunter. Apparently, everyone in Little Bethlehem did.

Part of the muddle had been resolved. She no longer had to worry about Crystal and Hunter being in love. About Hunter lying to her about that.

So where did that leave her? Back where she'd been that morning after she and Hunter had made love.

Everything was squarely in her lap again.

A sudden sharp cry came from the room where Enid and Dudley were.

"Mama," Crystal said. "I'll see to her. I'm still upset with myself that I let her make me leave yesterday. I'm not going to leave now until they're both recovered no matter what she says. Go up to bed, Sarah, and rest awhile."

She left the room.

Enid was laid low now, but that wouldn't last. As soon as she recovered, she'd be back trying to wrest control of Nicholas from Hunter.

Despite her crazy ravings two days ago, Enid *had* spoken the truth when she'd said Crystal wasn't interested in Hunter. So it was probably also true the judge was in favor of sending Nicholas to the boarding school.

It was quite possible she could make this happen.

The Cunninghams were powerful in the town, the county. Hunter could very well lose control of his adored son.

Unless he married again. Once more had a complete family. A wife who was a teacher, who could give Nicholas all the help he needed.

She loved Hunter. She loved Nicholas like a son of her own. It was within her power to stop Enid's plans in their tracks and make sure that Nicholas stayed with his father.

So your doubts have gone? her mind asked. *You can trust Hunter now? For the rest of your life? With your life?*

She swallowed. No, her doubts were still with her. Her mind still kept telling her that she'd never be able to forget what Hunter had done.

But she loved him and he needed her.

Was that enough to override the other things? She wasn't sure. How could she ever be sure?

She'd think about it some more. She'd consider it until Faith's annual gathering on Christmas Eve.

Then either she'd tell Hunter she would marry him. Or that they could never be together.

CHAPTER
TWENTY-THREE

"Faith!" Angela called from the parlor. "Come here and look. The Christmas cactus is blooming."

Hunter's mother, washing dishes in the kitchen, dried her hands on a dishtowel.

"Oh, praise be!" she called back. "I've been praying for that to happen. I know you're not supposed to pray for such little things, but I just couldn't help it."

"I don't see why there's any harm in that. I believe God's as interested in Christmas cactuses as we are," Angela replied.

"Well, it will certainly brighten my Christmas."

Hunter glanced at his mother and smiled as she hurried into the parlor, beaming.

It was hard to stay glum around the two of them. And he was going to do his best to appear cheerful for his mother's Christmas Eve affair. She enjoyed it so much. It was the highlight of the year for her. He'd do his best not to spoil it.

A knock came on the door.

"Hunter, will you answer that?" his mother asked. "Tell them I'll be there in a minute."

"Let me, Daddy," Nicholas asked. "Maybe it's Miss Sarah," he added hopefully.

"All right," Hunter agreed. He hoped it was Sarah, too. Then again, maybe he'd rather it wasn't. Being around Sarah was going to be a strain, considering the circumstances.

He hadn't seen her, except when he had dropped Nicholas off for another pageant rehearsal two days ago, since they were together at the Cunninghams. Not quite a week, but it seemed more like a month. She'd wanted time, and if it killed him, he'd give it to her.

But how much did she need?

Probably a lot more than a few days, his mind told him. *You'll have to be patient.*

Patience wasn't his strong suit. Action was. And lately, between Sarah and his business plans, his patience had been sorely tried.

That's just too bad, isn't it? Do you expect to come back here after all these years, after what you did, and have Sarah fall into your arms? You forgot all about courting her. You're lucky she's even considering having you for a husband.

He was. He knew that was true.

But still, when he loved Sarah so much, wanted her so badly, waiting was very hard.

He huffed out his breath. He was wound up like a spring.

A couple followed Nicholas back to the kitchen and

Hunter's spirits fell. Quincey and Millie Lawson. After greetings were exchanged, he led them into the spotless parlor, where his mother still stood by the Christmas cactus, as happy as if it were her newborn baby.

Angela dipped punch for the new arrivals, and Millie at once went over and began oohing and ahing over the plant along with the other two women.

"Doesn't take much to make a woman happy," Quincey commented, grinning at Hunter over his glass of punch.

Hunter forced what he hoped would pass for an answering grin. "I guess not. Mama's crazy about any kind of flower or plant."

"So's Millie."

Another knock sounded, and Nicholas ran to answer it. Hunter held his breath, then released it when he recognized Burt and Nellie Williams's voices.

Nicholas led them into the parlor, where they joined the others.

Nicholas tugged at his hand. "Daddy, where's Miss Sarah? Do you think she's not going to come?"

"Of course she's coming," Hunter assured his son, but he was beginning to wonder himself.

Surely, Sarah would be here. She wouldn't disappoint his mother and Nicholas, even if she didn't care how he felt. But what if she were sick? Or had maybe fallen and hurt herself?

His mind conjured up all kinds of disasters that could have happened.

He accepted a second glass of punch from Angela. If Sarah didn't arrive in another few minutes he'd go to her house to see if she was all right.

Another knock sounded on the door. Nicholas's face brightened. "That's got to be Miss Sarah."

He trotted off and Hunter held his breath as he heard the door open.

"Miss Sarah!" Nicholas cried joyfully. "Why are you so late? I thought you weren't coming."

Hunter let out his breath in relief. Then new tension gripped him. Maybe he didn't want to see her. See the look in her beautiful eyes.

"You didn't think I'd miss this, did you?"

Sarah's voice was bright and cheerful as she talked with Nicholas. Naturally, it would be. That didn't mean anything.

A beaming Nicholas proudly brought Sarah into the almost full parlor.

"Hello, Sarah." Hunter smiled at her, his glance finding her eyes.

She was smiling, too, of course. At least her mouth was. He couldn't fathom the expression in her eyes as she glanced back at him. It looked guarded, and wary, yet something else was in those hazel depths.

"Hello, Hunter. It's good to see you again."

Did she truly mean that, or was it just the usual polite remark? He couldn't tell.

Angela gave Sarah a glass of punch and general greetings were exchanged. Hunter wanted nothing more than to grab Sarah's arm and take her somewhere private. Where they could talk.

Where he could kiss her. Hold her in his arms. His body began warming at those mind pictures, then just as quickly cooled.

Sarah might never be in his arms again.

He couldn't stand that thought.

Sarah chatted easily with the other people. Hunter saw how much everyone liked her. Of course they did. Sarah was a wonderful person.

She'd be a wonderful wife and mother. Why couldn't she believe they'd be happy together?

Believe she could trust him with her life and he would be worthy of that trust.

"All right, everyone. It's time for the oyster stew and we need to sit down for that," his mother announced.

Millie Lawson sighed with pleasure. "I've been hungry for that all day, Faith. Your oyster stew is the best in town."

The other guests voiced their agreement and everyone trooped into the dining room, where the table had all its leaves in and was covered with a pristine white damask cloth.

A huge, steaming china tureen sat in the middle of the table, giving off a delicious aroma. Soon, all were served the rich, buttery concoction.

"Shame we can't turn out oysters in our cannery," Burt Williams said.

Hunter heard the proprietary note in Burt's voice as he said "our cannery" and smiled. Burt had enthusiastically accepted Hunter's offer to make him a partner in the fledgling enterprise.

"At least not until shipping costs come down a good bit," Quincey said. He turned to Hunter with a grin. "Think we can make any money canning the crawdads from the creeks?"

Good-natured laughter greeted his question. "We'd have a never-ending supply—that's for sure," Burt's wife Nellie put in.

Sarah smiled like everyone else, but she said nothing.

Hunter stole a glance at her where she sat across the table from him. What was she thinking? Was she as tense as he was? She didn't appear to be, but maybe she was just doing a good job of hiding her true feelings.

After the feast, everyone adjourned to the parlor again. Hunter managed to get a seat next to Sarah. Nicholas hastened to take the chair on the other side of her.

Impatience filled Hunter. Would he be able to find a private moment to talk with her today? He'd find one someway. She glanced his way, and again that strange mixture of emotions seemed to be in her expression.

He wished he knew what it meant. How she felt. And if she'd made up her mind yet.

But if he wanted Sarah as his wife, he had to wait. He couldn't rush her, he couldn't push her to hurry. He'd tried that and it hadn't worked.

And no matter how hard it was, he wanted her to be sure of her feelings. He couldn't live with distrust any more than she could. That would be no kind of a marriage for either of them.

Angela went to the old upright piano and began to play a Christmas carol.

Hunter was surprised at her skill. He hadn't even known she could play, but then Angela seemed to be good at whatever she turned her hand to.

Soon everyone's voice was raised in singing the beloved old songs. Hunter glanced at Sarah again, wondering if she was listening to how well their voices blended together.

Was she thinking, like him, that they belonged together, and always had, no matter what had happened in the past?

She suddenly turned his way again and he drew in his breath as her gaze lingered on his deliberately. Then she gave him a smile that lingered, too. Her arm was around Nicholas's shoulder, he saw. Curved protectively around his son's small frame.

Hope leaped in him. That had to mean something. Was she trying to tell him without words that her doubts were resolved and she would marry him?

As they finished a carol, a knock sounded on the door.

His mother looked surprised. "Now who could that be?"

"I'll go see," Angela said. Hunter gave her a curious glance as she got up from the piano stool and hurried out of the room. Her voice had held an expectant note.

He heard the front door open, then familiar voices.

"That's Dudley and Enid," his mother said, surprise in her voice. "Oh, my land. I would have invited them, but I didn't think Enid would be caught dead in my house."

Everyone's head turned, looking curiously toward the doorway to the hall.

In a few moments, Angela came back, followed by David Hopkins, who pushed a wheelchair in which Enid sat. Crystal had her father's arm, supporting him.

Of course, by now everyone in town knew about Crystal and David's courtship, but still the others present gave them bright, interested glances.

Crystal looked like a different person, Hunter thought, not able to push down a pang of envy. As did David. It was amazing what love could do for people.

Dudley moved to stand behind his wife. Enid's face was pale and strained as she gazed around the room. Dudley seemed a little shaky on his feet, and he'd lost a good bit of weight. His concerned gaze was on his wife.

"Enid, Dudley, how nice to see you. All of you come and sit down," Hunter's mother urged.

She was doing her best to be polite and gracious, Hunter saw, but it was a tremendous effort as far as Enid was concerned.

Enid shook her head. "No, we won't be staying long. We know we're not invited guests."

"I would have been glad to invite you, Enid," Hunter's mother said, a defensive note in her voice. "But I didn't think you'd come."

Enid glanced at her, her expression serious. "Thank you, Faith."

Hunter heard several indrawn breaths as if more than one guest was surprised at Enid's words. He was, too.

"I know everyone is surprised to see us here," Enid continued. She paused. "I have something to say to Hunter and Sarah."

"Do you want to go somewhere private?" Hunter asked at a loss for anything else to say.

"No. Everyone in Little Bethlehem will know by tomorrow anyway."

Again, Hunter heard indrawn breaths and suppressed laughs.

"First, I want to thank you, Sarah, for what you did for me last week. You no doubt saved my life. After the way I've treated you, I didn't deserve kindness at your hands. I'm deeply grateful that you could forget all that."

Sarah looked stunned at Enid's words. "Of course I'd do the same for anyone in those circumstances. You don't need to thank me."

Enid firmed her mouth. "Yes, I do. I've wronged

you, Sarah, and I'm sorry for it. I'm happy that things turned out all right for you, despite everything."

Hunter glanced around the crowded room. Everyone here, except Dudley, was staring at Enid in the same stunned way as Sarah.

Enid *was* like a new person, Hunter admitted. Had her near death experience changed her this much? Or would she revert to her old self once she was back on her feet and Dudley was restored to full health?

Dudley squeezed his wife's shoulder, as if he could read the thoughts of the others and was protecting her.

"That's not all I have to say," Enid continued. She fixed Hunter in her gaze.

"I've wronged you, too, Hunter, and I'm sorry for that. You've always been generous in sharing Nicholas with us. I had no business wanting more than that. You can stop worrying that I'll do anything to get control of Nicholas from you."

A relief so deep it weakened his knees swept over Hunter. His mouth stretched wide in a smile. "Thank you, Enid."

"I don't deserve thanks from either of you," she said, her voice faltering. Hunter saw how hard this had been for her.

Dudley squeezed her shoulder again. "I think we'd better go now, dear."

"Yes," Enid agreed.

"Oh, won't you stay for some refreshments and to join in the carols?" Hunter's mother asked.

Enid shook her head. "No, thank you. We're still a little under the weather and need to get back home."

Dudley cleared his throat. "Hunter, this isn't the time or place, but come around next week and we'll talk about your cannery. I hear you're offering partnerships. Would you consider another one? If so, I'd be mighty interested.''

Hunter stared at him for a long moment, beyond surprise now. Finally, he realized his mouth was hanging open, and he closed it. "I'd be honored to have you as a partner, Dudley," Hunter said.

He glanced at Burt and Quincey, his brows raised.

"I'd be honored, too," Quincey at once answered.

"So would I," Burt echoed.

Dudley smiled. "That's fine then. Merry Christmas to you all. We'll see you at the pageant this evening."

"Merry Christmas!" everyone answered back.

"We'll see all of you at the pageant, too," Reverend Hopkins said. He and Crystal helped Enid and Dudley out of the room, Hunter's mother following to let them out.

Hunter found it hard to believe what had just happened. In a matter of minutes, many of his problems had been solved with just a few words from Enid and Dudley.

Jubilance filled him. He turned to Sarah and Nicholas. Wanting to share his happiness.

Sarah's expression stunned him.

"I'm so happy for you, Hunter," she said, but her voice was stiff and strained. She didn't sound happy at all.

He didn't know how she sounded. As if she was relieved and sad and disappointed all at the same time.

But one thing he knew as he gazed deep into her eyes.

She hadn't decided she'd conquered her doubts and wanted to marry him. Whatever that half-hopeful expectant look had meant earlier, it was gone now.

Sarah gave him another stiff smile and turned her head away.

Hunter's jubilance died.

He no longer had to fear losing his son.

But maybe he'd lost the only woman he'd ever loved.

CHAPTER
TWENTY-FOUR

From her place at the back, Sarah glanced out over the crowded church. It looked as if everyone in Little Bethlehem was here tonight.

There was Faith ... and Dudley and Enid in her wheelchair, accompanied by Crystal and Reverend Hopkins.

The faces of the audience were expectant. There was a rapt hush over everything. This was one of the big highlights of the year.

Sarah wished she could share the feelings that seemed to emanate from the people sitting out there.

But she couldn't. Her mind kept going back to this afternoon at Faith's.

She'd struggled with her feelings since that day at the Cunninghams'.

This afternoon, when she'd sat there between Hunter and Nicholas, her arm around the boy, she'd felt good about her decision to tell Hunter she would marry him to keep Nicholas safe.

There was no longer any other pressing reason— her courses had come several days ago. She didn't carry Hunter's child. A small pang of disappointment had arisen in her and she'd firmly pressed it down. She wouldn't want to marry Hunter for that reason.

And you think this one is better? her mind had asked.

Yes. It wasn't a selfish reason, based on the necessity of not having a child out of wedlock.

This one is based on the same thing—fear. Marriage shouldn't begin with fear as its foundation.

She'd ignored that, too, trying to hold on to the sureness she'd made the right decision.

Then Enid had come, publicly apologized to Hunter and Sarah, promised not to interfere with Nicholas again.

Sarah's motivation for her decision had been swept away in an instant.

And all the doubts had come rushing back to fill the vacuum. She'd looked around at the happy couples in Faith's parlor, not only love but trust in their eyes, and she had known she couldn't go through with marrying Hunter.

Not until she was sure of his love. Not until she could trust him with all her heart.

Now she wished she could run out of the church, go home, and stay there forever. Even the thought of her school didn't comfort her as it usually did. As much as she loved teaching, it could never take the place of sharing Hunter's life. She would gladly give it up if all else was right between them.

But it wasn't. Maybe she'd never be able to forget what Hunter had done. Or trust him again.

She saw Hunter in the audience, sitting beside

Faith. He looked as miserable as she felt. What must he be thinking? Before Enid's arrival, she'd smiled at him warmly.

Later, she'd been cold and distant, and she had left the party early.

Worst of all, she couldn't explain her change of heart to him. It would only make things worse if he knew she'd planned to marry him just to protect Nicholas.

And because you love him. And want to share every day of his life.

Pain squeezed her heart. That didn't matter. Love without trust couldn't make a marriage work.

Someone tugged at her skirt. Sarah glanced down to see Nicholas dressed in his Wise Man's robe, a worried look on his face.

"What's wrong?" she asked, stooping to be at his level.

"I'm scared, Miss Sarah," he whispered. "There's too many people out there and they'll all be looking at me. What if I forget my part?"

She tried to think what to say to reassure him. Nicholas had been shy early on, but she thought he'd gotten over it.

"You were brave to take the part when it scared you, Nicholas," she finally said. "And now you must stick it out. I'm counting on you. All the people in the audience are, too. Life can be hard sometimes, but we can't run away from our responsibilities."

Nicholas looked at her and she could see the inner struggle going on inside him. At last he swallowed, hard.

"All right, Miss Sarah. I won't be a quitter. I—I'll do it."

Sarah smiled at him, squeezed his shoulder. "I knew you would."

He gave her a small return smile, then went back to where he was waiting to come on stage.

"You gave him good advice," Angela said, appearing beside Sarah.

The smile she'd managed to summon for Nicholas was fading, but Sarah revived it for Angela. "I hope it works."

"It will," Angela said confidently. "Just wait and see. Nicholas is like his father. When he has to shoulder responsibility, he does it."

Sarah's smile froze. "What do you mean?"

Angela looked surprised at the question. "Hunter made a bad mistake with Beryl. But he stuck it out. He didn't run away from the obligations of marriage and fatherhood."

"But . . . he'd promised me his love and he left me . . . ."

Angela nodded. "Yes. I said he made a bad mistake. But if he'd deserted Beryl and come back to you after what happened between them, do you really think you and he could have had a happy life together?"

Sarah stared at the other woman.

"Just think about it, Sarah," Angela said, her voice now soft and dreamy.

Somehow, Sarah felt she must do as Angela said. She turned her thoughts inward . . . .

Yes, she'd wished, desperately wished, Hunter would leave Beryl, come back to her, take her somewhere far away from Little Bethlehem, where they'd be blissfully happy . . . .

How could she have had that absurd daydream? And believed it? What a foolish girl she'd been . . . and stubborn, too. She'd refused to listen when

Hunter had tried to persuade her they could be married then . . . that they could have worked something out . . . .

Sarah trembled, feeling as if she were on the verge of a revelation.

"Maybe you've looked in all the wrong places to find trust, " Angela murmured. "Maybe you need to look inside your own heart."

Hadn't she ever done that? She thought she had a hundred times over . . . but maybe she was wrong . . . .

Yes, Hunter *had* proved he was a good man, a trustworthy man, by staying with Beryl . . . by sticking it out even if his heart wasn't in it . . . .

"That's right," Angela whispered. "It was there all along, but you just weren't ready to see it yet. None of us is perfect. Everyone should be allowed one big mistake."

"Yes," Sarah whispered back. "Hunter never did anything else to hurt me. He never lied to me."

"No, he didn't," Angela said. "Is that one mistake bad enough to make you distrust him for a lifetime? To live alone with only your pride for comfort . . .

"No," Sarah answered. "No, it isn't! But how can I find what I need?" She gestured out toward the audience.

"Look at all those happy couples out there. I watched them at Faith's house this afternoon. Dr. Lawson and Millie. Burt and Nellie. Enid and Dudley. And now Crystal and David. You can see the light of love and trust shining in their eyes when they look at each other.

"Do you really believe that nothing bad has ever happened between any of them? Or will never happen to Crystal and David?"

No, of course she didn't. How could she be naive enough to think that?

"Look at Nicholas," Angela said. "It's time for his part."

Sarah suddenly realized she hadn't been paying attention to the pageant when she was supposed to be there ready to help anyone if necessary. But everything seemed to be going along smoothly and they were almost at the end.

How had that happened so quickly? Where had the time gone while she'd talked with Angela?

Nicholas, standing with the other two Wise Men, knelt before the manger to present his gift to the baby Jesus.

"Here is my gift of myrrh," Nicholas said, his high young voice steady.

Sarah felt tears fill her eyes as she watched. Nicholas had done what he had to do . . . and done it well.

So had his father.

Trust was a leap of faith. Christmas was all about faith . . . and love . . . and hope . . . .

You could never have proof of it. You just had to take a chance.

She had to take a chance. She must forget her pride. Humble herself and admit she, too, had made mistakes.

Or lose the man she would love forever.

The pageant came to its end. Enthusiastic applause rose from the audience.

"I'll tend to the rest of this," Angela said. "Faith and I will take Nicholas home. You and Hunter have other things you need to do."

"Yes. Thank you, Angela." Sarah gave the other woman a grateful smile.

Angela smiled back. "I didn't do anything, except remind you of some truths you already knew."

The audience members stood up, stretched, and began talking to one another.

Angela disappeared toward the back of the church. Sarah watched her go, an odd feeling going through her. Angela . . . something about Angela she should know . . . .

"Sarah," Hunter said from behind her.

Sarah's heart leaped at his dearly loved voice. She forgot everything else but him . . . and herself.

His voice sounded tentative, as if he wasn't sure if she'd even answer him.

Sarah turned and gave him a smile. A warm smile. "The pageant went well, I think. Nicholas did his part perfectly."

His return smile was relieved. "I thought so, but then I'm a proud papa."

That kind of pride is fine to have.

"So you are. And a good one, too."

He blinked in surprise. "I'm glad you think so."

"Of course I do. And I should have told you so long before."

His surprised expression grew. "What's come over you tonight?"

She laid her hand on his coat sleeve, remembering the night they'd made love. How wonderful it had been to share herself with him.

"I don't know. Christmas, I guess. Hunter, can we go somewhere and talk . . . alone? My house? Angela said she and Faith would walk home with Nicholas."

Hope leaped in his dark eyes. "Of course."

Sarah reached down and touched his hand. His fingers closed around hers, squeezed tightly.

"But first we have to tell Nicholas how well he did."

"Yes, of course," Sarah agreed, leading the way to the back of the church to where the pageant members still milled around.

"Daddy!" Nicholas, his robe a little askew, hurried across to them. Faith and Angela, as well as the Cunninghams and Reverend Hopkins, were behind him. "Did I do my part good?"

Hunter looked as if it was all he could do not to pick his son up and hug him, Sarah thought. Instead, he stooped down and looked Nicholas in the eye.

"I can't imagine anyone doing it better."

Nicholas beamed. "I was scared, but Miss Sarah told me I could do it. That I had 'sponsibilities. So I did."

Hunter glanced at Sarah, his eyes warm and grateful. "You did, son, and you carried them out well."

"Let's go home now," Faith said. "I know a little boy who's tired and needs his bed."

"I'm not tired," Nicholas protested, then ruined the effect by rubbing his eyes.

"You did your part very well, Nicholas," Enid said. Smiling, she held out her arms. "How about giving me a hug?"

Nicholas smiled back and carefully leaned over the side of her wheelchair and hugged her. "How's your leg, Grandmama?"

Enid looked gratified at his concern. "It's getting better. I'll soon be up and around."

Dudley held out his arms and Nicholas hugged him, too.

Crystal and Reverend Hopkins held hands and beamed at everyone.

Sarah felt happy tears behind her eyelids.

Angela laughed merrily. "You two go on now.

Sarah, you'll be over tomorrow when we exchange gifts, won't you?''

"Of course," Sarah said.

They said their good nights. Then Angela and Faith took Nicholas to get out of his costume.

Sarah and Hunter made their way through the crowd still in the church, Sarah having to stop several times for parents to tell her what a good job she'd done with the pageant.

Sarah took a deep breath of the cold night air as they stepped outside. "Oh, that feels good!"

Hunter breathed deeply, too. "Yes, it does. Looks like more snow to me." He glanced at Sarah. "Ready to make a snowman?"

"I think so. It's been a while since we've done that together."

They linked hands and walked to Sarah's house in silence. Once inside, Sarah turned to him. "Would you like to sit in the parlor?" she asked primly.

Hunter gave her a serious look. "We can't do that until I know one thing. Has the Christmas spirit just gotten to you tonight, or are you trying to tell me something?"

She gave him an equally serious look. "I'm not trying—I *am* telling you something. If you still want me, I'd be honored to be your wife."

She heard his quick intake of breath.

"I'll want you until the day I die, Sarah. And then some. I love you with all my heart."

Happiness filled her to overflowing. "I believe you. And I love you with all my heart . . . and my soul and body, too."

He closed the space between them and took her in his arms, holding her close. Their lips met in a long, sweet kiss that promised more.

Finally, Hunter drew back a little. "I was beginning to think this moment would never come."

She rested her cheek against his coat, feeling completely at peace with the world. "So was I."

"I don't want to stir up any doubts, but what made you change your mind? A few hours ago I would have sworn you'd decided we could never be together."

"And you'd have been right," she admitted, wondering whether or not to tell him about Angela's part in her decision. Something told her not to.

"I . . . just had some kind of . . . awakening tonight. I saw things in a different way, realized for the first time what a hard time you've had over these last eight years. And how well you handled your responsibilities."

He lifted her chin and looked deep into her eyes. "Thank you, Sarah, for believing in me. For trusting me."

She felt as if his gaze were seeing into her heart and soul. "You're welcome. It took a long time but there are no doubts left. Only love and trust."

He scooped her up into his arms as easily as if she were Nicholas's size, then headed purposefully for her bedroom.

Sarah curved her hand around his neck. "I thought we were going into the parlor to talk."

He stopped and looked down at her. "Do you really want to do that now?"

"No," she admitted.

"Good," Hunter said with satisfaction. "We've got years to sit in the parlor and drink tea and talk. I have other things in mind for tonight."

"So do I," Sarah said, sighing blissfully.

Hunter set her down on the bed, stood back, and looked at her. Then he fumbled in his pocket and brought out a small ring box. He held the box out to Sarah.

She drew in her breath at the diamond that sparkled up at her. "It's beautiful."

"I've been carrying it around for a week, wondering if I'd ever be able to give it to you."

Sarah extended her left hand and Hunter slid the ring onto her third finger.

"It feels as if it belongs there."

"It does," Hunter assured her.

Their hearts and souls, full of promises, were in their eyes as they gazed their fill of each other.

EPILOGUE

Such a lot had happened this last year.

Sarah looked at her family gathered around her in Faith's parlor, her heart overflowing with happiness.

The Little Bethlehem Cannery was almost ready to start production. The four partners got along with each other and agreed on all the important issues.

Lorna Miller was Little Bethlehem's schoolteacher. She did her job enthusiastically and the town was satisfied with her work.

Despite the misgivings she'd had, Sarah didn't miss her job. She wondered how she could ever have imagined she wouldn't have enough to do. Besides her normal household duties, she still helped Nicholas after school. He seldom made his letters backward now, and he was beginning to enjoy writing and reading.

Crystal and David had been married for six months and were expecting their first child. Enid was busy helping Crystal sew a layette for the baby and ecstatic at the prospect of being a grandmother again. Nicholas visited her and Dudley frequently—and now willingly.

Enid's Christmas Eve personality change had lasted.

"I know this stitching isn't as fine as I used to do by hand, Sarah."

Faith gave her daughter-in-law an impish smile as she held out the long white garment. "But my sewing machine sure is easier on my hands and eyes."

"It's beautiful." Sarah settled the infant nestled in the crook of her arm more securely and leaned over and kissed Faith. "I'm sure Angela Faith will look beautiful in it at her christening."

Faith was another enthusiastic grandmother. Especially since Hunter and his family were all living in her roomy old house and she had unlimited access to her new granddaughter.

"I still say you shouldn't have named that baby after me. Oh, what a lot she'll have to live up to all her life!" Faith's eyes danced merrily.

"I think it's a good name," Nicholas said. He reached a hand out to his baby sister and grinned when she grabbed one of his fingers and held on tightly.

"So do I," Hunter agreed, his dark gaze meeting Sarah's in a tender look that lingered. "Mama, you're outnumbered, so you may as well stop complaining."

"Oh, I'm not complaining. I'm terribly flattered." Faith sighed. "I miss Angela. I wonder where she is. I still can't understand why she left so suddenly last Christmas and we've never heard a word from her."

"At least she took the tapestry bag I made for her

Christmas gift with her. She seemed glad to get it, too," Sarah said.

"She was," Nicholas agreed. "She said she'd used her old one for 'bout a hundred years."

Faith laughed. "It did look almost that old."

"I asked her why she couldn't stay with us for always," Nicholas continued, "and she told me there were lots more families that needed her help."

Everyone gave him a surprised look.

"Why, Nicholas, you never told us that before," Faith said.

"I know. Angela told me not to . . . for a while. She said you wouldn't understand why she couldn't communicate with you anymore." He frowned. "She said it was against the rules . . . and . . . her father wouldn't allow it."

"Her father!" Sarah said. "Why, I thought her parents were both dead. He would have to be pretty old, wouldn't he? Angela was about your age, wasn't she, Faith?"

Faith shrugged. "Oh, I don't know. Maybe. She always seemed sort of ageless to me. Not really young . . . and not old either."

"Angela, the mystery woman," Hunter said lightly. "Funny how she made people feel better by just being around her. And she always seemed to know what to do about everyone's problems . . ."

He looked at Sarah and their glances met and held.

Sarah's eyes widened and her mouth fell open.

Hunter stared at her in surprise, and his dark eyes also widened.

"What on earth are you two looking like that for?" Faith asked. "As if you'd just found out some wonderful secret?"

Then, she sat up straighter in her chair and swallowed.

"Oh!" she said.

"Tell me! Tell me!" Nicholas begged, his eyes shining with excitement.

Sarah reached out to him and drew him down between her and Hunter on the sofa and hugged him close.

"You already know," she said. "You're the one who told us."

Nicholas squirmed until he was comfortable. He sighed. "Why do grown-ups always say things like that when they don't want to tell you something?"

All the adults in the room smiled.

Little Angela Faith did, too.

Her very first smile, which immensely thrilled her mother, father, brother, and grandmother.

AUTHOR'S NOTE

Dear Reader,

Thank you for reading *Sarah's Christmas*.

I hope you enjoyed it! Christmas is such a special time of the year, and this was a very special story for me.

My next Zebra historical romance is *Promise Me Love*. Damask Aldon and Braden Franklin are falling in love. But Braden's promised to another. And he and Damask are fighting over Goose Creek Inn, which Damask's aunt left jointly to them.

Look for it in May, 2000!

I love to hear from readers. Write me at P.O. Box 63021, Pensacola, FL 32526. If you'd like bookmarks and a newsletter, please include a self-addressed, stamped envelope.

Elizabeth Graham

Put a Little Romance in Your Life With
Fern Michaels

__Dear Emily	0-8217-5676-1	$6.99US/$8.50CAN
__Sara's Song	0-8217-5856-X	$6.99US/$8.50CAN
__Wish List	0-8217-5228-6	$6.99US/$7.99CAN
__Vegas Rich	0-8217-5594-3	$6.99US/$8.50CAN
__Vegas Heat	0-8217-5758-X	$6.99US/$8.50CAN
__Vegas Sunrise	1-55817-5983-3	$6.99US/$8.50CAN
__Whitefire	0-8217-5638-9	$6.99US/$8.50CAN

Call toll free **1-888-345-BOOK** to order by phone or use this coupon to order by mail.

Name_____

Address_____

City _____ State _____Zip_____

Please send me the books I have checked above.

I am enclosing	$_____
Plus postage and handling*	$_____
Sales tax (in New York and Tennessee)	$_____
Total amount enclosed	$_____

*Add $2.50 for the first book and $.50 for each additional book.

Send check or money order (no cash or CODs) to:

Kensington Publishing Corp., 850 Third Avenue, New York, NY 10022

Prices and Numbers subject to change without notice.

All orders subject to availability.

Check out our website at **www.kensingtonbooks.com**